The
GOLDEN FLEECE

by Norah Lofts

A FAWCETT CREST BOOK

Fawcett Publications, Inc., Greenwich, Connecticut

THE GOLDEN FLEECE

THIS BOOK CONTAINS THE COMPLETE TEXT OF THE ORIGINAL HARDCOVER EDITION.

A Fawcett Crest Book reprinted by arrangement with Doubleday and Company, Inc.

Copyright © 1943 by Norah Lofts

Copyright © renewed 1972 by Norah Lofts

ISBN 0-449-23132-1

Printed in the United States of America

10 9 8 7 6 5 4 3 2 1

"**D**ON'T talk, darling. Just don't talk," whispered Roger, reaching for her.

Under the pressure of his hands, the warmth of his mouth, that treacherous current in Myrtle's blood began to run faster.

Almost reluctantly she unclasped her arms and began to push herself free. "Roger," she said in a small voice. "Don't. Wait. I want to talk to you. I must talk to you."

"What is there to say?" he asked, with his lips in her hair.

"Listen, Roger! We can't go on like this any longer . . . all furtive, I mean, and deceiving father . . . and . . . well, you know."

"I've been thinking the same thing, sweetheart . . . ," began Roger.

But it wasn't thinking, this frenzied struggle between the body's desire and the mind's reasonableness.

He loosened his hands, took hers, turned them palms uppermost and kissed them, one after another, slowly, lingeringly.

"Sweetest," he said, "I'd give anything in the world to be able to marry you! You must know that. But I can't. . . ."

Contents

MORNING

AFTERNOON

EVENING

NIGHT

MORNING

The
GOLDEN FLEECE

MORNING

The Fleece

There had been a slight frost during the night, and the grey of its breath still lay like a cloudy pall over the house and garden, blotting out the mellow red of the tiles and the green of the grass. Between the pallor of the shrouded earth and heavy sky the crimson leaves of the creeper on the inn wall and the bronze leaves of the beeches shone with a bonfire brightness.

Will Oakley, the landlord of the *Fleece,* stood on the step of the inn's back-door and shivered, sniffing the air and rubbing his thin, slightly tremulous hands together. No mistake about it, he thought, autumn had come. Four days before, when he had taken to his bed with one of his recurrent attacks of slight fever, the weather had been mild and damp, as though the season were lingering sadly, nostalgically, between summer and autumn. Now the change had come. Despite the dullness of the morning the air was crisp and exhilarating; and although he shivered, Will was conscious of a sense of well-being, as though the new season had revived a spring of life in his body.

He thought, with a wryness which showed in a momentary twist of his thin mobile mouth, that he was too old to be so responsive to the variations of wind and weather. A man of his age, forty-five next birthday, with two grown-up daughters, should be immune to the season's changes. But he knew, even as the thought went through his mind, that the year whose first day of spring left him unmoved, whose first breath of autumn did not

9

stir his blood, would be the year which found him, not only old, but dead.

Besides, he thought as he stepped into the yard, there were other reasons for his feeling of well-being this morning. He was restored to health, after an attack which had been slighter than usual; he had just paid back the last instalment of the money which he had borrowed when he bought the *Fleece*, and so was, for the first time in four years, clear of debt; the inn was prosperous and, thanks to Harriet, he had come downstairs this morning to find his small world orderly and efficient. He could remember the days, in the old *Dun Cow* at Lammingham, before Harriet was old enough to take charge, when the inevitable, almost rhythmic returns of his malady threw the whole house out of gear and made his recovery a nightmare of complaints from guests and staff, wasted food, muddled assignments of rooms, overcharges and bills completely forgotten. He was grateful for Harriet, and aware that he was being inexplicably perverse when he regretted the fact that she had, so unshakably and thoroughly, adopted the rôle of landlady. Twenty years of innkeeping had not fully resigned him to seeing his womenfolk in the kitchen instead of the parlour. Harriet dismissed this attitude as nonsense—as she dismissed so many other things. And in this, as in so many other things, he recognized that Harriet was right.

He stepped out, rounded the angle of the wall, and came in view of the great yard, already a scene of bustling activity: for this was "fitting" day in the country, the day when old tenancies ended and new ones began. Heavy wagons and lighter carts, piled high with farm gear and household furniture, were drawn up haphazardly while the men who had brought them so far on their journey were refreshing themselves after labours which had started before dawn, and fortifying themselves against further labours which would continue until nightfall. The place smelt and sounded like an enormous farmyard.

Hens and ducks squawked and quacked from crate and coop, and the dogs who helped the drovers to restrain the untethered bullocks, colts, pigs and sheep in some sort of order, barked and snapped in many keys. Joe, the potman, and the boy Davy who helped him, already a little breathless and flushed of face, were running about in their shirt sleeves.

As Will came into sight a local carter who had stopped rather early in his journey nudged another, a stranger, and muttered, "New landlord."

"Now," said a third man. "I woont call him new. Bin here a matter o' fower year."

"That is new for these parts," retorted the carter, unabashed, adding with a rueful regret in his voice. "Then thass fower year last summer since owd Job snuffed it. He was a rum un and no mistake."

"What like is this un?"

"Oh, so so. Not like owd Job. Bit stand-offish like."

"That doont do in a place o' this sort," said the stranger pontifically.

Will, threading his way across the yard, would have agreed with him. For the thousandth time he was conscious of his inadequacy. His part demanded that at this moment he should move freely among the men, dropping a word here, an inquiry there, venturing a mild joke and laughing extravagantly at any return witticism. Then he would be popular, as old Job Wainwright, despite his extortions, had been popular, and regarded—that most desirable thing in quiet country districts—as a character. Anything was forgiven if you were a character. But Will, faced with men, any men, in numbers, became self-conscious and awkward, and his knowledge of failing in what was regarded as his duty made him still more ill at ease. He could think of no casual remark to make even to those of the men who were known to him, so, with a few stiff smiles, he steered the shortest course possible across the yard towards the stables.

A stout red-faced farmer in a suit of good cloth and bright yellow leggings scowled as Will neared him, and fumbling in his pocket drew out and proffered, without a word, and with obvious reluctance, a shining silver florin.

"Pay the potman, will you?" said Will. "He'll know what you've drunk."

"I ain't drunk nothing, yit." The man's tone was ungracious.

"What's that for then?" Will jerked his head towards the coin, still tendered between a calloused thumb and finger.

"Standing yon wain in your yard," said the farmer, jerking his head in turn towards a wagon with bright blue wheels.

"Oh," said Will with a smile of understanding which lightened his face as the perfunctory grins of greeting had utterly failed to do. "We've stopped that charge. Didn't you know? Free standing for all customers. That's the rule now."

"Owd Job allust charged," said the farmer. His manner showed no pleasure—was, in fact, rather affronted—and although he had drawn out the coin very unwillingly he seemed equally reluctant to return it to his pocket. His whole attitude suggested that to him any change, even if it seemed for the better, must be regarded with suspicion and thoroughly chewed over.

"Well, I don't," said Will rather shortly, and proceeded on his way, while the farmer with a little shake of his head, and a vague feeling that he had been snubbed, pushed nearer the circle of the potman's ministrations in order to spend some part of the florin in brown ale.

"No call to be snorty, was there?" he asked plaintively of a bystander. "I ain't bin this way in *his* time. Thass five year since I moved out to Stradishall, and owd Job he charged me mortal that time. Fact I ony brought in one wain this time on account of what he charged me. Left tothers along the road with my missus. Nut that I mind

paying me dues," he added carefully that his confession
of thriftiness might be misconstrued and attributed to
poverty or parsimony, "ony I never could see why Job
arst the same for a little tumbril as a grut wain. And I'd
have arst yon chap to take a drink with me if he hadn't
gone off so huffy like."

"He's allust that way," said the local carter consolingly.
"He woont a drunk with you." (His eyes said, "But I
would.") "A queer chap is Mr. Will Oakley. Nut but what
he's straight like and nut half the twister owd Job wuz.
Still," he added ambiguously, "you knew where you wuz
with owd Job."

"Doont look a innkeeper neither," said the farmer discontentedly, beckoning Joe and ordering one pint, to the
manifest disappointment of the carter.

"No more he doont." The carter hitched his belt, preparing to move away. "Got a coupla wenches, too. Rigged
out like ladies and allust given the Miss afore their
names." He slouched off.

Another farmer, who had been listening, said rumina-
tively, "That's as may be. But owd Job ud have been out
here counting every mortal thing and charging fit to flee
you. Still, he'd a had a pleasant word while he was clawing
in the money. And there was allust a bit of gossip here-
abouts, what with his wimmin and all."

As though the word had loosened a barrier, a spate of
gossip began to pour forth as the drinkers who had known
the inn in the past reminded one another, or informed
strangers, what a wily old devil the previous proprietor
had been. They had hated him in his day because of his
exorbitant charges and the tricks he had played on those
who tried to evade them; but now they only remembered
the tricks which had victimized someone else and the
false façade of geniality which had been one of the old
man's business assets. Most of the comparisons they drew
were in Will's disfavour, and the fact that his discontinu-
ance of the standing charge had saved every man in the

yard some sum, ranging from two shillings—Job's mini-
mum—to about thirty, was entirely overlooked because
he had passed through the crowd without speaking.

Will was still pondering and still puzzled by the paraly-
sis which had overtaken him when, with a feeling of relief
he reached the stable and shut the half-door behind him.
But a stamping of hoofs and a glad whinny of welcome
distracted his thoughts, and he moved quickly to the end
stall, drawing an apple from his pocket as he went. Katie,
his own riding mare, a slim black creature with a strain
of Arab in her blood, leaned her head over the door and
nuzzled him with her nose before she accepted the apple.

Sometimes, in his moods of depression, Will indulged
in the childish habit of counting his blessings. He reckoned
Katie high in the list. He loved her, and she loved him in
her fashion, just as, he was sure, his daughters, Myrtle
and Harriet, did but he never worried about her as he
sometimes worried about Myrtle, and she was never dictatorial or inquisitive as Harriet was.

He kept Katie for his own pleasure and his own use.
He never hired or lent her however urgent the demand. It
was his habit, every day, between the hours of four and
five o'clock, when dinner was over and the inn's evening
guests still far on the road, to ride her as far as Winwood
Splash along the Norwich road, turn off on to a springy
sheep-nibbled turf of the Common and then, after a brief,
violent gallop, to saunter home along the leafy lanes of
Lownde Wood. Only his brief spells of illness broke the
pleasant custom, and at the end of them he always found
Katie brimming over with energy and high spirits which
must be dissipated upon the Common without delay.

On this Michaelmas morning, however, once her welcome had been given and her apple eaten, Katie gave no
sign of having lacked exercise for four days. She stood
listlessly, her head drooping a little and her usually restless feet quiet in the deep straw. Will entered the stall and
examined her closely. There were marks of sweat and mud

on her glossy coat, and one fetlock was slightly swollen and a trifle tender to his touch.

Instantly Will thought of Harriet. Once, only once before, another person had ridden Katie, and Will had raised a row about it; and on that occasion Harriet had said, "What fuss, Father. Don't you think it's rather a waste to keep a horse just for yourself?" Now, he suspected, Harriet had taken advantage of his illness and, more to show her authority than anything else, had given permission for the mare to be ridden. And if she had, he would have something to say. It just showed how much Harriet had taken to interfering. And he had never intended her to have any hand in the inn's running at all.

Even in that moment of anger, even as he raised his head and shouted angrily for the stableman, the cool just mind which governed most of Will Oakley's thoughts and actions reminded him again that Harriet was very useful, that he depended on her for many things, and that he had often been glad that the poor girl had found scope for her energy and undoubted ability. Nevertheless, if she had lent or hired Katie . . .

His furious thoughts were interrupted by the boy, Dick Stevens, until lately stable-boy, now promoted to full charge. He had called from the loft above in answer to Will's shout, and now dropped easily down the ladder, missing the last four rungs, and was standing at the door of the stall. He was a tall boy, with wide flat shoulders and a small waist, heavily girded by a leather belt whose steel studs caught the light. Looking at him, Will was aware, not for the first time, of his attractive appearance. His breeches were blue, and his shirt, originally red, had faded from sunshine and many washings to a dim pink shade, very pleasing to the eye. His skin was tanned, his eyes a light chestnut, his hair very black and thick. He had a ready and ingratiating smile. He was smiling now, and Will wondered, again not for the first time, why he did not like the lad more. He was industrious, civil and quite gifted in dealing with horses; his looks were pleasing and Will had never, in four years, detected him in any lie or bit of dishonesty. But he did not like him; had, in fact, given him promotion above his years simply because he did not like him, and therefore feared that not to promote him would be an act of rank injustice due to prejudice.

"You wanted me, sir?"

"Somebody's been riding Katie. Who was it?"

"Me," said Dick, without an instant's evasion or hedging, a fact that Will noted but which did nothing to allay his fury.

"What the hell for?"

"She was restive, Mr. Oakley, I coon't bear to see her. I only took her up to the Commons and give her her head for ten minutes."

Reasonable enough, Will thought.

"Your motives were probably praiseworthy, but it was sheer damned disobedience all the same. I told you before, didn't I? If it happens again I'll thrash you. D'you hear?" He added, as though seeking to excuse, in his own eyes, his petulance, "Now she's got a bad strain and I shan't be able to take her out myself. And why didn't you rub her down properly?"

Why not? Dick thought. If only you knew! But he said, politely and with a little plaintiveness:

"I'm sorry. Taking her out at all set me back a bit, and I was mighty busy." He entered the stall and bent to test the extent of the injury. "Thass nothing," he said with an air of genuine relief. "If I get a fomentation on that right away she'll be as right as rain to . . ." He checked himself on the verge of saying "tonight," and amended, "this arternoon."

"I hope so, for your sake. Get to work on her now."

"Right away, sir," said Dick willingly. Will, with a final pat for his favourite, left the stall and began an inspection of the stables which would have done Harriet credit. There was nothing with which he could find the slightest fault, and as he was on the point of leaving his sense of justice gave him a nudge which made him pause. The boy was only a youngster, after all, and the place was in apple-pie order, and though he had taken Katie out he had meant well by that, too. Why, then, had he, the master, a slight, unworthy feeling of disappointment at finding nothing which could be commented upon unfavourably? Why had he, always, reasonlessly, at the back of his mind, the feeling that Dick was not to be trusted? Effie Stevens now, the ugly little sister who worked in the kitchen, Will liked more than any of the maids. Without really thinking about the matter he knew, instinctively, that he would have trusted her with his life, if necessary. And his feeling about the brother was just as instinctive. All rubbish, he thought —probably Dick will rescue ten horses from a burning stable and Effie will steal a watch. What's instinct, any-way?

He turned round and called to Dick, now busy in Katie's stall:

"I'm pleased with the way everything looks." There, he thought, I've been fair: and he was turning away again, pleased with his own fairness, when, from a stall he had thought empty a long grey head protruded.

"Hi!" Will called sharply, "Boy! Why hasn't Mr. Moreton's beast gone home?"

"He said he'd call for it hisself," said Dick, coming to the door of Katie's stall with a brush in his hand and a slightly exasperated expression on his face.

"I don't care what he said. As soon as you've finished with Katie you can ease your itch for riding by taking it up to the Hall. If he thinks he can founder a horse and then leave it here for a fortnight eating its head off at my ex-pense, he thinks wrong. Before you go you can come to me and I'll give you a bill. And you're to see that Mr. Moreton has it."

"I oon't have much time today," said Dick, rather plaintively.

"You'll have time for that." Will's tone forbade further excuses.

"Very good, sir." A knowledgeable smile touched the boy's brown face as he returned to Katie's toilet. Old High-and-Mighty thought he had disposed of young Mr. Moreton, but Dick knew better. He knew other things, too. And if the old bastard could just have stayed indoors for another hour he'd have had Katie all spruced up and ship-shape. Fancy keeping a bit of lightning like Katie just to trot round the Common once a day. It was a wicked waste. Never mind, he'd wriggled out of that nicely and no harm done. Next time he'd know. No matter how late, or how tired he was, the mare must be properly fettled right away. As for the other matter, unless Mr. Moreton sent or called for the grey today, as he had arranged, Dick would turn it out on the Lower Meadow. Old Nosey would hardly walk that far today. He hadn't looked very spry, and there'd been enough doing in the inn to keep his mind off young Moreton.

But Will, out in the yard again, and this time genuinely oblivious to the men in it, was thinking of young Moreton, to the total exclusion of everything else. He had left the stable with a malevolent glance at the innocent grey horse, and the expression dwelt and hardened on his thin face.

That was a great disadvantage of keeping an inn, he reflected. A man in his private house might say to another: I don't like your face, or your manners, or your reputation, and I'll thank you not to enter my house again. He could then close his door, and any further intrusion could be rightly dealt with as an insult. But an inn was public; and although a drunken fellow or a trouble-maker could be summarily ejected, its doors could hardly be closed against a young gentleman of means and standing whose only misdemeanor, so far as the inn was concerned, was the fact that he had made advances to the innkeeper's daughter.

Most fathers in his position would have turned a blind eye; some would have encouraged the affair; for young men like Roger Moreton spent freely and where one came more were likely to follow. Besides, girls in inns were supposed to know how to look after themselves. But Myrtle was different. And Will was there to see that the difference was recognized and respected, even though the effort irked him.

Maybe, he thought—and his truculent expression gave way to more natural bewilderment—he had chosen badly when he had taken up this trade. Perhaps he should have thought forward to the time when the girls were grown, and when Harriet would take a perverse pleasure in working at a job she really despised, and when Myrtle's beauty would lead, almost inevitably, to this kind of nuisance. Perhaps he would have been wiser, when choosing his trade, to have taken a farm or a shop of some kind. But the fact remained that he had not thought forward. Twenty years ago, when he bought the *Dun Cow* at Lammingham, Myrtle had been just two years old, and Harriet only a few months; and he had gone, bull-headed, into the one trade that he thought he understood. His stepfather, a common, genial man whom he remembered with gratitude for his kindness, had kept the *Feathers* at Ludlow. His mother, though she had remarried in search of comfort and security, had always despised her second husband's business, and had done her best to make her son despise it, too; but Will had loved it. Between the ages of seven and sixteen he had shared and delighted in the bustling communal life, and had spent much time and ingenuity in circumventing his mother's schemes for rearing him as a gentleman on money gained by an ungentlemanly trade. She had certainly won a temporary victory later on. But later still, at the crisis of his life, he had turned naturally and instinctively to the rôle of landlord; and now, after twenty years of it, surveying his choice critically, he was compelled to acknowledge that he might have chosen worse. True, he lacked the touch of easy good-fellowship and the ability to suffer fools gladly, to cheese-pare here and exhort there, which would have made him at once richer and more popular. True, there were problems to consider where the girls were concerned; but on the whole it was a good life. And taken at the lowest basis it had kept the three of them in comfort for twenty years. That alone might be considered to justify his choice of trade.

As for Myrtle, he thought as he neared the door of the kitchen, he would be a fool to worry unduly. True, she had the kind of soft warm beauty which tended to make life difficult for its possessor; in many ways, in her looks, her impulsiveness, her careless good nature, she was her mother, the dead Clarissa, over again. The likeness often caused him a pang. But Myrtle had qualities which Clarissa had lacked entirely. She was capable of judgment, of shrewd observation. Harriet was inclined to treat her sister as though she were a twelve-year-old simpleton and often the treatment seemed justified; but Will, a less biased observer, knew that a portion of his elder daughter's mind worked exactly like his own, was detached, sceptical, reflective. It was out of place in so feminine and lovely a creature; but it might save Myrtle. He remembered how very well she had taken his embargo upon young Moreton. No tears, no sulking. It was time that that young gentleman was supplanted in her affections. And Will found himself hoping that eventually Myrtle's choice might fall upon someone suitable and eligible—say young Falkner of Willowbrook. He was personable and steady; he had had some schooling, a fact which should count with Myrtle, who was, surprisingly, bookish, and who had taken far more advantage of the expensive and rather ambitious schooling which Will had given both girls, than had the practical Harriet. And when old Falkner died, Robin would innherit the best farm within a radius of fifty miles.

The wry smile of self-derision which touched his lips so often, and which, misinterpreted, often made him feared at his weakest moment, showed again as he caught himself planning for Myrtle with all the worldliness of a scheming mamma; yet, remembering his own life, which had gone awry for lack of capital at a crucial moment, he told himself that, deny it how you would, the fact remained that a degree of security and a modicum of comfort were necessary for happiness in this life. And security and comfort were impossible without money, or money's equivalent. He had yet to meet the woman—or the man, for that matter—who could be poor and without prospects and at the same time happy and contented.

Actually that rare creature was within arm's reach of him as he opened the door of the kitchen and stepped on to the freshly scrubbed flags of the floor. She stood at a side-table peeling a vast quantity of potatoes in a wooden bucket, a young woman who had been born in poverty, reared by the coldest charity and forced to earn her bread by the hardest and most menial toil. When her capacity to perform her labours ended by reason of sickness or old age, she would be a pauper again, for she lacked the wits or the beauty which might have improved her state. And yet, until the July of the summer just past, Effie Stevens had been perfectly happy, unembittered by her past, undepressed by her present and unconcerned for her future.

Nobody within the walls of the *Fleece,* where she did all the heaviest and dirtiest work, regarded Effie and her happiness as in the least phenomenal. Her uncomplaining activity, her queer sweet smile and unwarying good nature, were as much a matter of course as her unprepossessing appearance, her clumsy shuffling movements and her exasperating inability to perform satisfactorily any job outside her own narrow routine. Most people, indeed, considered her half-witted, and would have attributed her capacity for happiness in circumstances not conducive to happiness to her lack of sense.

Other members of the staff with whom she came in contact—Mrs. Sharman, the cook; Dolly, Sarah, Clara and

Kitty, the other maids; Joe the potman; the boy Davy;
even her own brother Dick—treated her with contempt,
good-natured, indifferent, or spiteful according to their
nature or mood. Most of them at some time or another,
imposed upon her, a very easy thing to do, since she had
no sense of self-preservation and was foolishly generous
with the only things she possessed—an apparently inex-
haustible supply of wiry physical energy, and the steady
wage of four guineas a year.

She lacked the slightest trace of her brother's comeliness. She had a weak, rabbitty face with two good features
which were hardly ever noticed, her skin and her eyes.
Her skin had an unvarying flower-like pallor which
nothing—haste, confusion, the heat of the fire, indigestion
or sunshine—could ever tinge with colour; and her eyes,
darker than Dick's, were beautiful, very soft and gentle, so
lustrous that even the lids and long curving lashes seemed
to shine, and so set in an absent-minded, far-seeing gaze
that there was something slightly unhuman about them;
they were gazelle's eyes, especially when they were
startled. But no one save Harriet, who was unduly aware
of other people's complexions, had ever noticed her skin;
and no one save Will, who was oddly observant of irrelevant details, had ever remarked upon her eyes. Most
people saw only the colourless hair, the knobby forehead,
the prominent teeth, receding chin and the awkwardness
of her body. Her shoulder-bones protruded through the
thin print of her bodice, her hip-bones ridged the coarse
sacking apron, her elbows were sharp and ugly below the
bulge of her rolled-up sleeves and, at the end of her stick-
like legs, her feet were so long and so flat and so heavily
shod that they seemed to anchor this collection of awkward angles to the floor.

She looked any age; and except that she was senior to
Dick, she was uncertain, to within four years or so, how
old she really was. She and Dick had been orphaned early
in life, and the celebration of pauper's birthdays had not

been indulged by the parish overseers. She might have been as young as nine, or as old as thirteen, when, at the end of what seemed to have been an eternity of misery at the Poor Farm, where many of her contemporaries had succumbed to cold, hunger and ill-usage, she had been handed over to the tender mercies of Job Wainwright, who always had one or two juvenile paupers to do his most menial work. He was in high favour with the parish authorities because his paupers lived and throve—not through his kindly treatment, but because food, of a sort, if only other people's leavings, was always plentiful at the *Fleece*. As soon as Dick was old enough to be useful—an age attained early enough in the circumstances—he was set to work in the yard, and Effie was delighted to be able to share her food with him and to see to his clothes.

But life was hard and rough for Effie. She was consistently overworked, and it was nobody's business to speak to her kindly. She was very lonely, for even Dick soon showed plainly that he preferred the company of his own sex, and it was a repressed, miserable little drudge who, one afternoon, was bidden run all the way to Willowbrook and all the way back to fetch some butter which was needed. Notwithstanding the urgency of her errand, she halted on Goose Green because she could hear the sound of a fiddle and could see a small crowd. She edged forward timidly and stood watching the old man who was playing, and soon she had forgotten the butter in her delight in the lively jigging tunes. Even her tired springless feet in her heavy ill-fitting shoes tingled with the desire to dance. But soon, having drawn his crowd, the old man laid aside his fiddle and began to talk. Most of the crowd, disappointed and resentful at the music's cessation, drifted away; but Effie stood still, entranced. She was in her teens, at an emotional age, her empty little heart ready to welcome any occupant. So God came to Effie, there on the chilly Green, and took the place of the parents whom she had lost too early, the brother who had grown away

from her, the friends she had lacked, the lover she might
never know. The old traveling preacher, in simple homely
language, assured her that God was her Father, Jesus
Christ her loving Friend, and the Holy Ghost a Companion who would be with her always—even, she thought,
on the dark attic stairs where unknown fears assailed her,
and in the lonely passages which she dreaded. If only she
were prepared to be good she need never be lonely or
frightened again. And being good seemed at that moment
very simple and easy, largely concerned with not taking
food out of the pantry without permission and not sweeping the dirt under the mats. In return God would love her.

Since that moment, now more than seven years ago,
right up to the July of the summer just ended. Effie had
been blissfully happy. She was still poor, over-worked, ill-
clothed, tired and despised; but none of these things
mattered an iota. The darkness which had always terrified
her no longer held any terrors, and she was not lonely
any more. God had His all-seeing Fatherly eye upon her,
by night and by day; Jesus loved her, and she loved Him;
and if she could avoid sin there was heaven with all its
delights, imaginable and unimaginable, awaiting her when
she died. It was a philosophy of life which at that period
was being liberally dispensed by Evangelists all over the
country, bringing comfort to thousands for whom this
world held little, and reigning the people to their claims
for another half century.

Effie had never mentioned her secret, partly because it
was too precious to be lightly shared, partly because any
proselyting impulse that she might have felt was instantly
and automatically quenched by her knowledge that nobody would take the slightest notice of anything *she* said.
But there was a great difference in her work, after that
momentous afternoon, for she was conscious of God's eye
upon her, even when she was alone; He watched her as
she scrubbed floors and blacked grates and sifted cinders,
as she washed dishes and prepared vegetables. And He

never saw His new servant do a slovenly or careless job:
for, having no other sphere of well-doing, she served God
by serving first Job Wainwright and then Will Oakley to
the best of her clumsy dogged ability. She scoured greasy
pans for Christ's sake and polished brass for the glory of
God. And when Will had felt instinctively that he could
trust her with his life, his instinct had been as true and
accurate as a compass needle.

But early in the month of July of this year all Effie's
humble happiness and innocent contentment had been
swept away. The power of Evil, as though knowing that a
frontal attack would never succeed, and that no tempta-
tion could lure Effie into envy, or sloth, or dishonesty, had
performed a sly flanking movement and captured her by a
trick. Effie, bewildered, dim-witted, unresourceful, without
a friend to advise her, had been, despite her struggles, a
comparatively easy victim. God, though she felt Him still
watchful, had, so far, done nothing to extricate her from
the maze in which she stumbled, puzzled, prayerful and
distressed; and Jesus, though He loved her still, seemed
very far away; only the Holy Ghost and the voice of
Effie's conscience were unsparing of their attention. They
nagged her by day and by night.

Last night she had made one further fruitless effort to
break the bonds which held her, and, failing, had spent
hours in tearful prayer. This morning she felt heavy and
boneless; yet, although the tasks that confronted her
seemed too many and too heavy, she welcomed each one.
Work was her last bulwark against despair, and she still
held on to a childish hope that something might happen.
God might act before she had cleaned the great stove . . .
before she had scrubbed the wide floor. . . .

But she had finished scrubbing now, and the variegated
flags, grey and rose, primrose, ochre and cream, shone
spotless and slightly damp. Long before nightfall they
would all be soiled again; mud and manure, bits of straw
and stray dead leaves from the yard, grease from the

cooking and sawdust from the bar would mingle upon their shining surfaces; and tomorrow morning, at about the same time, Effie would set about them with her bucket and brush. And by that time how much further would she have plunged down the slope that led, inevitably, to hell?

She sighed heavily as she moved to the next task, the potatoes. She had barely started when the door opened and her master came in from the yard

As he entered, the sun, which for some time had been struggling with the layers of cloud, burst forth triumphant, and the open door laid a bright yellow oblong of light upon the newly-scrubbed floor.

Effie turned her face towards her master and towards the light. Her great eyes gave evidence of inward disturbance which would have flooded another girl's face with crimson, a disturbance that stemmed from two emotions, love and remorse.

She had fallen in love with Will on a day soon after his arrival at the *Fleece*. He had noticed her eyes one morning, and, arrested by their queer, incongruous beauty, had been led on to notice also how extremely thin she was. He had asked her, in the off-hand way that concealed his shyness, whether she had enough to eat. And that was the first time in all her life that anyone had shown so much personal interest in her. Moreover, his voice was far gentler than he knew, for he had already heard enough about his predecessor to be disposed to pity anyone who had served him. The simple question and the kindly tone had won Effie's devotion so completely that thereafter Will Oakley ranked close to the Holy Trinity in her affections. In fact, if the inn had changed hands a few years earlier, before the old preacher had taken his stand on Goose Green, Effie's story would have been very different and far less happy. Then she might have eaten her heart out in fruitless longing, made a fool of herself by unseemingly behaviour. As it was, having learned the lesson of adoration, it was an easy thing for her to love Will, and revere him and serve him without carnal longing as without worldly hope. So hopeless, indeed, was her love for him that she never even indulged in romantic daydreams of an impossible future. She accepted the fact that he would probably never speak to her except to give her an order or a vague kindly, "Well, Effie," when he met her point blank on the stairs or in a passage. And that was as it should be. Effie knew full well that the old man, Job Wainwright, had taken kitchen wenches, even gypsy girls, to his bed. But Will Oakley was so different from Job Wainwright that it seemed wrong to call them both men. The trivial, almost unconscious reforms which the new inn-keeper had introduced to ameliorate the lot of those who served him seemed to Effie the kind of thing that a saint might do if he were given power on earth.

She never lay down at night on the feather bed which had replaced the lumpy straw mattress of the old days without a feeling of gratitude which merged imperceptibly into a prayer for her master. And there was, too, the business of the print and flannel. Job had paid part—often the greater part—of his maid's wages in kind, buying the materials cheaply by bulk. Harriet, though Effie did not know it, had been in favour of continuing the custom; was, indeed, at the end of the year working out the amounts required. And Will had said, "Why bother? You and Myrtle have enough shopping to do without that. Give the girls an extra guinea and let them buy their own. They'll enjoy choosing it more than you will."

So Effie's wages had jumped from three guineas and a length each of striped print and grey flannel to four guineas. And since she could patch and mend or, when patching and mending failed, buy all the new material she needed for half a guinea, the new arrangement endowed her with a full ten shillings and sixpence every year. And thereafter many a beggar, soliciting scraps at the back door of the inn, had been surprised to receive from the sodden, scarred hands of the humblest of its servants a

whole sixpence or shilling, together with a sweet fleeting
smile.

This pleasing power to bestow alms, with a number of
other blessings, had come to Effie direct from Will. And
now, besides sinning against God, she was deceiving her
master; deceiving him, moreover, not in a vague, general
way, but in a matter which she knew concerned him very
nearly. So, as she turned towards the light and saw Will,
love flooded her warmly and remorse clawed at her with
sharp talons, and her eyes, if Will had noticed them this
morning, would have distressed him, so sad they were and
so distraught. But he passed her without a glance, went
to the big scrubbed table and said a few words to Mrs.
Sharman, who was stuffing the Michaelmas goose, and
then moved on to the dresser where Harriet was sealing
down and labeling the quince jelly which she had made on
the previous afternoon. The sharp scent of its boiling hung
ghostlike about the kitchen, mingling with the strong
odour of sage and onion. Will watched Harriet for a moment without speaking. As always, her movements gave
him pleasure. Even her simplest action had a delicate
precision, a neatness, an economy of effort which were
delightful. Her long white fingers moved over the paper
circles, the egg white, the labels, the scissors, with the grace
of dancers performing some complicated steps which long
practice had made easy. She never fumbled, never touched
an article unnecessarily, and as each gleaming pot, reddish amber in colour and clear as crystal, received its
white cap and its label, she pushed it into line with the
others with an orderly gesture which was, Will thought,
pure Harriet.

Even apart from her hands, Harriet Oakley was, from
the back view, a very trim and attractive figure. Her
hair, almost primrose in colour, was simply dressed for
the morning's business and drawn up from a smooth
white nape which ran in a lovely line to her slim shoulders.
She wore a dress of dark mulberry colour and, because

she was working, a small muslin apron whose wide strings, crisp from the iron which Effie had wielded at eight o'clock last night, encircled a neat round waist, and stood out behind in a stiff butterfly bow. Beneath the hem of the gown there was a glimpse of shapely ankles in white cotton stockings, and small well-arched feet in black velvet shoes.

There was nothing to prepare the observer for the shock which was inevitable when she turned her head. An exceptionally severe attack of smallpox had turned a pretty little six-year-old girl into a sight from which the sensitive eye must shrink. Even at a time when the disease attacked and marked thousands, so that an unmarked woman, however plain her features, was regarded as a beauty. Harriet Oakley was hideous. From the edge of her lovely primrose hair to her chin her skin was so pitted and pocked that its surface resembled coarse pumice stone. And although the lotions and pastes and powders which she applied so assiduously could, and did, to some extent conceal the damage done to forehead, cheek and chin, nothing could disguise or mitigate the distortion of her eyelids which were puckered and mis-shapen around eyes of a clear deep grey.

Her affliction had affected her deeply, more than heredity, upbringing or education could ever do. Moralists cast at beauty the reproach that it is but skin deep; ugliness, in a normal woman, has a deeper penetration. It had warped and twisted every natural instinct in Harriet Oakley's character. She knew that every person brought face to face with her for the first time must feel either horror or, in rare and hotly resented cases, pity, so she prepared for such reaction by adopting a brusque, arrogant and scornful manner. She had even come, in a passage of years, to take a perverse pleasure in the contrast between her figure and her face. Sometimes she would keep her back turned so that men—and there were always men in the inn—would see only a young attractive female and would approach, asking, in a voice that they reserved for such moments, some unnecessary question. Then she would turn quickly, exposing her mutilated face and answering in her sharp biting fashion, and seeming to enjoy the shock of surprise and disgust which resulted. This perverse and unnatural pleasure was always followed by a commensurate pain, and in the solitude of her room she had shed uncounted tears over her state.

But, since every human being has a deep need to be needed and admired for some quality within him, her affliction had had other results as well. It had made her energetic and almost uncomfortably efficient. She was as punctual, methodical and reliable as a machine. A proud streak in Will had prevented him from exploiting these virtues in her, and he had tried, with less and less success with each succeeding year, to keep her from taking much responsibility for the house's maintenance. But Harriet's efficiency acted like a force of nature, a flood or a gale, there was no withstanding it, and within certain well defined limits she was now mistress of the house.

Will stood for a moment watching her and thinking. Then he said, "It's a beautiful colour, Harriet."

"And it has set well," she replied, drawing his attention to the feature for which she, not Nature, was responsible. Then, without halting her hands, she said tartly, "You shouldn't have gone out without your top-coat."

"It's a beautiful morning."

"It's a villainously cold morning. And we're going to be busy. I don't want you in bed again."

No one would have guessed from her manner of speaking that during the four days just past she had tended him with the utmost care, or been tireless, ungrudging, even imaginative in her ministrations. "Will you drink coffee this morning, or rum and milk? That might forestall a chill."

He did not answer, and she glanced at him irritably. It was an infuriating habit which he shared with Myrtle, this absent-minded disengagement of attention. Here I am, thought Harriet crossly, concerning myself with *his* 'levenses and *his* health and he can't even take the trouble to answer. She followed the line of his stare and saw that he was looking at Effie Stevens as though he had never seen her before.

"That girl looks distinctly unwell," he said. "*Do* you think she gets enough to eat?"

"Of course she does. She always was a bag of bones. Some folks are like that. You couldn't fatten them if you tried. Besides, I believe she's daft. Last night I caught her in the backhouse ironing at eight o'clock; and ironing is Sarah's job, and always has been. And twice lately I've come on her mumbling away to herself. It sounded like praying." Harriet gave a kind of snort. Years of earnest childish praying that her face might get better had given her a poor opinion of the power of prayer.

"Somebody ought to see that Sarah doesn't impose on her," Will persisted, pursuing his own lines of thought. Harriet shrugged impatiently.

"I have told her before when I've caught her at Sarah's work that it's her own fault if she's imposed upon. *And* I had something to say to Miss Sarah, too, I assure you. Great fat thing, she's as lazy as she's high. I asked you just now whether you'd prefer rum and milk to coffee?"

"I know. I heard you. I'll have coffee as usual?"

Harriet pushed the last jar into place. There, said the gesture, that's another job done. The jars stood, ready to take their place upon the store-room shelf, side by side with the dark purple blackberry jelly, the scarlet strawberry jam, the green gooseberry preserve, and all the other delicacies which marked the seasons of Harriet's year. Except for the marrow ginger, which would not be made until the last week in December, the quince jelly was the last thing that would bear the date 1817.

Harriet rubbed her fingers on the checked cloth and, raising her voice, said coldly, "The jelly is ready to be

put away, Mrs. Sharman." The simple sentence recalled
to both women the old, sore subject of the store-room
keys. Until Mrs. Sharman's installation the keys had
been in Harriet's charge, and the old cook, lacking pride and willing to spare her ruined feet any extra
step, had been happy for them to remain there. But Mrs.
Sharman had regarded the custom as a slur upon her
honesty, and after an open attack had failed to gain her
possession of them, had embarked upon a wily war of
attrition which had resulted in her waking Will—not
Harriet—in the middle of the night and demanding the
keys in order that she might make some black currant
tea for a maid who was, she said, "corfing herself to rib-
bings." In the morning Will was irritable, "For God's
sake, Harriet, give her the keys, or get a spare set cut.
I'm sick of this business. What if she does slip a bit of
food home to her family now and again? It'd be better
than rousing you and me in the middle of the night."

Harriet was far from agreeing; but she knew exactly
when her father spoke to be obeyed. So she had handed
over the keys. But she then began ostentatiously to keep
a careful, exact account of everything that went into and
came out of the cool, airy room with the slatted window.
Nothing had ever been missed in the two and a half years
of Mrs. Sharman's reign; so it was more for the sake of
appearance than anything else that Harriet had moved
to the end of the dresser and took down a small black
book. Conscious of the cook's sardonic eye upon her she
entered the item, "Michaelmas Day, 11, twelve pots of
Quince Jelly."

Mrs. Sharman could also wield a pen, and was proud
of her skill with it, and frequently, beside her breakfast
plate, or pushed under her bedroom door, Harriet would
find a torn scrap of writing paper bearing some such
message as, "Out of store, 2 taters for late supper arter
youd gon," or "Give begar slice cold pudden wile you was
out." In fact, the more trivial the withdrawal the more

earnestly did she draw Harriet's attention to it. Will and
Myrtle, who shared what Harriet considered a childish
sense of humour, derived a great deal of amusement from
Mrs. Sharman's missives. But Harriet had neither forgotten nor forgiven the battle and her defeat, and could
sense the mockery behind the messages. They did not
amuse her, and unless they reached her in public she never
gave them a chance to amuse anybody else.

She wiped the fine nib of her pen and said, "We're
ready for our coffee now. And we'd like the raisin cake."
Then she led the way from the kitchen, and Will, after
another unesay glance at Effie, followed her.

The passage was dim. The door which led into the
kitchen was always kept closed, except during the serving
of meals, for, as Harriet explained when making the rule,
guests didn't want to smell food the moment they arrived.
The dining-room door, opposite the one to the kitchen,
was allowed to remain ajar, and the little light which this
allowed, together with that which fell from a long low
window near the ceiling at the far end of the passage, was
the only mitigation of the gloom. Harriet's remarkable
hair shone like a pale light as she tripped along ahead
of Will, and as he stared at it and at her little neck, he
forgot Effie and resumed the train of thought which he
had followed while Harriet dealt with the jelly. Pity took
him. It was an old emotion, but still poignant enough to
make him lay a hand on the smooth shoulder beside him.
Harriet misinterpreted the affectionate gesture in a manner
typical of her.

"You're tired already, Father. I told you you should
have had another quiet day."

He let his hand drop heavily to his side. "I'm not at
all tired. Don't harp so, Harriet. One would think I'd
never been ill before."

"It's this place," said Harriet, with more vindictiveness
than she knew. "This constant east wind is enough to
make anyone ill. And as for you . . . well, you never had

two bouts in a month at Lammingham, did you?"

"No. But I stood more danger of dying by starvation," said Will in the wry tone in which both he and Myrtle often made statements which either annoyed or puzzled Harriet. She was annoyed now.

"Don't talk nonsense, Father. I know it was awkward after the coaches started on the new road . . . but we could have managed. We could have moved into some small house, and Myrtle and I could have taught school or something." Her grudge against the whole manner of her life, a hankering after a state of gentility which she perceived to be desirable but would never now attain, showed in her words. "You need rest and comfort, not a great barrack of a place like this to run."

She hoped that here her father would interpolate some suggestion, complimentary to herself, that he did not run the inn single-handed; but he made none. Instead, leaning in front of her to open the door outside which they had halted, he said, half amused, half irritated,

"For God's sake, Harriet, don't talk as though I were sixty. I'm only forty-five. Myrtle, here's Harriet still bemoaning that I didn't turn you into a school-marm."

Mrytle Oakley had been lying on the rug before the fire, a book between her propped elbows, her chin in her cupped hands. As her father and Harriet entered she rolled over and scrambled into sitting position, her feet tucked under her.

"A fine school-marm I would make," she said. She looked down at the book. She had put it on the hearth and settled to read just after Harriet had said briskly, "Well, I must go and seal down my jelly." That must be half an hour ago at least, and she had not read a word. She had been thinking, and thirty minutes must have passed like one. She looked up at the painted face of the wall clock, whose relentless hands and wagging pendulum ruled Harriet's day.

"It's later than I thought," she said.

"It always is," Harriet commented dryly. And that was quite true. Myrtle would have been the first to admit that time was always playing tricks on her, slipping away in such a fashion that although she did not, in a week, do as much as Harriet did in a day, she was always late, always behindhand with such tasks as did fall her lot, always being caught with her stockings in holes, with the hem of her skirt falling down for lack of a stitch, with the petticoat which she needed to wear not even sent to the week's wash. She sighed, and then, blinking her beautiful short-sighted eyes in Will's direction, inquired:

"How do you feel, now that you've been out? I think you look a lot better."

"I feel it," said Will. He straightened his shoulders and smiled at her across the hearth. It would never occur to Myrtle to chide him for going out without his top-coat, or for going out at all. If you did what you fancied, Myrtle would hope it would do you good; and then she would say that you looked better for doing it, and oddly enough, you would *feel* better. And it was the same when you were really ill. You couldn't fully depend on Myrtle for a single thing; she was far more likely to bring you a branch of spindleberry than a bowl of beef tea, for instance; but she would sit on the bed and talk, rout out some old joke and make you laugh, and then, with a kiss which was as warm and sweet as the touch of the sun-opened rose against your face, declare that you looked better and drift away.

The coffee which Harriet had ordered arrived. She poured it out with neat dispatch and then, with her own cup balanced in her hand, sat down on the end of the sofa which flanked the hearth on one side. Will dropped into the big chair, which was regarded as his special property, and looked at the two girls as he sipped the scalding liquid.

Their relationship was very obvious, he thought, noting the fact anew because he had just been thinking of their mental diversity. The shape of their heads was alike, the curve of their long slender necks, the build of their bodies, the line of their hands. But Myrtle had inherited his colouring, an unusual combination of dark hair and very blue eyes, while Harriet, taking after Clarissa, their mother, had that peculiar pale golden hair and grey eyes. But Clarissa's eyes had been more like Myrtle's, Will reflected, aware of the slight pain with which he always remembered his wife: they had had that same softness, the lingering affectionate look which, when he saw it occasionally in the eyes of his daughter, often inflicted a sharp stab. Harriet's glance was always direct and straight. When she looked at you she was really seeing you—and often in no very favourable light.

The sun, late in breaking through, was now high enough to top the brick wall of the garden and shine into the window of the Little Parlour. As though it had called her, Myrtle turned towards the slanting ray and said, happily:

"It's a lovely morning after all. Dick said it would rain. 'Three frosts and then a rain,' he said."

"Where did you see him? You haven't been out," said Harriet. It was one of the characteristics—a very awkward one at times—always to know, or to inquire, or to wonder, about the whereabouts of her family.

"I spoke to him out of the window, while I was dressing," Myrtle expained.

"I'm annoyed with that boy," Will said, handing his cup to Harriet for re-filling. "He took Katie out yesterday and lamed her."

"He would!" Harriet's voice was terse with dislike. "If I had my way there are two people about here I'd get rid of—Dick Stevens and Sarah Cross. A pair of saucy, lazy, good-for-nothings."

"Dick isn't lazy," Will was forced to say, "but he is aggravating. I've told him once before about it." He gave a rueful laugh. "Now I've threatened to thrash him if he does it again. And I expect he will. I meant it when I said it, too," he ended, as though he rather wondered how he could have made so rash a threat.

"I should think you could do it. He isn't very big," said Harriet literally. Both Myrtle and Will gave another of their unaccountable laughs.

"I *know* I could, but I'd feel a remarkable fool trying to," Will confessed. "Let's hope he won't."

"I wouldn't count on it," Myrtle's voice was teasing. "There's something so specially compelling in doing what you've been told not to." A fool thing to say, she told herself angrily. Damn! Had her father noticed?

"Much you know about that!" Harriet snapped. "I shouldn't think you've ever taken an order in your life."

It was a symptom of her devouring jealousy of Myrtle's beauty to imagine that Will favoured her. In fact, it was Harriet who had first drawn Myrtle's attention to the fact that from being an odd, leggy child, all hair and eyes, she had grown into a very pretty girl—"just because you're pretty father lets you do as you like," Harriet had said in the middle of one of their quarrels. And although the words had been spoken six or seven years ago, they still formed the basis of Harriet's belief. She could not accept the fact that Myrtle, who never interfered or tried to order anything, offered to Will's mild authority no occasion for the rebukes which came her own way. She would have resented it hotly if Will had suggested some positive action to Myrtle, since that might have constituted a threat to her own activity or authority, yet, since Myrtle's idleness gave no reason for Will to tell her *not* to do things, and he was not the man to tell her to do things, Harriet considered that she was much favoured and the occasions when she herself had been given an order—as in the case of the store-room keys—had rankled badly.

As Harriet spoke, Myrtle, whose cheeks were coloured by the consciousness of her slip, shot an eloquent glance at Will, who caught it and then looked away uncomfortably. He had no very happy memory, or wish to be re-

minded, of the one time when he had given Myrtle a most
definite order. It had been a moment when their whole
happy relationship had been in jeopardy; and although he
had noticed what Myrtle had said about orders compelling one to disobey them, he had dismissed his first
thought as unworthy and reflected that had Myrtle dis-
obeyed him she would have put more guard on her
tongue now. In the moment when their eyes had met
after Harriet's snapping statement, he had seen the furtive
gratitude in hers, and at that instant they were so like
Clarissa's that he had winced.

Myrtle *was* grateful. He hadn't told Harriet then. She
had so often wondered, and the thought that Harriet
knew had made her sick with secret shame. For while
Harriet was jealous of Myrtle's unmarred skin, Myrtle
was not jealous, exactly, but terribly conscious of Harriet's superiority as a character. It was not lost upon her
that everyone—including herself at times—regarded Harriet as the elder of the two. Harriet had all the virtues
which greater age is supposed to confer, common sense,
a level head, method, balance and resource. Harriet had,
and had had for years, the ability to make Myrtle feel
young, raw, silly and worthless. Harriet could cook; her
embroidery was perfection; if she put on a patch it was
plumb straight and sewn with well-nigh invisible stitches.
Harriet never forgot anything, was never late or untidy.
In fact, Harriet was marvellous in the eyes of Myrtle, with
whom time and all material things played unaccountable
tricks, so that though she sweated over a patch it was
always crooked, and though she followed Harriet's recipes
meticulously her dishes were often unrecognizable. She
would have given quite a lot if she could once have
astonished Harriet, once have gained a word or glance
of approbation. And lately the idea that Harriet might
have been told about her and Roger Moreton, that Will
might even have talked over the affair with his sensible
younger daughter, had caused Myrtle considerable shame.

She knew that she had only to say, "Look here, Harriet, has Father said anything to you about me and Roger Moreton?" and Harriet would have said yes or no without a second's hesitation, for that was Harriet's way. But although she had often herself to ask it; she doubted whether she could never bring herself to ask it; she doubted whether she could even have pronounced that name in Harriet's hearing. So she could only wonder and worry and watch for any sign which Harriet might give. And now Harriet had said that about taking orders, and she had said it with such innocence, such a lack of innuendo that Myrtle knew Will had not said a word. So she shot him a glance of swimming gratitude, an emotion which, being genuine and heartfelt, was rapidly followed by scorching shame.

Will had dealt so gently with her, had seemed to share her embarrassment, had explained where another parent would have stormed; and he had not told Harriet; nor had he given any sign of thinking her foolish or immodest. Best of all, he had not restricted by a question or a glance her complete liberty of movement. And how had she repaid this delicacy, this affection, this trust? By the basest deceit. You couldn't deny it or whittle it down. It was deceit, of the grossest order. Hadn't she just thought "Best of all . . ." thereby implying that the kindest aspect of his treatment was the opportunity he gave her for deceiving him further? Could perfidy sink lower?

The vivid colour deepened in her clear cheeks. She imagined that Will was watching her, and, unable to meet his eyes, stared at the fire. She felt the hot blush reach the very tips of her ears. She couldn't bear it. She must escape, or she would cry, or go mad. Her voice sounded so unreal when she spoke that she thought both her hearers would notice it and exclaim, but they showed no sign of hearing anything odd about her, "I'm going to get some flowers." She went across the room to the bureau which stood between the two windows and rummaged in one of the drawers which was exclusively hers. With her back to her father she felt better, the hot flush died away; she had command of her eyes again. After a moment she could turn to Harriet and ask, "May I borrow your scissors, Harriet? I seem to have lost mine."

Harriet gave a kind of snort. Myrtle so often seemed to have lost things, which meant that she had put them down carelessly, or searched for them unthoroughly. She said, with blunt frankness, but not unkindly, "No, you may *not*. I don't want my scissors ruined. Your own are on the kitchen dresser, quite red with rust from all that wet stuff you brought in for Father." Harriet was pleased, as she always was, when, through her acute observation or retentive memory, she could extricate Myrtle or Will from some muddle of their own making.

"Oh, thank you," said Myrtle, genuinely grateful. "One day I'll do something for you, Sister."

She stood by the window, in the direct light of the slanting sunbeam. And the glow, which might have been so unkind to less youthful or perfect beauty, caught her cheeks, where the fading carnation of her blush lay on the smooth ivory skin, and her hair, wakening a multitude of colours in its cloudy blackness, and the vivid blue of her eyes. The impulse to escape, which had driven her to her feet, was over, and she stood for a moment looking out at the green lawn and the rusty gold of the beech trees and the pure duck's egg blue of the autumn sky. Her lips parted with pleasure, half derived from what she saw, and half from her thought. One day, if things went well, what might she not do for Harriet?

She could have her to stay for long, long holidays, help her to gratify her passion for costly clothes; perhaps even find something in London, where they knew everything, which would cure her face. And Harriet's scorn would turn to gratitude, and there would be between them the sweet companionship which there should be, between sisters, as there had been in the years long past when they were children together, before Harriet's trouble had turned her cold and hard.

Harriet was watching Myrtle; had seen the sun touch her, and the expression of dreamy pleasure set the final seal of her beauty. The old fangs of envy, sharpened, not blunted by custom, tore at Harriet's soul. She said—forgetting the days when, as the ugly little sister, she had hung about the fringes of a group of merry children, with Myrtle in the centre, and waited with passionate longing for Myrtle's unfailing gesture of inclusion, "I'll have Sister on my side," "Sister can be the fairy godmother," "Sister and I will hide from the rest of you," using the name which had been a pledge then, of a unity rooted in the blood, superceding all other claims—"You can do something for me now, Myrtle. Stop using that stupid name. You might remember that we are grown up now—at least, I have."

"I'm sorry," said Myrtle in a flat hurt voice. "I won't use it again."

She went out of the parlour. Harriet collected the coffee cups and the cake and piled the tray. Will, with a small, almost inaudible sigh, reached for his pipe and began to fill it. He was always pained by any evidence of friction between the girls, though generally he ignored it. On nine occasions out of ten his natural impulse was to side with Myrtle, which would only make matters worse, since it would confirm Harriet's conviction that Myrtle was his favourite. And when, as was often the case, Harriet's attacks upon Myrtle were due to the latter's untidiness and forgetfulness, he had another cause for silence, feeling himself rebuked as well, for he, too, was untidy and forgetful. But this morning, as he saw Myrtle's expression of pleasure change to the hurt of a snubbed puppy, and remembered how often of late Harriet had made some similar unkind and crushing reply to an innocent remark, he felt driven to protest. So, looking down at his pipe and speaking as casually as he could, he said gently:

"Do you find that name so offensive, Harriet? After all, you both call me Father, which is the equivalent, in my case."

"I find it intensely irritating," said Harriet, thinking—that's right, side with her, as you always do, as any man would. "It's all part of that ridiculous childish pose, like never remembering anything and calling you Daddy, and Mrs. Sharman, Sharry. You'd think she was twelve instead of twenty-two. Is she never to grow up?"

"In some ways, I hope not. There are plenty of grown up people in the world, Harriet, but few enough, too few I often think, like Myrtle. And I think the word pose is misapplied; she is, on the contrary, the most natural girl you would find. Isn't that true?"

"In a way, I suppose," admitted Harriet, with grudging justice. "If you call leaning half-dressed out of her window and shouting to the boys in the yard, natural behaviour. All the same, I have a name of my own and prefer to be called by it. As for the question of calling you Father, I often think that is deplorable."

The pipe, which Will had placed in his mouth and upon which he was making an experimental draw, jerked sharply.

"Why?"

"Well, it sounds as though being a father—which, after all, is only an incidental thing—was the most important. After all, you had a name before you had us . . ." She paused and her hands fluttered in a baffled, unconscious, beautiful gesture. "You know what I mean. I'm not clever with words, like you and Myrtle." She managed to inject the statement with uncomplimentary meaning, as though to be clever with words inferred crass stupidity in every other direction. She lifted the tray in a manner which showed that she had had enough of this particular discussion.

"All the same," said Will gently, out of the first blue cloud, "childishness is perhaps the one fault which should be checked kindly. Don't you think so?"

Harriet, with tightened lips, gave him a glance, lifted the tray and opened the door. She could not trust herself to speak. Always, always it was the same. Myrtle and her father were leagued together. Just because Myrtle was pretty she could be as careless and stupid and feather-brained as she liked; he would always support her. Whereas she, Harriet, could work her fingers to the bone, plan, contrive and organize until she was sick of the thought of food, and charges and room numbers, and candlesticks and keys, and it all went for nothing; just because her face was scarred. What would have happened here in the last few days if she, Harriet, had been as blessedly childish and blissfully natural as Myrtle? The place would have been chaotic. Why, when Myrtle went into the kitchen nobody took a scrap of notice, except to look up and smile and make some silly joke. One day Harriet would leave the pair, Will and Myrtle together, and see how they fared *then*.

But cold reason followed hard upon the hot spell of anger. How could she leave? Where could she go? No one would ever marry her; and who would employ her? She was doomed, damned, finished. Intelligence, ability, con-scientiousness and energy were all as nothing unless ac-companied by a degree of comeliness. That was the rule of the world, and the most unfair rule ever made. Better, far better never to have been born than to be marred like this. With whirling brain and breaking heart, Harriet tripped into the kitchen and gave everybody there a very bad half-hour.

Will, left to himself, smoked his pipe without enjoy-ment. He had, he felt, as usual, made matters worse by interfering. Better to have held his tongue. After all, Myrtle's hurt would have been healed by now, it was momentary, not concerned with essentials; whereas Har-riet's glance, flung at him without a word, had been eloquent of all the things she was too proud to say. Poor

Harriet; poor, poor girl! He would have given anything
to have saved her. He realized, as Harriet would never
have given him credit for realizing, that she was the last
woman in the world to bear with patience and fortitude
such a dire affliction. Harriet was born to be a wife and
mother. That had shown when, even as a little girl, she
had played with her dolls, pretended to keep house, and
begged to be allowed to cook. He could remember one in-
dulgent old woman in the kitchen at Lammingham, setting Harriet on a chair and letting her knead bread
in the big bowl that she could not reach from the floor.
If only Harriet had been just a little less ugly. . . .
Given a normal outlet for her instincts she would
have been such a happy, busy, efficient housewife,
such a careful, good mother. Dissipated among the needs
of a vigorous family her tendency to be dictatorial would
have been unnoticed, used in its proper sphere her in-
quisitiveness would not have been irksome. And—and this
was the first time that the thought had struck him—if one
girl must be irretrievably married, it would have been better
for Myrtle to be the one. The father in him, and the man,
shuddered before the thought of Myrtle's loveliness
quenched, but it was true, none the less. Myrtle had the
more pliant nature; she was interested in more things.
Scarred and pocked she could still have read her books,
gathered her nosegays, petted her animals, walked in the
woods and enjoyed the weather.

Dimly, and yet certainly, Will saw that what happened
to Myrtle would never affect her so completely as what
had happened to Harriet had affected her; she had more
ressources within herself. Harriet, denied the normal possessions of husband, home and children, had nothing left
. . . except the inn, which she hated even as she served it,
and her family, which she had outgrown. Poor Harriet!
He must remember in future, never to say anything that
might bring that look to her eyes. Many people must needs
love Myrtle. Harriet had only herself.

Myrtle had forgotten Harriet completely. The scissors were on the kitchen dresser, but they were no longer red with rust; for Mrs. Sharman, in the act of putting away the quince jelly, had noticed them and given them a brisk rub with bath-brick. In common with the rest of the staff at the *Fleece,* Mrs. Sharman liked Myrtle, who never thought of inspecting china for traces of bad washing-up, or corners for dust, or the ash-pit for ill-sifted cinders, or the pantry for left-over food to be economically and troublesomely recooked. Yet Harriet, in reflecting that Myrtle, left alone with the staff, would have been very badly served, had hit upon a cynical, if cogent truth. Little spontaneous actions of goodwill—such as the cleaning of the rusty scissors—were, indeed, often forthcoming, but if time pressed and one room had to be neglected, one bed given slovenly treatment, it was always Myrtle's room, Myrtle's bed. And if some chance had removed Will, who made up for his easy-going manner by sudden demands and flashes of irritability, and Harriet, who demanded good service always, Myrtle would have found herself starving in a welter of dirt and muddle, surrounded by workers whose affection for her did not prevent them from taking advantage of the very quality that endeared her to them.

She thanked the cook profusely, took the scissors and made for the back door. She could easily reach the garden through the gate from the yard, and she could look in at the stable on her way. Roger had said, "I'll leave him there until I come home again. It'll be about a fortnight. Then I'll either fetch him or send for him, and you'll know that I'll be in the loft at nine o'clock the same night. Will that do?"

It was one of several means of secret communications which had been made necessary by Will's embargo; and despite occasional pangs of shame, such as she had just experienced in the Little Parlour, Myrtle had found that they gave zest to the affair. Secret meetings, secret signs, these were the trappings of romantic love through all the

world, through all time. Myrtle's heart beat faster as she
leaned over the half door of the stable and peered at the
stall from which, for a fortnight, Roger's grey horse had
gazed at her. This morning no long grey head poked out,
and closer inspection showed that the stall was empty
and had already been cleaned. Myrtle stood still for a
moment with a great warm wave, part excitement, part
sensuous anticipation, washing through her body, melting
her bones. Then Dick Stevens came whistling out of a
far stall and, seeing her, paused and said, "Miss Myrtle,
would you give the master a message for me? Tell him
Mr. Moreton's man came for the grey the minnit he'd
gone. Master told me to take it up to the Hall and take the
bill, too. But the man wouldn't wait for the bill, he said
Mr. Roger woon't be home till later on today, but he'd
sent a message to fetch the horse. I hope I did right to let
it go?"

"Oh, yes, that's all right, Dick." Myrtle bestowed a
dazzling smile on the boy and turned away quickly. She
wanted to be alone to savour the moment's joy.

The yard was quieter now, only two men stood by the
water trough while their teams drank from it. They stared,
and a sheep-dog dashed out from under one of the wagons,
snapping and snarling as Myrtle came near. But she
noticed neither the men nor the dog. Her mind was far
away on the London road, along which, at this moment,
a young man was travelling. Her face was set this way, and
every moment, every lift of his horse's hoofs, every beat
of her own heart, brought him nearer. And he had remembered to give her the sign. Once or twice lately their
carefully arranged plans had gone wrong through some
omission on his part; and although he had sworn that
Myrtle had made the mistake she was convinced that it
was not so. Over many things she might be vague and un-
reliable, but when Roger named the day of their next
meeting she saw that day, both as a name and as twenty-
four hours, a visible, actual *thing*, with a kind of light on

it, and music in it, a special chosen sacred day beyond all possibility of mistake or confusion. So she was sure—though without rancour—that on those other occasions it had been Roger who had failed; but this time he had not failed. And tonight at nine o'clock they would be together again.

Now and again when she was thinking about herself and Harriet, she had perceived that part of Harriet's power lay in the fact that she was a whole person, single-eyed, single-minded. No part of Harriet ever stood afar off and criticized Harriet, or pointed out that there was a possibility that she was wrong, or that there was another person's point of view to consider. Myrtle envied her sister this unity of mind. For within herself she knew that there dwelt a voice which nagged and scolded, and presented her with the other person's point of view so vividly that when her shoes were ill-cleaned she would feel that Sam, the back-house boy, had been short of time, or not feeling well; so vividly that she knew all about Harriet's unhappiness over her face; so vividly that she had put up a piteously feeble fight when Will attacked her upon the subject of Roger. The inner voice—it was hardly conscience, since it did not concern itself much with right and wrong—chose this moment, as she let herself through the wooden gate into the sunny garden, to ask how she would feel were she Will, and were her daughter behaving as she was behaving. Suppose, asked the voice, everything went well this evening and Roger made her the definite proposal for which she hoped. Then how would she hide the fact that they had been meeting secretly? And how would Will feel about that? Or, suppose again, that was only another evening, sweet, torturing and abortive like the last they had spent together; was it to go on, dragging along down the weeks and months, involving her in so much deception that her whole life was a lie? You'll probably end, said the detached cold part of her mind, by being seduced in a hay-loft. That'll be a nice thing to remember, won't it? Even if nothing worse than a memory results.

The main part of her mind wriggled uncomfortably under the inquisition; but it had its arguments ready, facile, wellworn arguments. Roger loved her, she was sure of that. Only, of course it was very awkward for him, his people were wealthy and snobbish, they would not take kindly to the idea of his marrying Myrtle Oakley from the *Fleece*. But something would happen. At the very worst he would marry her and face the parental wrath, and once his parents had seen her they would realize that she was not just a common ignorant girl from an inn.

They could see that now, suggested the carping fragment of her consciousness, if only you ended this hole-and-corner business.

Then suddenly the two parts fused, and with unusual force of mind she determined that tonight should see the last of the secrecy. She wouldn't go on like this, deceiving Will and feeling like a leper. She'd go to the loft, but she wouldn't kiss Roger, nor should he touch her until they had come to some understanding.

Braced and cheered by this determination—which she had been making at intervals through the summer—she looked about the garden, feeling the tang in the air and the sense of well-being within herself of which Will, too, had been conscious. After all, she thought, Will would forgive her for meeting Roger if he could point out that the meetings had achieved their object. And although she hated deceiving him . . . well, he just didn't understand. He was old, and had forgotten, if he had ever known, how it felt to be so much in love with a person that the mere mention of his name upon a casual tongue could send strange hot currents through your blood. And could any reasonable man think by an order, however delicately given, to cure your madness, assuage your longing, lift you out of thraldom? Of course not.

But tonight should be decisive. Meantime the Michaelmas daisies stood bushy, heavy-blossomed, drenched with

dampness. The next frost would reach their sheltered corner and nip them off; but at the moment the sun was
quite warm on the red wall. And there, high up among
the glossy greeny-brown foliage were three late rosebuds,
all the sweeter for the touch of brown on the edges of
their pink petals. With a feeling of certainty that all must
go well on such a morning, Myrtle reached up and snipped
off the flowers. She would put them in a tiny vase and
stand it on Harriet's chest of drawers. Even Harriet must
love them. Harriet was rather unenthusiastic about Myrtle's floral offerings, and Myrtle thought that this was
because she sometimes, in setting them into place, spilled
drops of water or dew or rain on to Harriet's meticulously
polished furniture.

The odd thing was that Harriet, too, thought that was
the reason why she disliked flowers. Actually some dark
recess of her mind cherished a resentment against them
because their petals were smooth and flawless. Smooth and
flawless like the cheek of a six-years-old child before
damnation overtook her.

AFTERNOON

The Horseman

The two young gentlemen came out of the little wayside tavern where for an hour they had been drinking and gossiping and exchanging facetious remarks with the serving girl, and stood for a moment, staring at the rain. Then, moving side by side, they went to the hitching rail and untethered their horses. The shorter of the two, a darkfaced, merry-eyed fellow, suddenly smote his friend a heavy blow on the shoulder and said, in a rallying tone, "Cheer up, old man. One would think you were going to your hanging."

Young Mr. Moreton twitched savagely at his bridle.

"It's all very well for you to laugh," he said peevishly. "Change places with me, and *I'll* laugh my head off."

"Well, I dunno," said young Mr. Savile, more seriously. "Lots of fellows would change with you gladly. Thirty thousand isn't to be sneezed at, specially in these hard times. And after all, as they go, *as* they go, she's not bad."

"As they go," Roger Moreton repeated crossly. "As they go where? How'd you like to go to bed with her, Steve? Ask yourself that?"

Young Mr. Savile looked as much put out as his naturally cheerful cast of countenance would allow.

"The thing is, old man, that you can't have *everything* in this world. And you don't get thirty thousand quid for hopping into bed with your fancy. The wise man earns his money where he can and spends it where he chooses. And I don't see that you've made such a bad bargain."

"I didn't make it."

"Oh, well, of course if you'd sooner sit in the Fleet with only a few lousy trollops for company, you should have said so sooner. After all, I didn't gallop up to you and say I'd found you a raving beauty and an heiress into the bargain. You came to me and said that if you couldn't find a rich wife you were sunk. And I found you Miss Wilson. Seems to me you should be damned grateful."

Roger Moreton stared malevolently at the steadily falling rain. "I am grateful," he said, "in a way. But now that it comes to the point, and I know that she'll be sitting there when I get home, and all my blasted family running round looking like Cheshire cats. . . . It's no good, Steve, I can't do it. I'm coming back with you. I'll go and stay at Phiz's place. That'll put the duns off the scent for a bit until I have time to look around."

He jerked his horse's head round, away from Fulsham, and laid his hand on the saddle, about to mount. Young Mr. Savile smote him sharply on the elbow.

"Don't be a—fool," he said. "Phiz ain't a charity institution. Think what you owe him already. What's the good of looking round London when your pocket is empty?"

The ill-placed earnestness on his brown face lightened as he thought of a clinching argument. "Besides, what about your rustic charmer? She's waiting for you, ain't she? Come on, now, old man. Get along to Fulsham, give one wench a chaste kiss and the other whatever she's in mind for, and thank your lucky stars and your old friend Steve for arranging everything so pretty."

"Blast!" said young Mr. Moreton. "Yes, I've got to see Myrtle."

"That's right," said Steve, mounting nimbly, as though to cut short the argument. "And listen. I shall go back and bruit it abroad that you're engaged to marry Miss Wilson. That'll ensure all your creditors a good night's rest."

"Damn their eyes!" said young Mr. Moreton, hating all

the erstwhile servile and obliging people who had fed and housed and clothed and mounted him for a considerable space of time. "All right, Steve. I'll see you on Thursday."

"The worst will be over then, old man." He waved his arm and was gone, amidst a shower of mud drops from his horse's hoofs, eager to make his escape before his friend could again change his mind and suggest accompanying him.

Old Squire Moreton, back in his Fulsham manor, often said the most uncomplimentary things about young Mr. Moreton's friends and acquaintances in London. He would have been very considerably surprised to learn that his son's friends were as much concerned by his financial straits, and as anxious to see him safely settled, as he was himself. And his surprise would have been tinged with distaste could he have known that the impending betrothal to Miss Wilson, which he viewed with such relief and complacency, was entirely due to the guile and hard work of the, in his bigoted opinon, arch-rogue Steve Savile. That idle, careless young gentleman had, indeed, put more energy into getting Roger to meet Miss Wilson, and to be polite to her dull, wealthy old father, than he had ever put into a task before. And that was because, in common with the rest of Roger's friends, he was a victim to his personal charm and physical attractiveness, and, at the same time, tired to death of lending him money, of helping him to evade his creditors, of paying two shares of their mutual expenses, and listening to his interminable complaints about his father's parsimony.

The Squire knew nothing of Steve's back-stage activity; he only knew that after a long period of wild philandering and unwarranted extravagance and generally unsatisfactory behaviour, Roger appeared at last to be both sensible and fortunate that Miss Wilson and her father be asked to stay at the Hall; and at the moment when Roger was making his last futile gesture of rebellion, his father, his mother and his four rather dreary sisters, after a spell of frantic activity designed to put the best face possible upon the rather decayed splendour of the Hall, were nervously awaiting the arrival of their guests. And there was some truth in Roger's savage remark about Cheshire cats, for the whole of the Moreton family, from the Squire down to the third footman, whose wages had been owing for half a year, were rather like cats, who, after a long diet of skim milk, have at last sighted a brimming bowl of cream.

Steve Savile, riding back towards Barton Mills, where he had arranged his lodging (and also his bedfellow), was well satisfied with himself. He considered that he had given final, almost redundant proof of his devotion in riding, on this filthy afternoon, so far towards Fulsham. And he was not perturbed by Roger's awkward spurt; that was only a little nervous symptom, such as was often seen in good jumpers who would shy at the fence and then take it perfectly. He was quite sure that when he saw Roger again on Thursday everything would be all right and the charm of money already exerting its spell.

But young Mr. Moreton, scowling as he forged ahead through the rain and the mire, was not sure about anything. He had never been so undecided or so miserable in his life; he had never before been lonely. Now, even in the centre of his circle, he moved alone, remote, apart, separated from his friends by virtue of an experience which he knew they could never share or understand. He knew that from the way they talked. Steve for instance, hitherto such a kindred spirit, had in the last few days constantly repeated, in varying and picturesque phrases, the old adage about all women being the same in the dark. He had also, having wormed out of Roger in an unguarded moment, a bare and falsely light-hearted confession of his interest in Myrtle, made constant references to the rustic charmer, the Fulsham nymph and Roger's bucolic romance. And every word showed how far, how very far, he was from understanding what had happened to his friend. And, of course, you couldn't attempt to explain it all, and so risk scorn and mockery, you had to go on pretending that Myrtle was only just another passing fancy, just the girl from the local inn, just a partner for another lecherous little interlude.

And wasn't it the very devil that you should wish that Steve were right? Especially just now, when what you had known all along to be your one hope of salvation—a wealthy, infatuated wife—was within your reach. Wasn't it hell's own luck that at this moment the very thought of any other woman was hideously repulsive to you, and the one thing you wanted was to marry Myrtle Oakley and make a clean job of it?

As his horse plunged into the mud of the old low road that led into Slough Lane, young Mr. Moreton cursed the evening when, arriving in Fulsham late and knowing that nothing but cold meat and reproaches awaited him at the Hall, he had turned in at the *Fleece* in search of food and Dutch courage, and seen Myrtle, and lost both his heart and his head.

God! If only he liked he could have made a smashing retort to Steve's light-hearted cliches about the similarity of women. Why, Myrtle was like nobody on earth: and not, he thought angrily, just because she was the loveliest, most desirable thing he had ever set eyes on, but because she was also the most exasperating, unpredictable, ridiculous creature, at once amorous and cold-blooded, feather-brained and shrewd, yielding and calculating, lovable and infuriating. And tonight, after the family reunion, and the formal dinner with Miss Wilson looking at him yearningly, and all his damned family watching and grinning, he was going to meet Myrtle at nine o'clock in the hay-loft. And what the hell was he going to say to her? With a sudden hot throb of the blood he remembered a moment or two during their last meeting. He'd never been so shaken in his life. What had been a simple pleasure, as ordinary as eating and drinking, had suddenly become a dark, torturing necessity, a pivot upon which everything else in the world hinged.

Deep in his libidinous and yet romantic reverie he reached the mouth of Slough Lane, and passed, with only perfunctory attention, the coach which had stuck in the mud. Two female passengers stood on the bank, looking as miserable and bedraggled as hens in the rain. The male passengers were heaving and hauling; the straining horses smoked as they laboured and struggled under the lash of the coachman's whip. Just as Roger drew level with it the wheels, with a sucking sound, began to move in the gluey mud and the vehicle, slowly straightening itself, lurched forward. With the agility of a monkey the driver scrambled into his seat, shouting as he did so, "Get aboard, can't stop or she'll settle again." The passengers, with little runs and skips and hops, piled into the coach— all except one, a bent, decrepit-looking old man in sombre clothing and a wide Quaker hat. The last passenger to mount swung for a second in the doorway and shouted something to the old man, who shook his head and began to plod forward through the puddles. The last passenger disappeared inside and slammed the door. Driving his heel into his horse, Roger rode forward in order to enter the narrow lane ahead of the coach.

Slough Lane, Foxley Heath, Hunter's Corner, the crossroads where the *Fleece* reared its dark bulk, and then the Hall gates. He was almost home now. And at the thought of home and the welcome—so different from those which he had known of late—which awaited him, Roger's fair handsome young face darkened and hardened into lines of passionate obstinacy. He looked like a spoiled child, which at heart he was; for, born late to parents who had begun to despair of an heir, born with great physical beauty and high animal spirts, worshipped by his sisters, feared by his nurses and governesses and tutors, and then adored by a wide circle of friends, he had, in all his twenty-four years, hardly known the thwarting of a wish.

Lately, indeed, his father, harassed by his own financial trouble, had grown parsimonious and testy, given to loud expressions of a wish that his heir might take more interest in his ancestral acres and less in the Newmarket races and the gaieties of Town. Yet even this uncomfortable period had been swiftly brought to a close by Steve's ingenuity and persistence, and if young Mr. Moreton did what was expected of him and pledged himself to Miss Wilson and her thirty thousand pounds, he need never fear the Fleet again. His desperate parent had actually allowed him to languish in the gaol's hideous precincts for a week during the last summer, hoping it would teach him a lesson. And in a way it had, for it made him express the wish for a wealthy wife to Steve, and it had very helpfully paved the way for Miss Wilson when Steve found her. Indeed, it seemed that after all there was one thing and one thing only which young Mr. Moreton could not attain just for wishing for it, and that was the full possession of Myrtle Oakley. And then that damned fool Steve said . . . Roger's thoughts had completed the full circle and set off on the same track again.

The Chaise

Although his dream form had for five months figured in her worst nightmare, Julia Foxe did not recognize John Savory until, at her order, her driver had halted beside the old man, and she leaned forward and asked, "Wouldn't you like to ride?" Then, as he turned his head, pleased and surprised, and said, "Thank thee. It would be a great help," he was dismayed to see that the pleasant look on her pretty pale face was changing into an expression of horror and distaste. Why, he wondered, hesitating for a moment to enter the vehicle. Surely she could have seen from his back that he was neither young nor handsome,

had she been hoping for such a companion. Julia controlled herself quickly and said with an effort:

"It's Mr. Savory, isn't it? I don't expect you remember
me, do you? But do get in. It's a very wet day for walking."

She moved the small valise from the seat beside her,
drew her full black skirt into closer folds, and made room
for him. The chaise moved off again through the sticky
yellow clay of Slough Lane. The old man turned sideways
and studied his companion. His eyes were not what they
were, and lately his memory had been treacherous; but
suddenly as he peered at the small face, so white between
the black sealskin of the little cape and the black brim of
the plain hat, he remembered seeing the woman before
somewhere. And she had been crying . . . and there was a
child, or children, connected with it somewhere. Also,
very vaguely at the back of his mind, he had a picture of
his friend Joseph Steadman's barn. But the vital link was
missing. His failure to remember showed on his face and
he said:

"I'm sorry."

"I'm from Norwich," said Julia. "Mrs. Foxe. Julia
Foxe"

She thought sickly, as soon as she had spoken, that was
a mistake. He won't remember me unless I mention the
children, and I would rather not. Why didn't I just take
him in and not bother to mention that we had met before?

"I'm sorry," the old man said again. "Thee must forgive
me. From Norwich, too."

"Yes," said Julia gently. "I helped you, last May, with
the mill children in Mr. Steadman's barn."

"Ah!" There was relief in the sound. Of course, he
remembered now. This was the young woman who had
come with Susan Coke to feed and wash and clothe those
poor little victims of an iniquitous system. And that was
why he had remembered tears. She had been so appalled,
poor creature, that she had wept without ceasing; and

someone had said, "Mrs. Foxe might as well go home for
all the use she is." And Susan Coke had replied, "She has
a tender heart." And the other woman had jerked out,
"Something more than a tender heart is needed on a job
like this." Oh, yes, he remembered her now.

They were no longer alone in the comfortable little
carriage. Both the old man, who had known and fought
evil all his life, and the young woman whose first experience of it had broken her heart, saw, as they stared ahead
of them, those doomed children, paupers, used and tortured for the sake of the labour of their poor hands,
and then, when the mill had failed, driven off, brutally
turned adrift, who, in a little pack, like pariah dogs, had
followed the main road into Norwich and arrived there
one bright May morning when the weather, the flowers
in the gardens, the green budding trees, and the singing
birds had all been suggestive of the goodness of God. They
moved again, stunted, twisted, starved, through the memories of John Savory and Julia, just as they moved, night
after night, through the dreams that haunted the woman's
troubled sleep.

As though the words were being ground from her she
asked:

"Did you find homes for them? I could not come after
the first week. My own child was ill."

"Homes for some. Work for others. Seven died."

"Eight," said Julia in a strained, tormented voice.
"Eight. My little boy died, too." The pitifully thin veil of
politeness and normal social intercourse which had, after
that first glance, obscured the half-demented horror of
her eyes, fell away. She stared at the old Quaker, who,
schooled in experience of misery as he was, thought that
he had never seen a human face so wrenched with misery.

"He died," she repeated. "He died as those children
died. He was all I had. And I carried death to him, on my
hands, in my hair, on my breath. No, it was worse than
that. I carried death to him in my soul, John Savory, on

the morning when I went from that place. I killed him
with my mind. Shall I tell you what I thought as I took
him in my lap and put my arms round him and pressed
his smooth little face to mine. I thought that I had been
wrong to bring him into a world where such a thing could
happen to other little children, every one of whom had
been a baby, too, a little helpless precious child, ready to
laugh and crow and stretch its hands towards those who
tended it . . . just as Charlie reached his hands to me.
Such little dimpled hands, so trusting. And several of those
little ones had lost their fingers. I was so frightened, I
thought, suppose I died, and the investments failed, and all
Charlie's uncles and aunts died, too . . . then he'd be a
pauper child for somebody to work and starve and beat
and then turn adrift when they had no further use for him.
Only his money and his friends could save him. God
wouldn't. And I'd begun to teach him to say a little prayer
as soon as he could speak. I thought perhaps some of
those little children had been taught that very prayer. And
how had God answered it? So I carried death, though I
had washed and changed my clothes on account of the
sickness among those other children. But I thought that
this wasn't a fit world for such a rare delicate precious
thing as my little boy . . . and that thought was death
for him."

John Savory was seventy years old. He had, being a
philanthropist and a reformer, a vast and sorry knowledge
of evil in action. But he knew, too, knew with his very
blood, that the end was not yet; that this world where
cruelty and avarice and injustice abounded, was not the
only one. There was a Supreme Power, and it was good.
That was the core of his belief, and in that belief he had
lived and laboured. But for a moment or two after Julia's
outburst he sat silent. This woman was very sick of mind.
No out-pouring of sympathy, however genuine, no speci-
ous argument, no dry reiteration of belief could reach the

heart of such despair. So he was silent for a time. Then he reached out one of his hands, dry, gnarled, discoloured, an old man's hand, and laid it gently over hers which were clenched together in her lap.

"Listen . . ." he said.

The Coach

The chaise had followed the coach for a couple of miles, unable to pass on account of the narrowness of the road. Slough Lane was a track of great antiquity, the traffic of years had worn it so low that now the head of a mounted man barely topped its muddy banks. At infrequent intervals along its three-mile stretch the banks were broken by tracks that led off to remote homesteads or fields, and when conveyances met in the lane it was an unwritten law that the one which had most recently passed such opening, must back away and give the other passage. But for vehicles going in the same direction, there was no such rule. The first one through the lane's mouth at either end held the road until the farther end was reached.

At the end nearer the *Fleece* (still some miles away) Slough Lane rose steeply to debouch upon Foxley Heath, a place where coachmen whipped up their horses and cautious men, riding alone, loosened their pistols in their holsters. There had been robberies innumerable, and a fair share of murders done on this lonely stretch, whence a highwayman might swoop from any direction, hold up his victim, and be gone again towards any point of the compass.

The coachman was sorry that here, where the road gained the open, he would lose the company of the chaise, whose bright bay gelding, full of oats and impatient of the three-mile restraint would quickly leave the lumbering vehicle and its labouring team behind.

As the lighter vehicle swooped out in an arc, moved alongside for a moment, and then pulled ahead, the coachman looked at it with interest, then, wiping a spatter of mud from his cheek with his cuff, he said to his guard, "Well, I'll be damned! Did yer see that?"

"Naw," said the guard, who had not troubled to glance at the chaise. "What wuz ut?"

"Yon cranky old Quaker, picked up in that dandy turn out. He'll get to the *Fleece* afore us arter all." He spat copiously and shifted his quid. "Interfering old bastard. Let *him* try keeping to our time and see how he'd git on. He wholly riled me, George. I damn near put the whip acrost *him* the last time. Lucky I dint, maybe. He seem to hev fine friends."

"More likely some koindhearted folks took pity on the ould codger nading along in the rain," the guard suggested. "Arter all, he looked pretty harmless." He did not add that he himself had been a little sorry when he saw John Savory set down at the far end of Slough Lane, with the rain falling in torrents, the afternoon already growing overcast, and a good ten miles between him and the nearest house.

"Garn!" said the coachman, spitting again. "Noobuddy in their senses'd pick up a stranger whatever they looked like; not so near to Foxley. Why that Quaker business is just the sorta trick Jemmy Mace'd delight in. Noo, I tell you what. I reckon the owd chap knew he'd got a pal behind him, don't he woon't a bin so free with his 'I'd sooner walk than see the poor beasts suffer.' Poor beasts! What about us?"

He lifted his hat and swished it fiercely through the air over the side of his seat to free it from the weight of accumulated water. Then, replacing it, he shouted to his horses and flashed out with the long throng of his whip. Damnation to this rain, he thought. Coming like that after a perfect morning. He wouldn't have stopped so long at Ipswich *White Horse* if he hadn't made such good time earlier in the day, and been almost certain of equally good speed through the afternoon. How could you get along with the bloody roads just like porridge?

And at the far end of that blasted lane that cranky old fool must pipe up about being merciful to his horses! A nice fool he'd have looked if he'd left the coach in the bog because he wouldn't use his whip. As it was he'd have a job to get to the *Fleece* before the dead dark. Partly it was the fault of the near wheeler; it'd given out quite a bit before the bog in Slough Lane. This'd be its last journey he doubted. Might as well get the last ounce out of it. He raised the whip again.

Within the coach two of the corner passengers had also noted that the old man who had left the coach a little while before had not been left to foot it through the rain and the mire. One of them, a man to whom every other person in the coach had taken an unaccountable, instinctive dislike, had said with a titter:

"Ah, maybe the old chap wasn't such a fool. He's in good company now."

There were two women in the coach, one young and anaemic looking, one middle-aged, but giving the impression that she still cared for her appearance with some earnestness. As he spoke the words "good company now," the man in the corner let his eyes slide between their pouched lids to include both women in his glance, and somehow managed to imply that they were not good company now, never had been, and would never be.

Nobody made any reply to his remark. All the way from Ipswich he had been saying things in his peculiar high-pitched and yet broken-sounding voice, but by one of those mutual impulses which sometimes inspire a group of widely varied persons, all the other passengers had ignored him. There was something about him, about his doughy fatness, his huddled clothes, which though obviously new were very dirty, about his tittering laugh and restless shifty eyes, which repulsed everyone in some degree. Even the man with the handsome scarred face who sat next him, and who usually missed no opportunity for talk, ignored the fat man as far as possible.

That their late companion had been picked up by the chaise which had just flashed past was, however, gathered from Jonathan Smail's remark, and received with interest or pleasure according to the listener's nature. When he had refused to enter the coach again after its struggle with the treacly, axle-deep mud, and the vehicle had lumbered away leaving him, a stooping lonely figure between the high banks of the lane, he had done what he would have been glad to do, made everyone in the coach think a little and examine his own conscience. The thoughts had been very varied. "Nobody likes a horse better than I do, but that is carrying sentiment too far." "I don't feel that way myself, but if I did I'd do the same." "I agree with him, and I ought by right to be there trudging beside him." The reaction which was conspicuously absent was amusement, and the gap between Jonathan Smail and the other passengers widened when he laughed, a giggling high-pitched laugh with something of uneasiness behind it.

"Walk because a horse is whipped!" he cried. "That's the latest! He ought to have been where I have. Why, I've seen old men harnessed to ploughs instead of donkeys in the fields and beaten with canes till the blood ran down to their feet."

The plain young woman gave a scream, and as much colour as was native to the cheek of the elder one sank away, leaving the paint stark and obvious. The young man with the scar turned upon Jonathan and at last addressed him.

"Sir, I beg you to remember that there are ladies present." His words ran together with fluent ease, and his pronunciation was perfect; but there was something in his way of stressing his syllables which suggested that English was not his native tongue.

The fat man seemed less annoyed at being corrected than pleased at being noticed.

"Ladies! Ah, yes," he said with a sneer in his voice. "I was forgetting. Where I've been there were only women, and it wasn't the custom to consider their delicate feelings. Though, mind you, when it comes to whipping," he emphasized the word maliciously, "women can show men a thing or two. Why, I remember . . ."

"Your reminiscences are ill-timed and out of place," said the young man, just forestalling another cry from the pale girl. "I assure you, madam, that this . . . this person's chatter is not worthy of your attention. For one thing, it demands too much credulity."

"Have it your way," said Jonathan, unabashed. "I'm not telling stories for pence. I'm only trying to tell you that I've seen a whip wielded to better purpose . . ."

"Unless you will be silent, or will talk on some subject more fitting I will deal with you as soon as we alight." The young man spoke fiercely, and, unknown to himself, his muscular brown hand had sketched a threatening gesture upon the air. He expected, in view of the fat fellow's unabashed acceptance of former rebukes, some answering truculence. But to his surprise Jonathan seemed to shrink into the corner in a manner which one would have thought impossible for a man of his bulk. His small eyes flickered uneasily, and when he muttered:

"I'm sorry. No offence meant," his voice was cringing.

The young man held those flickering eyes for a moment in a threatening stare. Then he looked away with an air of contemptuously dismissing an unpleasant subject. The anaemic young woman perked up amazingly; it was the first time she had ever been so publicly championed, and she wished that she had seen fit to travel in her new bonnet of green grosgrain with the pink roses, at this moment wasting its sweetness in the darkness of her bandbox. But

the handsome scarred face was not turned towards her
again. After a slight interval the young man slewed round
in his seat so that he could survey Jonathan surreptitiously
while apparently staring out of the window. His gaze had
the interest of the collector of oddities faced with a new
specimen. That high voice, the fat, almost feminine figure,
the insolence, the trace of sadism in the voice, above all
the cringing reception of the mere threat of violence. And
then those spoken words of evidence, women with whips,
men harnessed to ploughs, professional story-tellers. The
pieces of the minute puzzle clicked into place. When next
the eyes of the scarred young man rested upon his
neighbour there was a curious pity in them, as well as a
certain contempt.

The rain fell more heavily as the afternoon lengthened
and a premature dusk closed upon the desolate countryside. The elder of the ladies opened her reticule, took out
a gentleman's watch on a short silver chain, looked at it,
held it to her ear, gave it a shake, and then dropped it
back again with a short impatient sigh.

"Surely we shall be very late," she suggested.

The young man produced his watch. "It lacks a quarter
to five," he said politely. "Not knowing the countryside,
I cannot say how much farther we have to go." The pale
girl cried with an eager bid for attention:

"I do. We've just rounded Hunter's Corner. We'll be
at the *Fleece* in about twenty minutes."

It was the woman who—contrary to the girl's hopes—
made a reply:

"Are you nearly home then? I wish I were. I've been
on the road five days, and I'm heartily sick of inn beds,
and inn meals. And to call one the *Fleece* is about the
most honest thing I've heard. I mean, they all fleece you,"
she explained, fearing that her joke, the first one she had
ever made, might go unappreciated.

The girl wished that she had thought of it, for everyone
laughed. Everyone except Jonathan Smail, who, in his

corner, had shifted as though the name of the inn had reminded him of something. Impeded by his bulk and the amount of clothing he wore, he fumbled in an inner pocket and drew out a small black book with a creased cover. He moistened his thumb on his tongue and began to turn the pages. Finding the one he wanted, he stared at it avidly. It showed, in minute scribble, a list of names which, linked together, covered every coach route in the eastern counties. Against all but four a heavy black cross had been scored. The first of the four unmarked ones was the *Fleece*, Fulsham. He knew the page by heart, yet he stared at it as though hoping that some addition or alteration might have been made upon it since he saw it last. Only five more. Four more throws in this desperate chancy game and then he was done. How had he ever hoped that so slight a clue could bring him to his goal? Nothing but guesswork to go upon at best. And yet it was a chance, the only one he had. Well, in twenty minutes, if that whey-faced trollop was right, he would know the worst.

By Jonathan's side the young man replaced his watch thoughtfully. Twenty minutes more. That would be five minutes after five. He could eat and rest for an hour. Then he must hire a swift horse. He closed his eyes and studied the map which etched itself against the darkness of his closed lids. Allow two hours . . . three perhaps, since he must allow for the bad going, the darkness and the unfamiliarity of the road. Three hours then, and he would have rejoined Henri, and they would be comparing notes, perfecting their plan, estimating their chances of success. For himself, he thought, as he fingered a small valise which lay on his knees, he had been very lucky. He had the money, good English money with which to bribe and bribe, pay and pay. If Henri had been equally successful with the shipmaster whose name had been given them, the most arduous, though least dangerous part of their plan was already accomplished. He was ashamed to observe that his heart had given a little fluttering jump of excitement.

Admittedly the plan, in its wild audacity and disregard of
risks, might partake of the nature of a schoolboy's prank,
but it would take a man's balanced coolness to carry it
out. There was no place in it for excitable hearts. The
memorized map of the terrain between the *Fleece* Inn and
the coast faded, and gave place to another, more a picture
than a map, although it was marked with lines of latitude
and longitude, with notes about currents and prevailing
winds and tides. But within and behind these geographical
details there was a purely emotional vision, a stark island
rising from a grey sea, prisoning within its narrow bounds
the man who had held a continent in thrall. Like a caged
eagle, he paced and pined, restless and wistful, and always
his eyes turned seawards, staring across the imprisoning
waters, seeking a sign, begging a word of hope. And who
should give it, thought the man with the scarred face, save
such as he, and Henri, and Jules, the young men, the
unknown ones whose names were not bruited about,
whose loyalty was steadfast because they had shared the
great dream, whose minds were mobile enough to conceive
reckless plans, and whose daring was sufficient to put
those plans into action. How else should they spend their
days, these young men whom the captive had forged and
tempered?

The hard lines of the scarred face softened suddenly.
Mon Empereur, he thought fondly, *vous serez libre, nous
vous le jurons*.

He opened his eyes suddenly and found himself staring
straight at the pale young woman whose eyes were dwelling upon him with a doting hunger. Caught off her guard,
she blushed hotly and looked down into her lap. Poor
girl, he thought, idly, no style, no chic, no appeal. So few
of them had, these English women—and what few did
possess it had blatantly copied his countrywomen.

The coach rounded the last bend and there, ahead at
the crossroads, the inn reared its great dark bulk against
the evening sky. The coachman gave his hat a final dash

over the side, straightened his drooping shoulders, gathered the reins more firmly, and gripped his whip, prepared to make his entry in style. The guard reached for his horn, drew a deep breath and then blew loudly, warning dogs and children and foot passengers out of the road, and sending a message to the inn that the Ipswich coach had succeeded in making another stage safely and that everything had better be in readiness.

EVENING

The Fleece

Harriet, as usual, was perfectly ready. At three o'clock precisely she had ended her last round of inspection and retired to her room. At twenty minutes to four she had emerged again, ready to face all comers, and dressed in a manner that showed that though she might stand in the hall, to receive the inn's guests and to do her best for them, she did it all of her own free will, and would tolerate neither patronage nor familiarity. This evening she wore a dress of russet silk, stiff and crisp. The bodice of it, which had severely tested the skill of Miss Phipps, the dressmaker, was cut just low enough to reveal its wearer's lovely neck, which was unmarked, and high enough to conceal the two scars which marred the perfection of her bosom. From its high waist it fell in straight folds to the hem, which was weighted by rouleaux of its own material, and stood out like the bottom of a bell. Every strand of her bright hair was brushed until it shone, and meticulously pinned into place. Her face was like a grotesque mask, so heavily (to close view so ineffectually) was it coated with paint and powder. She wore topaz ear-rings in her ears and a chain of gold, studded with the same stones, round her neck.

She was very nearly happy. The soaking wet afternoon had resulted in the house being crammed. Two families of farmers with several children and numerous dependents, who had expected to spend the night in their new abodes, had abandoned the struggle with the mud and the problem of keeping furniture dry, and had decided to seek shelter before dark. Several horsemen whose destinations lay a few miles in various directions had halted for comforting potations, and finding the inn comfortable and the stabling good, had settled in for the night. Mrs. Foxe, a lady by every one of Harriet's exacting standards, had been installed in the best room. And the Ipswich coach had arrived with a full complement.

For quite an hour Harriet had been happy, forgetful alike of her elegance and her affliction. The business of fitting in so many different people, the acumen demanded by the problem of who might happily share with whom, the meeting of all the demands made by travellers who were wet and cold, had engaged every atom of her attention and fulfilled to the utmost that deep need within her to be busy, indispensable, resourceful and slightly dictatorial.

She hung the slate, which bore a record of the guests names and the numbers of the rooms allotted to them, on a peg at the back of a little alcove in the hall. Below the slate, filling the alcove, was the Candle Table. It bore merely—and heaven help the person caught by Harriet depositing irrelevant articles upon its glassy surface!—a number of candlesticks, a box of new candles, and a little pile of pasteboard cards each plainly labelled with a number. Harriet never collected the candlesticks, never cleaned them or gouged out the stubs. But she always allotted them and, as in her other work, she had an unvarying system. At the back of the table were the plated candlesticks which were given to privileged guests who had impressed Harriet with their quality. In front of these was a larger number of more homely sticks of copper and brass. In front of these again were some common ones, pewter and pottery. And although she was not consciously aware of it, Harriet enjoyed allotting the various grades as much as she enjoyed anything. It gratified her yearning for power to give a polite person, even in a second-rate room, one of the plated candlesticks, while someone who had annoyed her—often unintentionally, perhaps by staring or even averting his eyes from her face—was doomed to have his superior chamber lighted by a candle in a pewter stand.

This evening she had few favours to bestow or grudges to make good, so beyond giving Mrs. Foxe the best stick of all (a silvered nymph bearing a torch), and the very polite gentleman with the scarred face the second best, she dealt out the numbered cards in strict accordance with the status of the rooms.

Suddenly, as she stood there with her back to the hall, she was aware of a cold prickling discomfort along her spine. She turned sharply, the last card poised between her finger and thumb. Close to her, only a few paces away, although she had not heard him approach, was a man. Just an ordinary man with a small valise in his hand; the sort of person, Harriet told herself angrily, whom one expected—indeed, hoped to see in the hall of the inn at this time of the afternoon. The entrance was brightly lit, a good fire burned in the grate and all around her there was the sound of bustle and human voices. There was nothing in the least eerie about the place or the time or indeed about the man himself. Yet Harriet, whose nerves were of iron, was suddenly and unaccountably frightened. The cold feeling chased down her spine, round her waist and along her stomach and down the insides of her thighs.

"Just a moment," she said, and turned under pretence of dropping the last card into place, and leant her hand on the edge of the table as though in search of support.

"I want a room," said Jonathan Smail in his peculiar broken voice. Harriet unhooked the slate and looked at it closely.

"I'm afraid you'll have to share," she said at last. "We're very full this evening."

"I want a good room," he repeated, as though he had not heard. "One with a fire. And a feather bed."

"I'm sorry," said Harriet. "I haven't a room left of any kind. I could put you a bed in number eleven. Mr. Roper is one of our regulars; he doesn't mind sharing, and there is a kind of partition . . ."

"I don't want to share. And I don't want a put-up bed, thank you, I've told you what I want."

"And I've told you that we're full up," said Harriet sharply. Despite herself, she cast a glance along the passage and up the stairs. Where was Will? He was always around when she didn't want him, always trying to push her aside; now, when suddenly and for no very good reason that she could think of, she did need him, he was gone.

"Are you the landlady?"

"No. I'm his daughter. I mean I'm the landlord's daughter. But he would tell you the same thing. He can't make rooms any more than I can. I know what I could do though. In race weeks when we're full like this we hire a room at a cottage just across the road. It's clean and very comfortable. I'll send across and ask the woman to light a fire for you. That's the best thing." She was glad that she had thought of the idea. Glad that this peculiar fat man would not be spending the night under his roof. Yet why, she wondered, forcing herself to look at him; he was certainly ugly, but not more so than dozens of men with whom she had dealt without interest and certainly without fear. And although he was intransigent in his demands, he could hardly be called rude. I'm as bad as Myrtle, she told herself scornfully, she's always getting ideas about people.

"I'll see the landlord," said Jonathan Smail. He set down his little valise and began to unwind the heavy muffler which was twisted about his neck.

"Very well," said Harriet, really annoyed now, her troublesome puzzling feeling swamped in a wave of irritation. Now, she thought savagely, he shall have nothing, neither number eleven, nor Mrs. Sharp's room, nor a bed put up anywhere else. He can sleep in a ditch for all I

care. And at that thought she felt the chill again. A ditch
was exactly the right place for him, and she knew why and
knew why he had afflicted her with that feeling. He was
like a toad, fat, bulgy, slow, and all her life she had
suffered from an unreasoning, incurable horror of the
things. That was it, she thought, those bright greasy eyes
with pouched lids, that shapeless lipless mouth, that dirty
doughy colour. He might have crawled out of a ditch, or
up from a dank dark cellar. Urgh!

But it was typical of her to feel better now that the odd
effect he had had upon her was explained. And as she
tripped along the passage in search of her father she experienced the more healthy feeling of fury. He had done
the unforgiveable, flouted her authority, scorned her arrangements, and sent her in search of Will, just as though
Will could arrange what she couldn't. As she paused by the
door of the tap-room, where she guessed that her father
would be, she reiterated her determination that the
stranger should enjoy no hospitality at the *Fleece*.

Harriet never entered the tap-room. She hated the smell
of it, and the way that men spilt their liquor on the white
scrubbed tables and spat on the sanded floor. To her it was
the epitome of the sordid side of inn-keeping. She now
opened the door a little way and peeped within, rather as
a person might peep into a cage of wild beasts. She was
glad that Will looked up as the door opened, and grateful
to him for leaving the bowl of punch that he was brewing
and coming directly towards her.

"What is it, Harriet?"

"A man, Father. He wants to see you. You must come."

"Very well. Just a second." Will turned back and spoke
to Joe, and then joined Harriet, who had drawn back
into the passage.

"Listen, Father," Harriet began as soon as the door was
closed. She spoke rapidly, impulsively, more like Myrtle
than herself. "He's *horrible*. He came after I'd arranged
all the rooms. And he wants a room to himself and a fire

and a feather bed. I tried to make him share, or to have a bed put up somewhere, or to go to Mrs. Sharp's. But he won't do anything. You send him about his business, Father, please. Don't *try* to fit him in, for my sake, Father, please."

"Why, Harriet!" Will exclaimed in astonishment. "What's come over you?"

"I don't know. But he's horrible. He makes me shudder. He's like a . . . you know."

Will knew. It was well known in the family as Harriet's one weakness. She never even spoke the word, and the sight of it on a page drew her attention like a magnet and made her shudder.

"Poor old man," he said lightly. "Still, you wouldn't mind his going to Mrs. Sharp's, would you?"

"I'd like him to sleep in a . . . in the rain," said Harriet viciously.

"He wasn't rude to you, was he?" Will asked, looking at her closely.

"Oh, no, not rude. Just horrible."

"I'll soon dispose of *him*, then," said Will, resolving to send the man across to the cottage.

"Thank you," said Harriet, quite fervently. And then, in a more normal voice, "I shall be in the kitchen if you want me."

The stranger who had so oddly affected Harriet had moved close to the fire, and stood with the red glow painting his face and the front of his long heavy coat. He turned his head as Will entered the hall from the passage, and Will saw at once what Harriet had meant. There was something unmistakably reptilian about the wide doughy face. It inspired Will to extra civility, for probably Harriet's revulsion had been beyond her control, and, after all, the poor fellow couldn't help his face and his needs merited as much attention as anybody else's.

"Good evening," he said affably. "I'm told you want a

room. I'm afraid you've chosen a bad day. But we can fix you up over the road very comfortably."

A look of incredulous surprise, followed by one of utter delight, dawned on the wide face. Will was astonished. Harriet had made that very suggestion—and, anyway, the surprise and the delight were disproportionate to the occasion.

"V . . . very nice, I'm sure," said Jonathan with a splutter. Then, throwing back his head he let loose a burst of laughter, high, tittering, crazy.

"You do good business," he said delightedly.

"On occasions. Today, for instance. A pouring wet Michaelmas. Much of the time we're slack enough and you could have your choice of rooms."

The man laughed again. And all at once Will knew that he had heard similar laughter before, not similar in sound, for the laugh which he remembered had been a roar, not a bleat, but there had been the same note in it, a kind of secret gloating as though the amusement arose, not from something funny, but from some other person's discomfiture. Yet, in this case no one had been discomfited. There was not even that poor excuse for the fat fellow's merriment, Probably he was a little crazy, and perhaps Harriet had sensed the fact.

The laughter ceased abruptly. "Pray don't apologize for being busy," the man said. "I'm delighted to see it, delighted. Congratulations on your daughter, too. A comely wench if it wasn't for her face."

So he *had* been rude to Harriet, and she had been too proud to complain. Will's thin yellow hands clenched.

"Keep your tongue off my daughter," he said shortly.

The fat man smiled, and again Will was reminded of someone who had smiled in just that way, cruelly, mirthlessly. When he spoke again his manner was made harsher by the memory:

"You'd better find your own lodging. We've nothing for you here."

"The name over the door is Oakley," said the fat man with a low caressing note in his broken voice.

"What of it?"

"I never knew a Will Oakley. But I knew Mike Latter, and he wouldn't have turned an old pal out in the rain."

So that was why the laugh and the smile that seemed familiar!

"Jonathan Smail," said Will. Loathing and horror and fear were in the words.

"That's right," said Jonathan with a deadly pretence at heartiness. "I grant you I've changed a bit. A lot has happened since you and me were messmates. But I thought you'd remember Jonathan."

When Harriet entered the kitchen Mrs. Sharman was giving the great goose a final basting. She raised her flushed face and gave the girl a malevolent look. Why in the name of wonder, she thought furiously, couldn't that one go and sit in the parlour like the lady she pretended to be? Always buzzing round like a mucky owd hornet! A certain amount of nervousness mingled with the cook's resentment. Under Harriet's stare her hands lost their usual cunning and became clumsy, indecisive of action, as though they, too, were conscious that the chit of a girl watching them had hands which could perform any action more quickly and efficiently. Just as Harriet could never forget or forgive her final defeat in the long battle for the keys, so the cook could never live down the memory of the day when Harriet had notably defeated *her*. For on one occasion during that struggle Mrs. Sharman had played what had seemed to her a trump card. On an afternoon when it was certain that at least twenty people would soon assemble in the dining-room expecting to be fed, she had taken to her bed in a dudgeon, just after Harriet had locked the store-room for the last time and carried away the keys. She had left the kitchen in a state of utter confusion, the fire unstoked and the chickens, which should, in a few minutes' time, have been roasting in the oven, undrawn and only partially plucked.

She was happily certain of two things. None of the maids—except Effie, who didn't count, anyway—would give Harriet anything but the most drudging and perfunctory help. And within thirty minutes at the most Harriet, staggered by the magnitude of the task left to her, would come to her senses and with apologies and pleas for help, would make her peace with the one person able to see things straight.

But time passed, and the first person to approach the room where the penitent and anxious cook was counting the quarter hours, was Effie, stumbling along under the weight of a heavy tray, which Harriet, with a nice sense of malice, had piled with a meal exactly like that which was being served punctually in the dining-room. Mrs. Sharman stared at the slices of chicken perfectly cooked, exquisitely carved, at the curls of bacon, just crisp enough but without a trace of chippiness, at the bread-sauce, smooth as cream, and at the roast potatoes, floury balls within a thin golden casing. Then, without a word, she lifted the second cover. Anyone could roast a chicken, she told herself, but a sponge pudding of the kind which she made took an artist. She looked at the pudding and then replaced the cover, despair in her heart. It was perfect. Light and spongy, the jam precisely one inch deep at the bottom, the white of egg browned to a turn at the top.

She had come down next morning expecting to be given her notice; but Harriet had merely asked whether she felt better and then ignored the whole episode. But it had left its mark on the cook who, ever afterwards, was to know a tremulous lack of confidence when forced to ply her trade under Harriet's eye.

This afternoon, though beyond that first angry state, she ignored Harriet's presence, she felt the heavy basting spoon turn awkward in her hand. A drop of hissing grease flew out and touched her wrist scaldingly, and she swore under her breath. But she set the weighty pan back in the oven safely, slammed the door, and then, pivoting nimbly on her feet, turned to face Harriet.

"Thass no good you coming in here to tell me to hurry," she said, sensing that Harriet was about to question whether the goose would be cooked in time, and reckoning that attack was the best form of defence. "Short-handed I am, tonight of all nights, and thass a downright shame. If I'd known about it sooner I should have had something to say, I can tell you."

"You seem to have something to say as it is, Mrs. Sharman," said Harriet in the cold nasty voice which made her so much feared in the kitchen. "What is the matter? Why are you short-handed?"

"You may well ask! You're the one as said Sarah could go off today. Michaelmas Day, and wet into the bargain."

I said no such thing," said Harriet, genuinely shocked. "Why. . . As though I . . . How dare she? Where has she gone?"

"Home," said the cook laconically, growing calmer in the face of Harriet's agitation.

"Home? She must be mad!"

"With *your* permission, she say, saucy as you please. Thass a nice thing to hear at two o'clock in the arternoon, ain't it?"

"But I *didn't* say it," said Harriet, her voice rising in a crescendo of denial.

"Effie," said the cook in a voice of doom.

Effie was engaged in what she called trying to get forrard. She had collected all the cooking utensils, the bowls, basins, spoons and whisks which Mrs. Sharman had flung down as she finished with them, and was washing them in a bowl of water already scummed thickly with grease. She had known for days now that this moment would come, must come, and yet, at the sound of her name, spoken in that tone, her heart began to race suffocatingly. She said, "Yes, mam," in a faint, choked voice.

"Come here." There was no escape now. Despairingly she lifted her hands from the bowl and moved across to where the cook and Harriet stood watching one another like wrestlers searching for a new hold. She twisted her hands in a fold of her apron, partly to dry them, partly to conceal their unsteadiness.

"Now," said Mrs. Sharman, happily, "tell Miss Harriet what you said to me when I had that argle-bargle with Sarah."

"I said," repeated Effie sickly, "that Sarah had the right of it acause Miss Harriet towd her she might go."

"Thass right," interpolated the cook. "You see, *I* said nobody in their senses could of said it. Not on a day like this. But Sarah brazened it out. And I should of sent and arst you myself ony Effie here pipes up and says that you did say . . ."

"All right, Mrs. Sharman. I'll get to the bottom of this. Now, Effie. You know perfectly well that I never said anything about Sarah going home today."

"But you did, mam. I heard yer."

"When?"

"A long time ago, mam. 'Bout Whitsun that wuz. Sarah, she say to you, Kin I go, she say, to see my owd mother some time while thass still so as I kin get through the water-splash? And then you say, Yes, you say, you kin go a Michaelmas." Effie paused with the air of one who has repeated faultlessly a hard-learned lesson. Her great dark eyes fluttered from Harriet's face to the cook's, from the table to the floor, but there was nothing new in that; and although her face was as white as the white-washed wall behind her, both her interrogators knew that that was her normal colour.

"Well," said Harriet, after a second of speechlessness from sheer astonishment. "Of all the crazy things I've ever heard, that is the craziest. As though I would promise that great lazy girl a holiday four months ahead. What nonsense! For one thing, I never dreamed that she would be here at Michaelmas. I didn't intend to keep her . . . and I shouldn't, but that girls are so difficult to come by these days."

A queer expression showed through the agitation of Effie's face. It was as though she knew that she had failed in some mission and was in terror of some immediate retribution. She said, as though her life depended upon Harriet's believing her:

"But, mam, you did say it. You must of forgot, it being so long ago. That wuz Whitsun time, I remember acause I was ahulling gooseberries for the fust time. And the sun wuz a-shining in at that there door, and you wuz a-wearing your lilac gownd. I remember it all as clear as anything. And afterwards, Sarah, she say to me, thass the way to git a holiday, she say, speak up for yourself. Whyn't you arst for one, too? But I tell her, I ain't got nowhere to go to. And then s'morning Sarah say, I gotta go, she say, don't my owd mother'll wholly be disappointed. I bin telling her Michaelmas every time I sent her a message by owd carrier."

Harriet's cold grey eyes fixed themselves in a stare directed at Effie's face; and Effie's strange deer-like ones were caught and held by the stare, so that their unwonted steadiness, combined with their palpable earnestness, did much to shake Harriet's self-confidence. After all, she reflected, the girl had nothing to gain by lying, and she certainly hadn't the wits to invent such a sustained and circumstantial story. The gooseberries and the lilac gown. . . . Vainly she drove her mind back, but there was nothing.

"Well," she said at last, "if I ever said such a thing I have completely forgotten it. And it's not like me to forget anything. It's a pity, Effie, that with a memory so much better than mine, you have to be reminded so often about cleaning the candlesticks."

Effie seemed relieved rather than distressed by this shrewd thrust.

"All right, get back to your work. I'm afraid you'll have to help in the dining-room tonight. So make yourself tidy and change your shoes as soon as you finish that job. And now, Mrs. Sharman," said Harriet, turning to the cook, "I can only say that I'm sorry about all this, and I *do* apologize. Is there anything that I can do to make up. Just tell me and I'll do it."

"Oh, no, Miss Harriet, I can manage, thank you." While unwillingly acknowledging the impulse of justice which had prompted Harriet's offer, the cook's only desire was to get her out of the kitchen.

"Nonsense, Mrs. Sharman. You must miss Sarah. Come along. Tell me exactly what she would have been doing had she been here at this moment and I'll do it myself."

The cook, who lacked Harriet's method and who had not the vaguest idea of what the absent Sarah would have been about at that moment, was almost in tears.

"I've done it all," she cried. "There's no need for you to do anything, really, Miss Harriet." Only for God's sake, you smug-faced ugly bitch, get out of my kitchen, do, before you send me daft.

"You don't seem to have missed . . ." Harriet began, when the door opened sharply, and there was Will, looking ghastly and beckoning her.

"Effie," said Mrs. Sharman, in a kinder voice than she generally used to her minion, "take this key and go to the storeroom and bring me a bottle of cooking brandy that's on the second shelf under the hams." She was pleased with Effie because she had assisted in Harriet's defeat; and she needed the brandy because what with one thing and another her nerves were on edge.

Effie lifted her hands through the thick crust of grease which had formed on the water as it cooled and went quickly into the store-room. Once safely inside it she put her sodden red hands together and shut her eyes. "Oh,

dear God, do please forgive me," she prayed. "All them
lies. I couldn't help it, dear Lord. Please, you'll hetta
forgive me because I am in such a fix. And please God
don't let me hetta do no worse, for Jesus Christ's sake.
Amen."

"Be quick Effie," called Mrs. Sharman, banging a sauce-
pan back on the stove.

Effie opened he eyes, seized the bottle, and then, staring
madly around, lighted upon a dish of cold meat pasties.
She snatched two and dropped them into her apron
pocket.

"You'll hetta look quicker'n *that*," said the cook taking
the bottle, "if you're going to serve in Sarah's place."

"I doon't like the dining-room. They stare so."

"That's what Sarah likes," said the cook, tilting the
bottle. "I'll tell you what, Effie Stevens, that mawther that
you make such a fuss on ain't no better than she should
be. And I'll tell you another thing. Thass my bounden belief she's in the famliy way already. All that fat ain't
natural."

Had the cook been regarding Effie at that moment she
would have been startled to see an expression of utter
horror upon her pallid features. She might even have
been tempted to include Effie in her supsicions, for there
was guilt as well as horror in her look. And when she
spoke it was with such an agonized frenzy of repudiation
that it might well have been her own honor she was de-
fending.

"Ah, no, mam. That ain't true. You marn's say that,
Mrs. Sharman. Sarah ain't like that. She ain't that way."

"Oh," said Mrs. Sharman dryly, "and what makes you
so sure, pray?"

In succinct, homely terms, Effie told her why she could
be certain that Sarah, despite her size, was not pregnant.

Will, who had so often offended by leaving the kitchen
door open against Harriet's wishes, was the one who, this

evening, drew it shut. The light from the candles in the wall
sconce shone on his face, and Harriet thought—sadly and
yet with a certain satisfaction in her own prophetic
powers—I was right, this day has been too much for him.
His face, especially around the nostrils and mouth, was a
yellowish white, and all the grooves and lines upon it
looked darker than they had done ten minutes before, as
though someone had traced each one with a thick soft
pencil.

"You're feeling poorly," said Harriet, and this time it
was she who reached out the sympathetic hand.

"No, no," he said. And in spite of her sympathy she
was a little disappointed. It would have pleased her to have
had this full house to command for a few hours. "What
gave you that notion? I'm all right." His voice certainly
sounded quite ordinary, and she said:

"Oh, well, perhaps it was the light. You wanted me?"

"Yes, Harriet. I want you to do something for me."

"Well?"

"I know it means putting you about at very short
notice, but . . . would you mind sleeping in Myrtle's room
tonight?"

"Yes, I do," said Harriet instantly. "If we have to share
a room—and I don't see why we should—she can come
into mine. Her room is a shambles; it makes me quite
sick. Besides . . ." the logical corollary of his suggestion
smote her, "who's proposing to use my room, I'd like to
know?"

"Well, you see, my dear, it's like this . . ."

"You haven't gone and promised that *awful* man my
room, Father?"

"It was all I could do, Harriet. You see, he turned out
to be an old acquaintance of mine."

"Old acquaintance! But . . . but . . . I've never seen him
before."

"Maybe not. But I'm older than you, you know. I had
acquaintances before you were born."

He was pleased to hear his own voice, light and ordinary. Above everything, he must keep Harriet out of this. She was so inquisitive, poor girl, so apt to seek interest and drama in the affairs of other people.

"Well, old friend or not, he can't have my room. I'm surprised at you for suggesting it."

"I've got to make him comfortable," said Will reasonably. "And I've done more than suggest. I've promised." His voice took on the note which both the girls recognized as a sign that further argument would be wasted. "So if you'll just take out the things that you need for the night. . . ."

"I shall take everything," said Harriet hysterically. "I couldn't ever like my room again after he'd been in it. What's his name?" she asked inconsequentially.

"Smail," said Will with reluctance.

"It should be Snail. I could belive that he'd leave a slimy track all over everything. Oh, Father, all my lovely things! Must he have it?"

"I told you, I've arranged it. Do be sensible, Harriet. It's only for one night. He can't hurt it. And it can all be cleaned."

"I'll never go in it again."

"Well, we'll talk about that afterwards. Just now I want you to get your things out, see that there's a good fire for him, and then forget all about it. I'm going to ask Mrs. Sharman to send us a supper into the Little Parlour, and I want you to see that we're not disturbed."

"You won't be by me. Nor by Myrtle if she once sees him. I thought you were particular about your friends, Father."

"I am. But it doesn't do to set too much store by appearance. Besides, people change a great deal in twenty years."

"He hasn't." Her voice was vicious. "He always was a devil, I am sure. And he'd just delight to think he'd got my room. After I didn't want him even in the house . . ."

There were tears in her throat. Will heard them and his heart smote him. Harriet hadn't cried for years.

"If I could think of something else," he began hesitantly. Then the memory of his own predicament came to him, and he thought, my God, as though I hadn't enough to think about just now. So he said harshly, "But I can't. So go now and get your things. I must see about some wine."

"Give him the best of *that*, too!

The furious words came out so jerkily that she knew she would be crying in another minute. She turned abruptly, tore open the kitchen door, ran across the width of the room and made a rush for the back stairs which opened out of a corner beyond the dresser. As she went she could hear, from somewhere in the house or the yard, the thin sweet scrape of fiddle playing a merry tune. It was like a mocking comment on her defeat.

For to Harriet her room was something more that the place where she slept, stored her clothes, and performed her complicated toilet. In a world where so many of her arrangements depended upon the co-operation of other people, where so many good plans were brought to nought by fools or by factors over which she had no control, her own room was the last place where her wishes were undisputed, her choice final, and her power absolute. The store-room, which, in a private house, would have been the pinnacle of her achievement, was here vulnerable to Mrs. Sharman's attacks; the inn as a whole was at the mercy of the public; the Little Parlour she must share with Will and Myrtle, neither of whom was tidy or methodical. But in her bedroom Harriet had, quite literally, a place for everything and everything in its place. No picture ever hung askew upon its walls; no ornament varied its position by so little as an inch. Until about a year ago the cleaning of the room had been the bugbear of a succession of chambermaids. Then Harriet had taken on the task herself. The cupboard by the fireplace held her own broom, dust-pan, sweeping brush, clean dusters, mops and polishing cloths. Every morning she rose very early, made her bed, and swept and dusted the room. Every Saturday she indulged in a form of spring-cleaning, polishing pictures and glass, beating rugs, changing her bed-linen, washing her window.

The room itself, though not very large, was attractive. Its walls were panelled and painted cream, and the window, which was tall and painted at the top, had a surround of coloured glass panes which, when the sun shone, scattered a broken pattern of ruby, blue amethyst and orange upon the walls and the polished floor. Its appointments bore evidence of Harriet's industry and taste. She had chosen, hemmed and hung the curtains of the bed and at the window. She had assembled, piece by piece, the serpentine fronted chest of drawers, the Dutch tallboys, the small library table which bore a rosebud-patterned inkstand and a matching tray of quill pents and penknife, and, snugly fitting under the stone window-sill, the squat dower chest, black with age and polish, which, although it did not conform to Harriet's idea of elegance, was cherished by her because it held, very tidily, several oddments which were too bulky to be laid in her neat drawers.

The serpentine chest with its graceful carved apron and dazzling brass handles served Harriet for a dressing table. Over it hung a long narrow mirror with a frame of encrusted gesso work painted gold and blue and dull scarlet. On the chest's glossy top stood a pair of three-branched candlesticks, and midway between them was a box of Chinese lacquer in which reposed Harriet's modest pieces of jewellery.

The two small top drawers were devoted to toilet articles. The one on the right held hairbrushes, combs, curling rags, all scruplously clean and neatly arranged. The left drawer held Harriet's secret things, and was always locked; for she was morbidly sensitive about the lotions and pastes and unguents, the paint and the powder with which she endeavoured to repair her complexion.

There were dozens of things in that locked drawer, many of them substances for which Harriet had paid considerable sums of money, tried hopefully and then abandoned in disgust. Yet, even after their uselessness had been proved, she suffered from an inability to throw them away. Now and again she would dive into the remotest recesses of the drawer and bring forth some long-discarded pot or packet and try the contents again.

On this darkening afternoon, having locked the door of her room and lighted the six candles. Harriet stood for a moment with both hands pressed, palm downwards, upon the chest's glossy top. The tears which had been in her voice were in her eyes now, brimming against the thickened lids and spilling over to make ruinous tracks down her painted cheeks. But as she stood there she made a desperate effort for control, and no more tears came after a moment, and by the time that the candles were burning steadily and clearly she was mistress of herself again. She withdrew her hands, straighened her shoulders, and moved to the cupboard by the hearth. From it she lifted a plain wooden box, fitted with a padlock. Setting it, with the lid open, upon a chair near the chest, she unlocked the left-hand drawer and began to move its contents, one by one, into the box.

The thought went through her mind that it was very stupid of her to preserve so much rubbish. Some of the stuff had been so long in the drawer that it had deteriorated with age. This would really have been an opportunity for making a clearance; but she could not afford the time necessary for deciding what to keep and what to throw away. So the jars and the bottles, the pots and packets, followed one another into the box, skilfully fitted by Harriet's fingers so that they should not tilt or spill.

Over one packet, however, she hesitated, balancing it on her palm with a gesture of indecision and distaste. The sight of it always shamed her slightly. It was neatly wrapped now in a piece of tissue paper; but she knew that inside was the original wrapping, a screw of dirty calico, and within that was a handful of greenish-grey powder, made from God knew what horrible ingredients. It was, to Harriet, the final proof of her folly and weakness.

Last autumn, almost a year ago, Joe the potman had been afflicted by an outcrop of painful and unsightly boils, and one day, when he was complaining about them and saying that nothing did them any good, Clara, one of the dining-room maids, advised him, in Harriet's hearing, to visit old Mother Fenn, the local wise woman. She backed up her advice by giving a list of the almost miraculous cures which the old dame had worked, the warts charmed away, the love philtres that had been successful, the threats of blindness averted. Four days later Joe, able once more to turn his head without wincing, confessed that he had taken Clara's advice and was glad he had done so. More than that he seemed unwilling to say.

Reluctantly and shame-facedly, Harriet had begun to make inquiries about the old woman. She chose Effie as her informant, partly because Effie had lived in Fulsham all her life, partly because Effie, of all the maids, was the least likely to gossip, or to speculate as to the reason of the questions.

Effie described the sybil as a "wholly owd, wholly mucky owd woman," and said that she reckoned most of the tales about her were lies. She at least knew one mawther who hadn't done herself a mite of good by visiting the old crone. But she did tell Harriet exactly where the woman lived, and did not, to Harriet's great relief, seem to regard the questions as in the least interesting or extraordinary.

Harriet, with unusual procrastination, shelved the matter in her mind. But, after the fashion of subjects once brought to one's notice, the matter of Mother Fenn's cropped up a few days later, this time upon Myrtle's lips. Myrtle was notably credulous, and given to gossip. Joe's sudden recovery from his boils had engaged her attention, and she had gone very thoroughly into the—to her—fascinating question as to whether or not Mother Fenn were a witch. With very little prompting from Harriet, indeed, expecting at each sentence's end to be sternly rebuked for talking rubbish, she told Harriet all she knew about the old woman. How old she was, so old that several doddering old fellows in Fulsham swore that she had been grown up and the mother of a child when they were still little lads. So old that they found no difficulty in believing her own claim to be able to remember the suicide of that Squire Morton who had committed suicide when something called the South Sea Bubble ruined him.

"That was 1720. I looked it up," said Myrtle. "So if she was say, ten then, she's well over a hundred now. Yet she's quite active. Joe said she was out in the woods after roots and things when he went to see her. That's quite astonishing, isn't it? And as for her cures, they sound uncanny."

"Do you believe those tales?"

"Not absolutely. But it's difficult to believe that people would go on making up stories like that over such a period of time, don't you think, Harriet? And Joe is cured, after trying so many sensible things. You can't deny that. I swear that if ever I get a wart on my nose I'll go to her straight away."

Two days later, choosing a bright sharp afternoon for the purpose, Harriet, without a word to anyone, and taking a carefully planned roundabout route, penetrated to the heart of the autumn woods and found Mother Fenn at home.

She was ashamed of herself for her credulity, and for the weak, sly hope which would persist in making itself felt. And she considered that she paid for her silliness by the disgust with which the old woman inspired her. The cabin was filthy in an indescribable way, the old woman more repulsive than Harriet could have imagined, and her manner was rude beyond belief. She had listened to Harriet's faltering explanation, which had sounded so fantastic in the circumstances, and then, with a coarse chuckle and a prodding forefinger (caked with filth and terminating in a long, curved, coal-black nail), she had croaked:

"Now then, duckie, you be honest and don't waste my time. Is it your face or your belly giving trouble?"

Harriet had shrunk away from that terrible hand, and at the question had swung round and begun a dignified retreat, but the old woman had caught her by the elbow and, certain now that it was for her complexion that Harriet sought her skill, began to pour out such promises, so many stories of faces far worse than Harriet's which she had cured, that despite everything the tough undying hope began to revive again.

"Thass a cure, duckie, a sartin cure. I promise you that. Ony thass dear to buy. Dear to make, and dear to buy." She had taken careful stock of her customer's clothes and manner and priced the cure, this time, at five shillings.

Harriet handed over the coin and received in exchange the screw of dirty calico and some final instructions how to use the powder within it. Carrying the thing delicately, she had sped home and, behind the locked door of her room, examined the cure. That night, before going to bed, she had tried it. The greenish-grey powder had dissolved completely in water, and she had, shudderingly, applied the resulting lotion to her face. It was as worthless as Mr. Davidson's Complexion Restorer, as unmiraculous as Mrs. Tobers' widely advertised New Skin Paste. In the morning, after one half-hopeful, half-ashamed glance in the mirror, Harriet had wrapped the remaining powder and the bit of cloth in tissue paper and pushed in into the back of the drawer which held so many other memorials to dead hopes.

Now, packing it into the corner of the wooden box, she made up her mind that tomorrow, before she settled into whatever new room she chose, she would destroy it, together with most of the other things from the drawer. At present she had no time. She laid the Chinese casket on top of the cosmetics, closed the lid of the box and fixed the little padlock.

By this time the tears had dried on her cheeks and the first pang of her angry pain was beginning to subside. To-morrow she would insist upon everything in this room being carried into another, probably, if she could manage it, the one where tonight Mrs. Foxe was sleeping. That was the nicest room in the house. It had three cupboards instead of two, and one of them was big enough to take the washing-stand, which in this room was hidden by a screen. By tomorrow evening she would have all her lovely things around her again and this hour's misery would be forgotten. Though she would not have forgiven Will for his perfidy or his favouritism.

The worst of it was, she reflected, as she dragged two capacious valises from the cupboard, she was really much fonder of her father than he was of her, so when the relationship between them was strained, she suffered more than he did.

Fresh tears, springing from a softer source than their predecessors, came into her eyes as she thought about Will. He exasperated her very often, but she was ex-tremely fond of him, intensely anxious for his good opinion, and genuinely concerned for his health. She would have given anything to have been his favourite daughter, as she considered Myrtle was, and amidst all her strivings after perfection in housekeeping, all her economics, personal activities and slave-driving propen-sities, there was the unformed but vital hope that one day something would happen which would open Will's eyes and make him see her value.

Even now, as she opened one drawer after another and lifted the neat piles of clothes—sorted according to kind and interlain with little bags of lavender and violet root—into the yawning valises, even now, in a way, she was helping him. There were very few women who could be relied upon to vacate a room after four year's occupation, and leave it fit for a fresh occupant at a moment's notice.

The old feeling of superiority, the mainspring of her existence, came to her support, as, closing the filled valises, she dragged a chair to the side of the bed and began to unhook the curtains. It would spoil the look of the room, but she cared nothing for that. She did not intend to have *that* creature's breath sullying her curtains.

Abruptly her mind reverted to Smail and to Will's astonishing claim that he was an old acquaintance. She realized the force of her father's remark about having had friends before he had a family; yet it was difficult to imagine that at any time, however remote, he could have been friendly with that nasty fat man. And as she pondered the matter she thought suddenly, for the first time, and with a queer little pang, that she really knew very little about her father, except what she knew as a matter of experience. He never talked about his past. Her own memory began at Lammingham *Dun Cow,* and for all that she knew he might have lived there for years before her birth, or moved there when she was very small. He had never mentioned the subject, and until this moment in the middle of unhooking her curtains, she had never given it a thought. But now her mind, suddenly set working, presented her with a number of questions. Was there, for instance, some mystery about their mother? Was it possible that Smail might be a connection of hers? Once or twice, when they were very young, she and Myrtle had asked questions about Clarissa and had received discouragingly short answers. Their mother was dead, and she had been beautiful. That was all they knew. And they had decided that Will had loved the dead woman so dearly that he could not bear to talk about her, even to them. For years she had not been mentioned. But now, as Harriet mounted the dower chest and slid the window curtains, rings and all, off their pole, it occurred to her for the first time to wonder whether this silence was quite natural.

Suppose there were some mystery about Clarissa. Suppose that awful fat man turned out to be—oh, horror upon horror!—some kind of relative. She shuddered away from the thought, everything in her mind, fastidiousness, snobbishness, possessiveness, outraged and aghast.

But of course it was nonsense, she thought, leaping nimbly from the chest with the curtains trailing in her hand. Smail was merely someone whom her father had met at some time, probably in the course of business, and the mere fact that he had asked for supper to be served to them alone in the Little Parlour went to show that he knew, as well as she did, that this old acquaintance was not a fit person to introduce to one's family. In essentials, Will could be trusted.

She put the folded curtains into the cupboard, stripped the bed and added the bedclothes to the pile, rolled up her own rug, a natural fleecy sheepskin, and forced the door close and locked it.

Moving from that cupboard to the one that matched it on the other side of the hearth, she paused by the bell pull and tugged it so sharply that the peal of it startled everyone in the kitchen and brought Effie scuttling upstairs at a breathless gallop.

Harriet unlocked the door and walked back to the cupboard where her dresses hung, each on its hook, the better garments shrouded with covers of butter muslin. She spoke to Effie as she lifted down dresses and hung them over her arm.

"Run down and send one of the boys, Sam or Davy, up here to me at once. And tell Kitty that this room is to be made perfectly ready for use, fire lighted and everything. Be quick now. And Effie, you heard what I said about helping in the dining-room. Don't forget to change your shoes. Hurry now."

Effie turned and scampered away. Without troubling to close the door again, Harriet studied the stripped apartment and then, satisfied that she had removed everything except the furniture, began to decide what the boy should carry and what she would take herself. But one part of her mind was still busy with the thought of Smail; and now that her misery over Will's favouritism was abating, her curiosity, which was as ingrained and violent as her jealousy or her passion for tidiness, began to wake and stir. A vague, but very attractive, plan began to form at the back of her mind.

Myrtle had finished her hair. Out of the clutter of ribbons and pins, pots without lids and bottles without stoppers which littered her table, the two tall blue and white candlesticks rose stem-like, each with its blossom of flame. Not far away, on a small table a thick carriage candle in a battered tin holder afforded extra light, for Myrtle was nervous and hated shadows in corners.

The room smelt slightly catty, for Myrtle's pet tabby had lately had kittens, and although she performed this business twice a year with the greatest ease and speediness. Myrtle always treated her like an invalid. She and the three kittens were installed in a box lined with flannel, near enough to the bedside for Myrtle to touch the striped head comfortingly during the night. A blue dish which had contained rabbit meat stood empty beside the box, the bones, licked clean, strewed the mat, and Myrtle, on her way to the cupboard to get out her best dress, had caught her foot against a pie-dish full of milk and sent half of it flying across the floor. There were clothes on the bed and on both chairs. Not one of the drawers in her chest was properly closed, bits of various garments protruded from them, and all the drawer rims were dusty. A bowl of moribund flowers stood beside the carriage candle; they were not quite dead enough for Myrtle to throw them away happily. The new bunch, some of those gathered this morning, filled the ewer, awaiting more permanent arrangement.

In the middle of the confusion Myrtle moved, serene,

happy, perfectly at ease. Tonight her appearance, which
so often lacked the finishing touches which Harriet considered so important, was unusually trim. A heap of
underclothes and stockings, hastily discarded upon a
chair, showed how many different garments had been tried
and found to lack some integral part, before Myrtle had
assembled a whole outfit that was beyond reproach. She
had left the faulty clothes out in the open because she
fully intended to deal with them next day. She was genuinely shocked to find how many buttons and tapes were
missing, how many ruffles were ripped from their founda-
tions, and how many unmended holes there were in her
stockings. Tomorrow she must spend the day with her
needle. And even that dreary prospect had no power to
depress her this evening. For with the passing hours of the
day her excitement and her hope had mounted steadily.
The self-reproaches of the morning were forgotten. She
was going to meet Roger, and tonight all would be well.
She was quite certain of it.

In the cluttered room she looked as lovely as a flower.
Her new dress was of soft hyacinth blue, made from the
same pattern as Harriet's, but with rouleaux covered with
velvet the colour of red clover. From the low neck and
short puffed sleeves her throat and arms showed milky
white and perfect, and she had brushed and twisted her
cloud of dark hair until it hung about her forehead, ears
and nape in glossy curls, like the pelt of a black lamb.

Usually she was not aware of her loveliness; indeed,
until lately she had sometimes thought that Fate had made
a grave error when it decreed that Harriet should be ugly
and she beautiful. Ugliness would not have worried her so
much. There were so many things that one could still do
with any face—read, walk in the woods, have a lot of
pets, take interest in the inn's guests, and make up stories
about them, argue, good-naturedly, with Will. Harriet
cared for none of these things. Harriet was really a
woman who was born to be married; she should have had

a man to work for and several children whom she could
have ordered and questioned and put into clean clothes
every day. In happy circumstances, all Harriet's energy and
attention to detail, and all her love of power would have
established her as a benevolent autocrat. So really, Myrtle
thought, Harriet should have had the face which would
have gained her a husband quickly.

But since Roger had come into her life Myrtle had regarded her beauty with more respect. He seemed to value
it so highly. That critical part of her mind which was so
obstreperous sometimes regretted that, and had once
driven her to say to Roger, "I shall be old one day, you
know, and ugly like everybody else." That had been a
mistake, as most attempts at mental honesty were, she had
discovered. And after that the critical ego had been silent,
though it had sometimes writhed under the feeling that
men put beauty too far above other things.

However, as she settled the last curl and turned from the
mirror and went to the box to stroke the kittens once
more, she was satisfied that tonight she did look what
Roger had called her, "a lovely little thing," and she was
quite happy. Because whatever that carping critic in her
mind might say, Myrtle knew that she had a great deal
to compete with in the way of loveliness. Roger spent
most of his time in London, and when she pictured the
world in which he moved there, she peopled it with im-
possibly lovely ladies who moved with stately grace up
and down marble staircases, or floated swan-like through
the measures of a dance. And they were all like Harriet—
neat, trig, complete to the last button; and they had
Harriet's self-assurance, and could get service from
menials, and knew what to say to cooks. They were all,
in fact, far more suited to Roger than Myrtle could ever
be. Yet he said that he loved her, and she was quite certain that she loved him, and once they were married she
would alter. Perhaps Myrtle Moreton would have powers
and abilities which Myrtle Oakley lacked.

The cat reached up in an affectionate gesture and began to sharpen her claws on the new gown. Myrtle put her down gently and was straightening herself when an urgent tapping sounded on her door.

"Come in," she called.

"I can't," said Harriet's voice. "My hands are full. You must open it."

Myrtle flung open the door and stood gaping in astonishment at her sister, who carried a big box in one hand, two pairs of shoes in the other, and whose arms were draped with coats, cloaks and shawls. Behind her was the boy, Sam, carrying two valises and a hat-box.

"Why, Harriett . . . !"

"I'm desperately sorry," said Harriet hastily, "but you'll have to take me in. My room is let. I'll explain later. Come in, Sam. Put the things down . . . there . . . yes, that will do. Now you can go, I'm sure you're busy. And don't forget to tell Kitty to get that room ready immediately. Tell her I shall come along and look at it in a quarter of an hour."

She slammed the door behind the boy and then turned back to Myrtle, renewing her earnest apologies.

"You know I wouldn't have chosen this myself, don't you?"

"Isn't there anywhere else you could go?" Myrtle was ashamed of her ungraciousness; but really, to have Harriet spending the night here would complicate things horribly. Harriet would wonder if she came in late, and in the darkness and the sweet confusion with which she always left Roger it was difficult to be certain that she hadn't a wisp of hay somewhere, or her hair all disarranged. It couldn't have happened more awkwardly.

Harriet upon her part, was thinking of what her feelings would have been had Myrtle suddenly arrived with all her belongings at *her* door. She thought that she could understand Myrtle's feelings; and, at the same time, as she smelt the cats and saw the frantic disorder of the room, she felt sorry for herself as well.

"I'll never forgive Father for this," she said bluntly. Then, "No, I'm sorry to say that there isn't a spare inch anywhere, except in number eleven. And I couldn't very well share with Mr. Roper, could I? But *he* could, or he could have gone to Mrs. Sharp's if Father hadn't gone crazy and promised him my room."

"Promised who?"

"A perfectly horrible person who came in just after I'd fixed everybody in. He was revolting to look at, and as rude as could be, in a quiet way. A little mad, too, I think. I went to fetch Father to turn him out, and then it appears that he's an old friend of Father's and so has to have my room. I said I'd never go in it again; nor I will. I've brought as much as I can."

"Heaven knows where you're going to put it all," said Myrtle vaguely, but with great earnestness lifting the bunch of flowers out of the ewer. "Who is the friend? Mr. Greenwood?" Her vivid little face lightened hopefully. If Will had his friend Mr. Greenwood, the Yarmouth boat-builder, to sit and yarn with it would compensate for having Harriet in her room: one of her watchers would be accounted for.

"Oh, Myrtle," said Harriet wearily, "why won't you listen? I just told you that the man was as ugly as sin, and rude and mad. And then you say, is it Mr. Greenwood? You might know that I shouldn't leave my room for ever because a nice man like Mr. Greenwood had slept in it. This person's name is Smail. I've never seen him before, and I've never heard Father mention him. Have you?"

"No, never," said Myrtle, with more assurance that her faulty memory warranted. She gazed wildly round the room again, and this time lifted the pile of underclothes from the chair and crammed them into a drawer which promptly protested against such overloading by refusing to close at all. Myrtle shoved at it so fiercely that the open hat-box on top of the chest tottered and fell off, shedding, not the bonnet that Harriet expected, but a shower of red rose hips, crimson hawthorn berries, pink spindle and black privet clusters.

"Oh, my God!" exclaimed Myrtle in despair, falling upon them and clutching them together, "I was going to try to make some permanent posy thing with these . . . in little low bowls, you know, with some Honesty and bits of cypress." She glanced up and saw the expression of long-suffering on her sister's face. "Honestly, Harriet, I am sorry about the mess. I would have cleared up a bit if I'd known you were coming."

A pang of self-reproach tinged Harriet's exasperation. Not for the first time she was conscious that Myrtle, for all her careless muddle, possessed a generosity of spirit which she herself lacked. Here she was, for instance, greeting intrusion with apologies, not reproaches.

"Never mind," she said, with unusual resignation. "It's only for tonight. And it's absolutely Father's fault, Myrtle."

"Yes?"

"You don't think he's still feverish, do you? Sam told me another funny thing. Some old couple were at the back door just now, absolutely sopping wet, playing a fiddle and begging. And Father invited them to spend the night in the hay-loft."

"Oh, no!"

"Oh, yes! I suppose he wants them to set the place on fire. Luckily Dick objected. He said the last time somebody slept there the hay was kicked all over the place. So tonight we've got two tramping fiddlers in the haunted attic." She paused, puzzled by the frank relief that shone on Myrtle's face. "In the morning I suppose they'll be gone, and half the silver with them. I can't think what Father was doing. First this Smail person, and now tramps!"

She would have welcomed some word of agreement from Myrtle; a good mutual grumble would have relieved

her feelings. But Myrtle, as ever, was quite unsatisfactory.

"Imagine going sopping wet to sleep in that attic," she
said with a shudder.

"A long sight better than a night in the rain."

"Well," said Myrtle, abandoning all hope of ever re-
storing order among her possessions. "I think I'll go down
now and see if there's anything I can do. Make yourself
at home, Harriet. Shove my things anywhere."

"The cats as well?" asked Harriet with a flash of hu-
mours. Myrtle, on her way to the door, laughed. "No,
save my pussies." The mother cat, as though unwilling to
remain in an unsympathetic atmosphere, sprang from the
basket and began to follow her mistress.

"She wants to go out. Really, she is the cleanest cat I've
ever had," said Myrtle delightedly. "Come on then, Tabby.
And Harriet, when you come out, leave the door open,
will you? Then she can get back to the kittens."

"Your watch is here." There was ample comment upon
Myrtle's strange attitude to her belongings in the simple
sentence.

"Oh? Well, push it in a drawer, will you, there's a
dear."

On account of the cat Myrtle turned left instead of
right outside her own door and went in the direction of
the back stairs. As she left the wide main corridor she
could see, through the little lobby which gave Harriet's
old room a special privacy, two maids at work within,
making the bed anew and laying out fresh towels. Then
she left the front part of the house, turned the corner,
and tripped along a passage flanked with secondary bed-
rooms, and came to the top of the stairs that ran down
into the kitchen.

There was a hanging lantern on the wall, and it shed
a pale glow over the top stairs, leaving the bottom in
shadow. Someone was moving on the lower stairs, so
Myrtle stood aside at the top, waiting. The cat ran lightly

ahead, and there was an exclamation as she collided with the slowly moving body which was mounting the stairs.

"It's all right, Jerry," said a hoarse female voice. "It's nubbut a cat, and ye didn't hurt her. Come on now, luv! Best foot forrard."

Slowly there came into view a tiny old woman bundled in a wet shawl which shone like silk from the water on it, leading by the hand an old man who had once been tall, but was now so bent that except for the sharp upward tilt of his head his face would have been parallel with the ground. The light from the lantern fell on his face as he climbed the stairs, and Myrtle could see that his eyes, old and milky, fixed and expressionless were the eyes of a blind man. Blindness was implicit in his grasp of the hand of the little woman, too, blindness and utter trust like the trust of a child.

From the sodden folds of the shawl the woman's face looked out like the face of a bird from a nest. She had bright beady little eyes and brown weathered skin puckered with a thousand wrinkles. The wrinkles shifted and some of them deepened as she smiled at Myrtle.

"I'm sorry, lady," she said with cheerful apology, "didn't know you was waiting. My old man here, he can't see so well. That make him a bit slow."

"I can't see at all," said the old man in a quavering falsetto. They were on the top stair now, full in Myrtle's view. They were so ragged, so wet, so utterly pathetic that Myrtle could have cried. She could see the bulge under the shawl where the woman was sheltering the fiddle, and she could perfectly well understand why Will had been prompted to offer them shelter.

The little old woman possibly mistook the meaning of Myrtle's grave horrified scrutiny. She said cheerfully:

"It's all right, lady. We was invited in. The gemmum said we could sleep in the attic, and he towd me which one."

"It . . . it isn't very nice," said Myrtle, who had never seen it.

"That'll be nice to us," replied the woman staunchly. "We ain't used to luckshery. Give us a bit of a roof over us and we'll be as right as a trivet."

"Have you had any supper?"

"No," said the blind man promptly. "Nor we didn't have no dinner on account of the rain. Nubbuddy'll harken to the music in the wet."

"Look," said Myrtle, a little hesitantly. "If you go down again and say I sent you . . . say Miss Myrtle sent you . . . and ask to sit by the fire in the backhouse, I'll come down myself in a minute or two and find you something to eat."

Hoarse voice and quaver chanted a unison of thanks. The little woman turned her charge about and began to pilot him downstairs again. Myrtle heard the man say:

"Who was that, Lindy? The landlady?"

"No. That was a lady."

It seemed to Myrtle unbearably touching that they should have names, and use them to one another, just like any other couple. Lindy and Jerry . . . such endearing little names, too. And borne by such sad wrecks. They had been babies once, and maybe their mothers had chosen their names with love and joy and pride, and speculated on what their children would do in the world. And they had come to this. . . .

It was the kind of thought which often occupied Myrtle's mind and was responsible for her not listening, a trait which Harriet found most annoying.

She stood at the top of the stairs now and wondered what more she could do for the fiddler and his wife. Well, the answer to that was simple.

Turning sharply she retraced her steps to the corner of the main passage opposite the alcove of Harriet's room. Here, huge and glossy, stood the linen press, it shelves piled with sheets and blankets and quilts and pillowcases.

Being part of Harriet's care, it was in apple-pie order, each article with its kind. Myrtle studied the shelves for a moment. No. The couple probably went to bed in their clothes, so sheets would not be appreciated and might be ruined. Blankets? Yes. She tugged, from near the bottom of the pile, two thick red blankets with black borders; and, from halfway down the quilt pile a heavy wadded cover, old but clean. She was, quite genuinely, unaware that both piles, so roughly assaulted, were now ready to pitch forward and fall out when next the press was opened. She pushed the door close upon the resisting mass and sped back to the top of the kitchen stairs.

Here, from the narrow landing lit by the lantern another flight rose at right angles, steep, narrow and pitchy black, and as she stood there Myrtle began to reconsider her impulsive decision to make the haunted attic more comfortable for its pathetic guests.

She knew that at the top of those dark stairs there were several rooms; one or two of those nearest the stair head were occasionally let to guests of humble standing. The others were occupied by the staff of the inn. Mrs. Sharman slept alone; the maids shared their apartments. At the far end of the attic floor, in the remotest corner of the old building, was the attic which no one ever entered.

The story of what had happened in that deserted room was only dimly remembered by a few old people in Fulsham; but garbled versions of it had entered into the living folk lore which is always being made in country places. There was no one now under the *Fleece*'s wide rambling roof who had known Ellie Roon, or Hester her daughter, or Tom Drury, whose name had once been a thing to shudder at. Will Oakley had found among a pile of old papers the bill which promised the award for the little highwayman's arrest. He had thought it interesting, but Harriet had called it rubbish, and had dealt with it accordingly. And even Will had not known the true connection between that yellowing paper and the attic which no one would enter. Nevertheless, there was, in Fulsham, the definite belief that the attic floor of the *Fleece* was haunted; and the belief was fostered by the stories of nervous maidservants who declared that at certain times a low moaning cry could be heard, accompanied by restless footsteps like those of a person who sought for something. Will and Harriet dismissed the stories as nonsense; but Myrtle never heard the matter mentioned without a chill of the spine.

And now, at this hour of the evening when the attic floor would be emptied of people, and when the first floor itself would be but sparsely populated, she was pledged by her own impulse to mount those stairs and enter the very room itself. And it was all very well for her father and sister to make fun of the story; after all, everyone had his weakness. Harriet would grow pale and turn back if a harmless reptile crossed her path; Will had once confessed to a similar feeling for spiders. So why shouldn't she be aware and frightened of the supernatural?

It would be easy enough, she thought, to go down to the warm bright kitchen, see that the poor couple had their supper, and give them the bedding to arrange for themselves. But somehow that seemed banal after the pleasant idea she had had of sending them warm and fed up to the waiting bed in the attic. Besides Harriet might be nosing about, and she would protest against the use even of coloured blankets and cotton quilts by dirty wet tramps. And then the little pair, Lindy and Jerry, would feel badly. It would be so much simpler to go up the stairs and make the bed as she had planned. If she let a stupid fear deter her she would be ashamed for ever more. And it was only just six o'clock, and she could take the lantern.

So, acting quickly before fear could get the better of her, she hooked down the lantern, clutched the bedclothes firmly, and began to climb the stairs.

It was utterly silent upon the attic floor. She was horribly conscious of the space dividing her from the safe company of other people; horribly aware of the deserted sleeping chambers on either side of the narrow passage. It seemed as though the silence had personality, alien, menacing. The noise of her own footsteps was an affront to it. She found herself trying to walk quietly; only then she could hear the thudding of her own heart. Harriet's right; I *am* a fool, she thought, a fool to come here and a worse fool to be so scared.

But she kept on, drawing upon an obstinacy which can, in some circumstances, be a substitute for courage, and at last she pushed open the stiffly moving door.

When she had said that the attic was not very nice she had imagined it as any ordinary room would be after a long period of disuse. She was not prepared for the scene of utter desolation which the beams of her lantern revealed. At some period of time the attic had been open to the out-of-doors, and birds had fouled the floor and the shelf upon which young Hester had kept her books. Now the birds and the rain were excluded, for damp had seeped through the floor to the ceiling of the bedroom below; so the window through which Ellie had flung herself screaming, the window which she had smashed in the last moment of her humble harassed life, was boarded over roughly. But the bed where Ellie had borne Hester, the bed which Hester had left in order to let Death into the house, and under which Tom Drury had spent his last hours, still stood mouldering by the wall. It was past her power to make it usable. Myrtle saw at a glance. Fungi, sinister and unhealthy, sprouted in the folds of the indistinguishable bedding, and the dampness had rotted the cover of the mattress, so that the straw with which it was stuffed protruded in several places.

Poor little pair, she thought. They'll have to sleep on the floor after all. So I can't make the bed and surprise them. I might just as well not have come. It was so exactly the anticlimax which might be expected of any plan of hers that her lips curved in a smile which was half amusement and half self-mockery. I never have any luck with *stuff*, she thought, disgustedly. Now if Harriet had had this idea there'd have been a new mattress pushed on to the landing yesterday.

Ruefully she laid the blankets and the quilt on the floor in the corner. As she stooped something flashed in the lantern light, and when she had reached out her hand and taken hold of it she discovered that she had found a guinea. It was marked with the date of its minting, 1760. Interest, rather than avarice, prompted her to hold the lantern lower and to inspect the floor carefully. Near the bed, just below one of the bristling outcrops of straw, lay a crown piece and a penny. She picked them up and then turned her attention to the mattress. Was it possible that she had stumbled upon some miser's hoard? Was it even within the bounds of reason that the whole story of the haunting had arisen through the desire of the hoarder to keep people out of the attic? Myrtle's romantic mind seized upon the idea with avidity and a certain relief.

Setting the lantern on the seat of the broken chair near the bed, she explored the rotten mattress with fingers that moved eagerly yet fastidiously. The first sharp tug released a shower of coins. Guineas, sovereigns, florins, and four-penny pieces fell tinkling and went rolling upon the uneven boards of the floor. Now free from fear and shaken with excitement, Myrtle gathered them together into a square of cloth torn from the old damp bed-clothes.

Most of the coins were of gold, as bright and shining as they had been when Ellie Roon's worked-scarred hands had tucked them away; the silver ones had blackened, and the few coppers were green with verdigris. Staring at them, with her eyes wide in wonder, Myrtle could see how it was that money which lay at the root of so much misery and evil in the world, had attained its ascendancy over the minds of men. The bed was useless, the mattress rotten, but the money, outlasting both its hoarder and its hiding-place, was as good as ever. It could be taken out and spent tonight.

So far as her not very thorough inspection could inform her, it seemed that no coin had been added to the hoard since 1765. No later minting had its representative here. For fifty-two years, then, the secret had lain undisturbed. And whose was the money? How had it been acquired? Why had it been hidden in this unlikely place? And why had it never been claimed?

Myrtle stared at the heterogeneous collection of coins as though they might answer the questions that crowded into her mind. But the money, like the attic, held its secret. In itself it was as lifeless, as insignificant as any pile of coins taken from a till or a cash-box. There was nothing about it to inform even Myrtle's active imagination of what blood and tears, what toil and self-denial, what love and humility, scheming and terror had gone to its getting. How badly it had been earned, how sternly saved, and what tragic happenings it had caused—these were secrets still. Ellie Roon had lived and sinned and suffered and died; and she had taken her story with her.

Slowly Myrtle drew the corners of the square of cloth together and tied them as a cook ties a bag-pudding. What a surprise for her father and for Harriet! And all because she had met that little couple on the back stairs. Suppose she had not sent them down again. The little woman's bright eyes would not have missed that coin on the floor.

At the thought Myrtle grew still and thoughtful. Perhaps Fate had meant the tramps to find the money; perhaps the wet afternoon, and Will's generous impulse, which Harriet had thought so crazy, had all been part of some slowly maturing plan with which she, from the best of motives, had interfered.

On the other hand, if Fate were capable of bringing the fiddler and his wife here, and of causing Will to invite them into the attic, it was hardly feasible that it would have allowed Myrtle, at the last moment, to frustrate its intentions. No; if it were destined that the hoard should be found this evening, it was clear enough that she, Myrtle Oakley, who had never entered the attic before, and who had violated a deep instinct in order to do so now, had been chosen to be the finder. Besides Will had bought the *Fleece* as it stood, "with contents." And he could do with the money, as Myrtle well knew. There had been lean months at Lammingham before the move was made, and the purchase of the more flourishing business had demanded all his savings, as well as the sum gained by the sale of the old one.

Myrtle began to take a more practical view of her find. But even as she speculated upon what the money—she reckoned it close to two hundred pounds—would buy, she opened the knot and took out two of the golden guineas. The pathetic couple should go away that much richer at least; and if Will chose to give them some further reward for their unwitting service, well, so much the better.

She took the lantern in one hand and the heavy poke in the other and made for the door. She was just over the threshold and into the passage when a gust of the autumn wind, flinging itself upon the old house and entering the top storey through a hundred cracks and crannies, swept down upon her in the form of an icy draught which was like the very breath of fear. It was as cold as well-water about her ankles; it laved her bare neck and arms and thrust chilly vibrating fingers through her hair. The flame of the candle within the lantern flickered and bent, and although it did not go out, the smoke from it had so blackened the glass that the tiny light became muted and strange, more terrifying than darkness.

And then, as she forced herself forward on feet that seemed to be weighted to the floor, she heard what she had, subconsciously, been expecting and dreading to hear—the sound of a low, suffering moan, and the slow regular pacing of feet. She knew, as she stiffened into immobility, that this was the moment which she had dreaded all her life. The faintness which had always come upon her with the recounting of any uncanny story, her senseless fear of the darkness, her unwillingness to mount those stairs and her awareness of the silence and remoteness of the place where now she stood, had all been pointers, warning that this moment was awaiting her somewhere, sometime. It was as though some part of her had always known that she would one day stand, helpless, terrified, exposed to an onslaught of some pre-destined evil. Her mind reeled drunkenly, thinking that it was for this that the tramping couple had come, and been asked in, and inspired her with pity; it was for this that she had found the money, so that she might be delayed and incautious. Now she was trapped in this haunted place, in this eeerie light, hearing moans and footsteps where no natural sound could be. What next?

Perhaps because of the very keenness of her fear she neither fainted, nor cried out, nor fled. There was, for an unmeasured moment, nothing in her except the realization and the expectation of horror. It was without relief, without surprise, that she saw, at the far end of the passage, between the attics inhabited by the maids, first a faint luminous glow and then, outlined in it, a shadowy female figure. She stood motionless, awaiting its approach, and it was another second or two before she realized that the ghostly footsteps and the foosteps of the woman in the passage did not coincide. The figure with the candle moved with a rapid shuffle; the footsteps of the unseen were slow and regular.

A vast feeling of relief filled her, freeing her lungs, her blood, her limbs and her reason. Of course . . . it was a human figure; one of the maids; in fact, it was Effie Stevens, and she was stopping by her own door, the third from the head of the stairs.

Myrtle called "Effie!" And Effie withdrew her hand from the door and spun around, showing a face of fright as great in its degree as the more deadly horror which still blanched and stiffened the countenance of her young mistress.

"I'm so sorry, Effie," gasped Myrtle, now able to move forward and cover the distance between them, "I wouldn't have frightened you for the world. But, oh, I have been frightened myself. I heard it, somebody walking and moaning. . . ."

"Oh, no, Miss," said Effie with a terrified glance. "Thass ony the wind, you know. That howl in the roof up here, time there's a gale."

"Listen, then," said Myrtle, and the two young women seemed to hush their breathing, as within the sanctuary of human company and friendly candlelight they listened for a sound from the world of the unseen. Then:

"I doon't hear nowt," said Effie stoutly. And Myrtle, although she knew that the noise had been audible and had now stopped, thought suddenly that Effie must, every night of her life, face those stairs and that passage and spend the night on this horrible floor. So, with commendable self-control, she forced a sick pallid smile.

"Nor do I," she said weakly. "It must be what you say —just the wind. But you see. I'm not used to it. It startled me horribly and made me imagine things. I'm so sorry, Effie. I hope I didn't frighten you."

"That ony give me a bit of a turn like when you spook," said Effie generously. "Not knowing you wuz up here, you see. But thass all right, Miss Myrtle. You get along down now. Up here ain't nice at night for them as ain't used to it."

"I'm going now," said Myrtle. She passed Effie, who pressed herself against the wall to make room, and hurried down the stairs, not noticing that Effie had turned again and watched her out of sight before she again ventured to lay a hand on the latch of her door. She was down in the warmth and brightness and bustle of the kitchen before she noticed that through all her dreadful experience she had retained her clutch on the poke of coins. The two that she had separated and held in her hand were glued to her palm by the cold sweat of terror. She paused by the kitchen dresser and opened the drawer full of oddments like string and skewers and nails, and pushed her bundle well to the back of it. The wrapping was not very stout and she did not want to break it and shed a Danæ shower in front of her two poor protégés.

They were pressed close to the hearth in the back kitchen. Mrs. Sharman had already supplied them with bread and cheese and a slice of pie apiece; for when she heard that Myrtle had sent them down and was coming herself to give them supper, the cook had thought—ten to one she'll forget it and then break her silly soft heart about it for hours. So she had guarded against Myrtle's bad memory and managed to find time to make a note for Harriet: "Harf a loaf, harf pound cheese, 2 peeces Pie for old cupple miss mertel arst it."

Lindy got to her feet and brushed the crumbs from her lap when she saw Myrtle.

"Here's the lady, Jerry," she said, and the blind man swiveled round and made the gesture of touching the hat which his wife had removed from his head and put to dry in the hearth.

"We've had a good meal and we're grateful," he said.

"Oh," said Myrtle. "I was coming down sooner but something stopped me. I'm glad you've had your supper. Look . . . have this, will you? It'll get you some supper tomorrow, too."

Colour flamed into her white face; she loved giving people things, but sometimes, as in this case, she was embarrassed by the act. She thrust the two guineas at the old woman and said "Good-bye" very quickly, and was hurrying away to escape being thanked. But the woman, after a hasty, stupefied glance at the shining coins, called after her in a sharp, urgent voice:

"Lady! Stop a minnit. There's summat I want to tell

ye. T'ain't just because you give us this, though thank you kindly, I'm sure. I was saying to my old man here, wasn't I Jerry?"

"You was saying a lot of rubbish," said the blind man tolerantly.

"T'ain't rubbish! Not when you've got the eye like I have. Lady, I've got a seeing eye, and it don't work for money and it don't work for just the asking. But it worked for you, out there on the stair as plain as daylight. And I was telling him about it time we et our supper, so these has nowt to do with it."

She seemed alight with an earnest desire to convince Myrtle that she was offering her something that was not to be bought.

"What is it?" asked Myrtle gently.

"I could see that you was going to be lucky, my dear. You're going to have a stroke of real good fortune right soon. Only maybe you won't see that it's good, and you may hev to cry a bit over it. But it is good, take my word. Only first, you're going to be faced with danger. And maybe that won't look like danger any more than the other look like good luck. But that's a real danger, my dear, don't you make any mistake about it. Run from it, scream out, save yourself somehow."

She stopped, as though exhausted by the force of her exhortation. Myrtle thought, with astonishment, of her find and her fright. Really, it was marvellous, the way the little old woman's words seemed to be already fulfilled.

"You mind me now," said Lindy earnestly, "and get away from the danger whatever you do."

"Don't worry," Myrtle said. "I think you have got the eye, or whatever it's called. And I think that all this has happened already."

"It couldn't have. I only just saw it now, on the stairs."

"That's what I mean. I've had good fortune, and I . . . think I've been in danger since then."

Lindy's puckered little face fell into line of disappointment and displeasure.

"This is still to come," she said, almost as huffily as if Myrtle had expressed frank incredulity. "Whatever's happened to you just lately, this is to come, and I'm warning ye. You should give heed to me."

"Do no such thing," quavered the blind man. "Lindy's seen a mortal lot of things in her time, but I'll bet she never see us with a roof over us and good meal in our bellies tonight."

"I can't see for myself!" She turned to vent her ruffled feelings upon her husband. "If I've told ye that once I've told ye a thousand times. Nor for anyone belonging to me. Nor for money. Nor for being asked. But for all that I've got the seeing eye, mock how you will. And the lady here'll be sorry that she didn't heed me afore she's much older."

"Oh, but indeed I will," said Myrtle soothingly. "I'll remember it all. There's to be some luck that won't look like it at first; and then some danger."

"The other way about," said Lindy shortly. It was easy to see that where her belief in her talent was concerned she was a true artist. Neither gratitude for past favours nor hope for more to come was allowed to mitigate her attitude. In genuine contrition Myrtle cried, "Of course, the other way around. Now, can you see something else? Am I going to be married?"

"I told ye, I can't see for asking," said the little woman, not yet wholly appeased. "But as it hapens, I did see it the moment I laid eyes on ye. Yes, you'll be married, right enough. And you'll never want for worldly gear." Her voice softened, "Nor you should. For the hand that's open to give will often catch Fortune's eye and come back the richer."

"Well," said Myrtle, "thank you very much. I've never had such a nice fortune told for me. I'll often remember you."

"Remember to cry out in the nick of danger," said Lindy——but kindly this time. "And thank you for all that you've done for my old man and me." She smiled and bobbed. The blind man, judging that the conversation was closing, added his word of thanks, and again raised his hand towards the place where his hat usually rested. Myrtle, with her mind already detached from the pair, swept them both with a vague sweet smile and darted away. There was, somewhere in the back of her mind, an idea that she had promised to help somebody who was short-handed. But she had forgotten about it. And the idea that Harriet would be angry with her troubled her slightly. Why?

Harriet was angry. She attacked Myrtle as soon as she saw her in the manner which so often denied the difference in their ages, making Harriet seem like the sensible admonishing elder and Myrtle a silly recalcitrant child.

"Where *have* you been? You said you were coming down to see if you could do anything to help. And here I've been with that fool of an Effie in the dining-room instead of Sarah, and Father shut away with his friend and Mrs. Sharman snapping and snarling, and you nowhere to be seen. I do think you might help just a little on an evening like this."

"Oh, I will. I'll do anything. I've been pottering about. I'm sorry. What did you want me to do?"

"Nothing now. It's all done. But you could have overlooked Effie setting a table."

"I know. I am sorry, Harriet. But you see, I met those poor little old people on their way to the attic, and thought I'd just take up some bedding for them. And, Sister, what do you think I found?" She reverted, in this moment of excitement, to the childish name.

"I don't know. Some rubbish, I'll be bound." Harriet turned aside to attack Effie. "You've been a mighty long time changing your shoes. And your cap is crooked. And . . . oh, come here!" With hands which even impatience could not render clumsy or wasteful of movement, she straightened Effie's cap and re-tied the strings of her apron. "There, get along now and do your best, for goodness sake."

It occurred to Myrtle that her secret would keep a little longer. After all, she would not tell Harriet until after she had told Will. Harriet's "Some rubbish, I'll be bound," was very damping; she didn't deserve to hear something exciting.

"Where is Father?"

"In the Little Parlour with his friend Smail."

"Oh, good! I'll go and have a look at him."

"You can't. Father said specially that they weren't to be disturbed. So as well as being turned out of my room, I have nowhere to sit . . . when I do get time to sit down."

"But I've something to tell Father, and something to show him."

"I suppose it'll keep. Of course, go if you like. But he said that they were to have supper in there alone and were not to be disturbed."

Sometimes Harriet's voice sounded like a saw, Myrtle thought.

"Oh, all right then. I won't go. As you say, it'll keep. I'll see if I can help Effie."

Yes, that's the way, thought Harriet, regarding Myrtle's back, stay out while all the real work is being done and then go peacocking about in the dining-room so that everyone can stare and think how pretty you are. And then, oh God! why do I always have such horrible thoughts about her? She's the kindest person I've ever known, and the loveliest, and she's modest and patient and generous. Why must she have this effect upon me? I do love her. I'd do anything for her, and yet I always act and think as though I hated her.

Standing there, alone for the moment, midway between the bustle of the kitchen and the bustle of the dining-room, Harriet sighed and pressed her hand to her head with a

gesture of weariness and despair which she would not, for
the world, have had anyone witness. There were a few
occasions when her self-imposed activity and self-incul-
cated anxiety resulted in nervous tension which seemed to
her the prelude of madness. For a moment or two,
at such times, with an ache in her head and a nagging pain
in her back, she would feel that life had defeated her. All
her activities seemed trivial and senseless; nobody loved
her. Myrtle appeared to, but then Myrtle loved everybody;
and Will pretended to simply because he was her father.
The inn was hateful, and would get on just as well without
her. She might as well be dead.

These phases lasted only a short time. Her good health
and excellent nerves soon re-asserted themselves, and there
she was, as busy, as completely engrossed with trivial
routine, as ever. But the moments were there, nevertheless,
poignant and revealing.

This one passed; but for once her mood of depression
and its resultant physical weakening, had been overlooked.
Georges Marguerat, having finishing his hasty meal, came
quickly out of the dining-room, searching for Harriet,
whom Effie had pointed out as the landlady. Effie made
no distinctions between landlord's wives and their other
female appurtenances. She had started to work at the
Fleece during the period when Job Wainwright, with his
consciousness of his waning powers inflamed by Hester
Roon's treatment of him, had embarked upon the wildest
and most transient sexual adventures in all his long
career. To Effie each succeeding mistress had been "the
landlady," and it was natural that she should now regard
Harriet as the occupant of that position.

George Marguerat had seen Harriet on his arrival. She
had been then in the midst of a perfect exhibition of efficiency, level-headedness and resourcefulness. It was a
surprise to the young man to come across her suddenly
with her straight shoulders drooping, her hand pressed
to her forehead, her whole posture eloquent of weariness

and despair. It prompted him to accost her with especial consideration of manner.

"I'm sorry to trouble you . . . but I need your help."

Harriet was herself again instantly. But she had noticed his manner, and as she raised her eyes to his face she noticed something which had escaped her attention in the busy moment of reception. Just as her face wore scars over its original beauty, so his hadsome face was marred by a puckering gash which on one side pulled his eyebrow upwards and his mouth down. Of course, in a man it did not matter much, if at all. He was a handsome person still; but, combined with his deferential manner, she found his physical defect comforting. It was as though they were two people of the same kind and tongue who had met in an alien land.

"Anything I can do I shall do with pleasure," she said, with an obligingness which was only slightly a matter of habit.

"It is about a horse. I require a good horse, reliable, yet speedy. I have to make a two-hour journey which is very important. I would undertake to send the animal back safely tomorrow morning. And I would, since I am unknown to you, deposit any sum you cared to name, to be re-claimed, with suitable deductions, of course, by the man who would bring it back tomorrow."

"Yes. That is quite all right," said Harriet. "We keep horses for hire. I'll get the ostler for you."

"Unfortunately, I have already seen him. All the horses are out, bar one, which I understand is never hired in any circumstances."

"That's Katie," remarked Harriet with a smile. "She's my father's own mount. He wouldn't hire her. I know." She twisted the ring on her finger, and the young Frenchman noticed that her hands were as lovely as her face was grotesque. She had style, too, that indefinable quality which makes clothes more than garments or decorations. He gave her a smile which would have turned the head of the pale girl in the coach. It inspired Harriet's resourcefulness.

"I'll send across to Willowbrook," she said. "They'll lend a horse if I ask."

"How long will that take?"

"Not more than half an hour."

He glanced up at the clock on the half-landing.

"I canot wait," he said, mastering his impatience. "If you remember, I did wait some time for my meal. It is imperative that I reach my destination on time." He smiled and waited. And Harriet responded exactly as he had hoped.

"Perhaps you might have Katie. I can't ask Father because he is not to be disturbed. But I'll take the responsibility myself." It was the kind of thing she loved above all to say. And to say it while at the same time obliging this polite, handsome, charming person was particularly gratifying. "Yes," she said more definitely, "you may take Katie. But you'll be very careful of her, won't you? And send her back early tomorrow. Or I shall be in terrible trouble." She smiled, a conspiratorial smile, which, although it twisted the painted mask of her face, did also light up her fine grey eyes.

"I'd better see Dick and tell him myself. He honestly wouldn't believe you if you told him you'd hired the mare."

"I can hardly thank you," said the young man. "And I will see that no reproaches come your way through me. I am an experienced rider, and careful." He smiled, a memory of cavalry charges flitting through his mind. How amusing for the gods, to see him here pleading his fitness to be trusted with an inn-keeper's precious steed! Very amusing for him, too, to think that this never-to-be-hired Katie was going to carry him one stage back towards the cavalry charges again. The warm flood of excitement and impatience flooded him again.

Harriet mistook the smile for pleasure in having the

matter of hiring a horse settled, and she smiled back. For a brief second their glances met and held and an incandescent glow of feeling—obscure, doomed never to be recognized or named or fully understood—shone between them. Then, impulsively, he lifted one of her hands to his lips, laid a fleeting kiss upon her fingers, murmured another word of thanks, and then turned abruptly away to the row of pegs where he had hung his hat and coat.

Ten minutes later, seen off by a surly and infuriated young ostler, Georges Marguerat took the road to the coast, blessing his luck—and Harriet, who had been Luck's lackey for an hour—with each easy elastic stride of Katie's legs.

NIGHT

Myrtle

Supper was ended and the activity of the inn was running down, like a wheel that revolves more and more slowly until it ceases to spin at all. The maids were starting their final tasks, warming sheets with hasty thrust of long-handled warming pans for such guests as felt the cold, running hither and thither with cans of hot water, laying the last logs on the fires.

In the kitchen Mrs. Sharman sat like a priestess who has, once again, successfully conducted a complicated and sacred ritual. A pair of purple felt slippers were easing her tired feet; her sleeves were unrolled for the first time since the morning; and before her upon the tidied table was a large plate piled with food and a pewter pint mug of ale with a cauliflower head of froth.

It had been one of the busiest evenings she could remember, and she was well satisfied with it.

"Warm my bed while you are about it," she said in a lordly manner to the scurrying Effie. "After all this running about I feel the cold upstairs. Leave the pan in. I shan't be long."

"I've to clear the table in the Little Parlour yet," said Effie with a harassed look.

"Let Kitty see to my bed then."

She did full justice to her food and liquor, but was not disposed to linger over the meal. Ten minutes later, when Myrtle peeped cautiously into the kitchen from the passage door, it was empty and she was able to move

unseen across the width of it and let herself out at the
back door.

Escape had been made far more easy than she had
dared to hope. As the dining-room emptied and the guests
began to disperse she had dreaded that Harriet would say
something about going up to the shared bedroom since the
Little Parlour was closed to them. But Harriet, whose
movements were never questioned by Myrtle, had actually troubled to say, "Don't wait about for me, Myrtle.
If you want to go up, do. I'll take care not to disturb you."

"Oh, I shan't go to bed just yet. I shall be about somewhere for quite a while," said Myrtle deliberately vague.
Harriet did not bother to ask where the "somewhere," or
how long the "while" might be.

That was most unlike Harriet, who, even at her busiest,
seemed to find time to ask awkward questions. But then
Harriet had been rather preoccupied all through the
evening. Whatever was on her mind had not sweetened
her temper, she had snapped and snarled and chased the
maids rather as though she were a sheep dog engaged in
folding a herd of particularly foolish and obstinate sheep.
But two or three times Myrtle had caught her standing
still, lost in thought, with a peculiarly in-drawn, planning
look on her face. And when she had finished speaking to
Myrtle she had turned to Effie and said, "Has Mrs. Sharman gone to bed yet?"

"She wuz jest about off," said Effie distractedly.

"Well, I want the key to the store-room. Ask her for
it, will you? If she *has* gone you must go up and fetch it
for me."

And that *was* just like Harriet, thought Myrtle, making
her escape; to choose nine o'clock in the evening of one
of the year's very busiest days, to make a raid upon, and
probably some quite revolutionary rearrangement in, the
Holy of Holies. Myrtle beat a hasty retreat before she
could be dragged in to assist.

And here it was at last, the moment to which she had

been moving forward for a fortnight; the moment for which she had yearned and longed.

She splashed across the yard, the puddle water cold on her ankles, the bell of her skirt lifted high on either side. The critic in her mind remarked upon the stupidity of wearing one's best clothes and spending so long in curling one's hair in order to cross a wet yard to a tryst in a dark hay-loft. But the feminine, instinctive Myrtle knew that there was confidence to be gained from the knowledge that one looked one's best, and in that bedrock of the mind where neither evasion nor self-deception is possible, she knew that she had need of confidence.

She entered the stable warily; it was not so late that Dick was sure to be abed. It was possible that he and a crony or two might be dawdling by the fire in the harness-room at the end. But the place was silent and in darkness, so, at the foot of the rungs which made a perpendicular ladder against the stable wall, Myrtle halted for a moment, trying to steady her breathing which her anticipation, and the slight nervous dread which shot it through, had shaken. Then she began to climb. Still some rungs from the top she said, very softly, "Roger," and from the loft came the sound of hay rustling as the young man rose from the place where he had been waiting.

He came to the edge of the square opening in the loft floor and said, "Darling!" in a thick, urgent voice which she had not heard before. Then, before she could release her hold of the top stave and nimbly step to the side, he seized her, so quickly and clumsily that for one horrible second her feet swung, unsupported, over the hole, and she had to clutch him tightly to save herself from falling. As soon as she felt the floor beneath her again the momentary fear passed and she said with a little laugh, "You almost had me down."

"No, no," he said, in that same queer voice. "I had you safe. I wouldn't let you go. I'll never let you go, Myrtle."

He held her still, just as he had lifted her from the ladder, and now, tightening his clasp, until it was painful, he bent his head and began to kiss her—not the gentle, lover-like kisses with which he had greeted her on other occasions, but in a hot, fierce, almost angry fashion which frightened her. Once or twice before, especially at their last meeting, he had kissed her almost in that way towards the end of their time together, and she had taken it as a sign that she must go. She had always been able to plead that it was late, that Harriet or her father would be waiting, and she had always hurried away, as much afraid of herself as of her lover. And now the two-edged fear was upon her in the first moment.

She made an effort to force things into their normal pattern. Leaning her head backwards and drawing her mouth free, she said:

"It has seemed a long time. A whole fortnight."

"A fortnight of hell," he said. There was still that queer thick slur in his voice, and as he spoke the reek of brandy on his breath told her the reason.

"You've been drinking," she said impulsively.

"Yes," he said in a rough, brutal voice. "I've been drinking. The old man opened his heart and his cellar. And when that damned dinner was over, with all the mopping and mowing and the grinning and leering . . . well, I just helped myself. What's wrong with that? I'd earned it, hadn't I? Blast the lot of them!"

"What dinner, Roger? Who grinned and leered at you, darling? Have they been horrid to you again?" She knew that of late his welcome had been anything but kind, and he had told her, more than once, that it was only in order to see her that he came home at all these days. "Come and sit down and tell me all about it."

He led her, willingly enough, back to the piled hay where he had been sitting. The scent of it, the ghostly perfume of all the myriad little flowers that had gone to its making, rose around them as their weight pressed the soft piles. He had released the painful clutch in which he had held her, and Myrtle drew a long breath of relief. It was all right. She had been stupid to be frightened. He had been drinking, but he was not drunk. She reached out and took his hand. "Tell me all about it," she repeated. But he drew his hand away, put both arms around her again and bore her backwards against the hay.

"I don't want to talk," he said. "I only want you . . . like this. I've thought of nothing else, Myrtle. Thought of it. Dreamed of it. I've . . . there's . . . nobody else, Myrtle. Nobody else matters a——in hell!"

"Roger!"

"Well, it's true. Let's have the truth for once. Let's be done with humbug."

"Something has upset you."

"Don't talk, darling. Just don't talk."

Under the pressure of his hands, the warmth of his mouth, that treacherous current in her blood began to run faster. And for a space of time, not to be counted in moments, but in the rapid thunder of their heartbeats, they lay pressed together. There was something almost inhuman in this contact of vibrant bodies, lost it seemed to every sense save that of touch, deprived by the darkness of the power of sight, and forebearing, of their own will, from speech. They might have been the first man and the first woman who, newly emerged from quadrupedant state, had just discovered that arms could enfold, hands clutch and cling. But, since an age-old process of evolution divided them from that primeval moment, the power of thought was at work with them, and although the close held flesh was fusing towards unity, darkly, within the separate shells of their contiguous skulls, the lonely streams of consciousness, which could never fuse, never unify, were busy about their separate and secret thoughts. Roger, drunk with wine and with this more heady draught, groped and blundered, wondering what to tell her, whether to tell her at all, whether it would not be better to snatch at this moment's pleasure and leave the rest to chance. Myrtle thought more clearly, for the cynic in her mind was making a desperate bid for mastery, and, after a wild struggle, gained it and said distinctly—It is what I always suspected: seduction in a hay-loft. Very nice!

Almost reluctantly she unclasped her arms and began to push herself free. "Roger," she said in a small voice, "don't. Wait. I want to talk to you. I *must* talk to you."

"What is there to say?" he asked, with his lips in her hair. "What's the use of saying anything?" But the grip of his arms slackened and Myrtle sat upright, and reaching out found both his hands, which she folded between her own.

"Listen, Roger! All this fortnight I've been thinking. Darling, you mustn't mind what I'm going to say. I don't mean it nastily. But you were cross when I left you last time, weren't you? And I knew why. In fact, until this morning I wasn't quite sure whether you would ever come again. And now, I do think, I know it doesn't sound a very nice thing to say, but I do think the time has come when we can't go on like this any longer . . . all furtive, I mean, and deceiving father . . . and . . . well, you know what I mean, don't you, darling?"

There was a pleading note in her voice as she ended the faltering little speech. It was very difficult, like trying to say a few intimate things to a stranger. Perhaps she had spoken too soon. On the other hand, she had been forced to speak at once. For the Roger whom she knew, despite their short acquaintance, the gay, spirited person who had charmed her, had never been in the loft at all this evening. From the moment when he lifted her from the ladder there had been between them the question which, on former evenings, had only reared its troublesome head during the final moments, the bare and inescapable question of passion's assuagement, the question which had the power to make them enemies rather than lovers.

She sat still, hoping for some reassuring, understanding

answer, dreading an outburst of anger. But his first words were comforting.

"I've been thinking the same thing, sweetheart . . . if you call it thinking."

It wasn't thinking, this frenzied struggle between the body's desire and the mind's reasonableness, between the urge to do what one wanted and the need to do what was expedient. It wasn't thinking; it was a form of torture. And it wasn't ended, God damn it! although up at the Hall his father and old Wilson were indulging in an orgy of self-congratulation, and his mother and sisters were swarming all round Miss Wilson, whom he must now call Dorothy, and looking on her as though she were a combination of Rescue Society and Thorley's Bank. The core of the problem wasn't even touched yet . . . though Myrtle's faltering little speech had opened the way to it.

He felt muzzy in the head, too, and regretted being so free with the brandy. If only he could think a little more clearly. . . . Suppose he promised, here and now, to marry Myrtle. He'd have her then, tonight. And tomorrow some damned lackey from the Hall would come down and spill the news. And that would be the end. He was not a student of character, and had never before been interested in the personality of any of his mistresses; but he had gone sufficiently far towards falling in love with Myrtle to know that she would never forgive deception so flagrant. The only alternative, and the only hope of making the kind of semi-permanent arrangement which was all he could hope for now, was to be frank with her and offer her a dishonourable proposal, trapped out as romantically as possible.

So he loosened his hands, took hers, turned them palms uppermost and kissed them, one after another, slowly, lingeringly.

"Sweetest," he said, "I'd give anything in the world to be able to marry you! You must know that. But I can't, Myrtle. That's the devil of it, and the thing that has been worrying me all along. You see—no, wait a moment, let me make it clear—you see, my old man is devilishly hard up. I thought at first it was stinginess, but I see now it wasn't. Back in the summer, when I was being dunned for debt, I asked him for money. He hummed and hawed so long that I spent a week in the Fleet, and it wasn't pleasant. He sent the money at last, but I've only just learned that he had to sell Falkner some land to raise it. And I'm still in debt to my ears. And so . . . well, all I could do . . . only thing, best for everybody except me . . . To put it quite bluntly, Myrtle, I've got to marry somebody with money, a lot of money. S'matter of fact, she's up at the Hall at this minute, name of Wilson, oldish, over thirty I reckon, swarthy, hellish dull, but good for thirty thousand pounds. And I've got to marry her."

Myrtle's hands, gone genuinely limp and cold, withdrew themselves from his. A sound, neither cry, nor sigh, nor word exactly, came from her lips. Roger, momentarily wise, made no move to touch her but hurried on in his slurred voice, saying the thing which, to his not-quite-sober mind, seemed a reasonable and brilliant piece of inspiration.

"It was partly for your sake, too. As you say, what's the use of meeting up here for an hour, once a fortnight, once a month? We're in love, we've got to be together, properly. As we are we could never do it, nowhere to live, nothing to live on. But once I'm married it'll be a different story. . . . I'll set you up properly, house, allowance, every-thing. *She* won't be in Town much, she prefers the country —all dull women do. So, you and I, Myrtle . . . it'll be just like being married. We'll have such good times, and I'll look after you just as though we were married. I know the very house, darling! I could take it on Thursday, and if we were careful . . . yes, I see no reason why you shouldn't come up at once . . . Saturday, say. Well?"

Myrtle sat utterly still, completely silent. The two en-tirely different women who had lived in the one body and called themselves by a single name, and each had her turn at pretending to be Myrtle Oakley, stepped away from one another and across an immeasurable space, began to bandy arguments.

The sentimentalist said, "It can't be true. It will break my heart. I never dreamed that he could say such things to me."

"Rubbish!" said the cynic. "I knew it all along. I've told you over and over again. No good could come of it. You're very lucky that it wasn't worse. Get up now and leave him. Be dignified, and glad that you spoke when you did."

"But I love him. And he must love me—a little. After all . . . they say half a loaf. . . . I should see London. I've always wanted to. And I could sleep with him. I've always wanted to do that, too. And I'm sorry for him . . . having to marry someone he doesn't care for."

"Half a loaf, indeed! Now if you're going to start proverbs, what about eating your cake and having it? That's what he wants to do. As for seeing London, *how* would you see it? More secrecy, more furtiveness. Gossip, winks. 'Roger's fancy-lady, hee-hee-hee!' What friends would you have? And what security? What would become of you when he tired?"

"He wouldn't tire. I'd make it my one object to keep him. After all, that was the way Nelson and Lady Hamilton lived."

The cynic said vehemently, "They had no choice. The two cases are not comparable. Do you for one moment imagine that if Nelson had met Emma when they were both young and completely free, he'd have said, Look here, I love you very much, but I'm going to marry for money, and if you're agreeable I'll give you some of it as an allowance? Of course he wouldn't. Of course, if after all your high-falutin' noble notions you want to be just a man's plaything and live on the money of a woman you're deceiving and robbing, do it. But be clear about the issue and, above all, face the future squarely. Ask yourself where you'll be and what you'll have in twenty years' time when your looks are gone, when you should have a man bound to you by respect, by experience and trouble shared, by work done, and by a family reared."

"I know," whispered the sentimentalist. "I know, you're always right. But if I say no. What shall I have then? And I do love him."

"A common trouble. Most women love some man who doesn't love them. But they live it down and forget. It's a pity to ruin a whole life to gratify a passion that is partly a romantic dream, partly a very natural animal passion, and partly . . . well, shall we say vanity?"

"Well?" It was Roger, wondering at her silence, waiting for her answer. Oh, to be able to let one or other of them speak. Oh, to be a whole, single-minded person, like Harriet. Oh, to be able to be sentimental without evoking the cynic's scorn, or to be cynical without hearing the sentimentalist's weak reproaches. But they are *you*, Myrtle Oakley; *you* have to give the one answer, speak with the one mouth; and whichever you choose *you*, as one indivisible person, will have to follow the path to the end.

She said weakly, "Oh, Roger! Isn't there any other way?"

"You heard what I said. I explained it as well as I could. What else can we do?"

And suddenly a fact, which both the sentimentalist and the cynic had overlooked, flashed into Myrtle's mind.

"Roger, listen! . . . She isn't the only one with money. . . . Oh, nothing like thirty thousand pounds . . . not even one. But I have some money, too. I found it. I suppose it belongs to Daddy really, but he'll give it to me for a wedding present, I'm sure. Couldn't we take it and pay what you own, and then *earn* some for ourselves. I know I'm not very handy, but I would try . . . and perhaps if I got away from Harriet . . . she does everything so well that it never seems worth while to try very hard. . . . You see,

I might. . . . And we're both young and able-bodied. . . .
Couldn't we try something else, before you committed
yourself . . . and me?"

"How much have you got?"

"About, almost, oh, I should think there is about two
hundred pounds."

Young Mr. Moreton gave a bellow of laughter whose
echo rang among the dusty rafters of the loft and was
silenced, and rang in Myrtle's mind, and was not silenced.

"My dear simpleton," he said, "it wouldn't pay my
tailor!" His voice changed. "No, my sweet. It's no good.
There's no other way than the one I have told you. And
believe me, it is the best. And you know, it's not such an
outlandish way. Most people do it. I mean most men marry
to please their families, or to get money, or to keep a job,
and then they . . . Well, where's the difference? Only a
few words chanted by a parson." Something told him that
he was on the wrong track. He groped in the darkness for
her hands, and holding them firmly, said, "Myrtle, I love
you; you love me. We want to be together, and I've told
you the one way. My sweet, say yes . . . and we'll be
together on Saturday!"

Laughter . . . my dear simpleton—that was what he
really thought her, in his heart—my dear simpleton, and
the laughter ringing on and on. . . .

"I'm sorry, Roger. I can't. Not especially, not because
I want some words chanted by a parson, or because . . .
Oh, how can I make you see? The whole idea is wrong.
Your marrying her deliberately, like that, and then plan-
ning to spend her money on me. We shouldn't be happy,
and it wouldn't last. It couldn't."

"Don't say that, Myrtle. Think it over, don't answer
now. Look, I shall be here until Thursday. Take your
time and think it over."

"It's no good, dar. . . . It's no good. I have thought.
And I know it wouldn't do. I . . . I have enjoyed our
times together and I was . . . was fond of you, but I'm

just not the right person for that kind of life. So I'll say good-bye, Roger. And I hope . . . I hope you'll get to like her better and be happy."

The hay rustled as she rose to her feet. And the wave of madness which had been lapping at the brain of young Mr. Moreton for some hours, a wave compounded of disgust with his life, and with himself, desire for Myrtle, and for freedom, distaste for poor plain Dorothy, and for expediency with all its demands, swelled with his final ingredient of disappointment, rose and broke. This, he thought, was what you got by being frank and honest. This was virtue's reward. He saw, quite clearly now, that he'd been a fool to mention Dorothy and her money and his plans. He should have taken Myrtle, just now when she lay limp and quiescent in his arms . . . and done his talking afterwards. She'd have been glad then of any offer. Fool, fool, fool! But it wasn't too late. Coldblooded, calculating little bitch . . . it was always a mistake to talk to women. He'd heard Steve say so again and again. There was only one thing they understood. And she should have it. Before she went from here she should have it; and if it didn't bring her back begging for another helping, well, it shouldn't be his fault.

He reached up and put his arms around her thighs, dragging her down. Half in the hope that he had changed his mind and that she would hear him say again that he would never let her go, Myrtle made no resistance, and when, a second later, she realized that he had indeed changed his mind, and in what fashion, it was too late. She was already down upon the couch of hay, and the enemy in him had her again in hand.

For a moment she struggled weakly and then lay still as the old dread magic of touch began to work again. Sight left the closed eyes, speech deserted the sealed mouth, the ears were deaf in the thunder of the blood. The cynic and the sentimentalist, as though aware that they had no place here, departed together, and there lay, for a moment which had countless ages within its measure, only a nameless, mindless woman, without past or future, without thought or reason, only a rapt, quivering female thing, instinctive, receptive, desirous, awaiting the moment of the final conquest.

It was to this lost, atavistic Myrtle that the voice spoke; the one voice which, since it was already forgotten and had sunk so far through the layers of consciousness that it had not deserted her with real mind and memory, could now, in these dark places, make itself heard.

"Remember," it said with startling clarity, "to cry out in the nick of danger."

Twisting her head, Myrtle freed her mouth and screamed, long piercing screams which went vibrating among the rafters and piercing the silence of the sleeping stable. The third of them had hardly died away under the throttling pressure of Roger Moreton's hand before, from the bottom of the ladder, a boy's voice, fiercely concealing its nervousness, shouted, "Hi! What's going on up there?"

Myrtle, who had never hurt any living thing in all her days, twisted her head and sank her teeth into the wrist of the hand which was strangling her. It loosened its grip automatically. She drew a hissing breath and cried, "Dick! Dick! Help me! Myrtle!" And with the ease of long practice the boy swarmed rapidly up the staves.

She was still sobbing violently when, leaning on the boy's taut young arm, she stumbled into the empty kitchen.

"Promise," she gulped, repeating what she had been saying all the way cross the yard, "promise not to tell anyone, please, Dick. I feel so ashamed. I could die. I'll make it worth your while not to tell."

"I oon't say nothing, Miss Myrtle. I never did like him. He ain't good with a horse. You can always tell."

She loosened her clutch on his arm and staggered across to the dresser. After two or three weak tugs she succeeded in opening the drawer.

"Some of it was mine," she said, while Dick, watching her in bewilderment, saw her hands fumble about behind the snarls of string and the boxes of nails. "Here, take it," she said, and thrust into his hands a handful of coins, carelessly gathered, as one might gather a handful of corn for hens.

Dick's shallow brown eyes gleamed greedily, but he said stiffly, unwillingly, "Thass a lotta money, Miss Myrtle. There ain't no need to gimme all that. I oon't tell nobody."

"I know. I know. It isn't for that, Dick. It's for gratitude."

"I dint do much," said the boy. He fingered his bruised jaw reminiscently. "I had wuss biffs than that in my time."

"Don't talk about it," begged Myrtle. "Don't think about it. Just take this and go, Dick. And try to forget it."

He stuffed the money into his breeches pocket. "There ain't no need for you to feel bad, Miss Myrtle," he said attempting to comfort her, to banish that look of white misery from the face whose smiles he had valued. "All of us makes mistakes at times. Lots wuss than that." There was a thread of bitterness in his voice. "Well, good-night, Miss Myrtle. And thanks for the—you know." He patted his pocket. "You can count on me being mum as the dead."

"Thank you, Dick. Good-night."

She turned towards the door of the back stairs. Her heart was broken, her pride slain, and shame, scorching as fever, nauseating as physical sickness, penetrated to the last recesses of her being. She was ashamed of the hope she had held, ashamed of having deceived Will, and most of all ashamed of that last desire to yield. She knew now exactly what she was, and she must go on for years living with this unspeakable self-knowledge.

Heavily, slowly, with a stifled sob now and again, the woman whom Myrtle Oakley had become that evening mounted the stairs down which the girl had tripped so lightly only that very afternoon. Away on the half-landing at the front of the house the tall clock chimed the hour, and Joe the potman, with many sleepy yawns, began his round of bolting doors and testing window fastenings.

Will

Effie piled the last load on the big brass tray and heaved it into place with its rim resting on one of her prominent hip-bones. If Will had been in a position and a mood to notice her he would have been concerned by the look on her face. Her eyes were mad now; they had been growing more and more crazy as the moments of the evening sped away. Neither her own goodwill nor all Harriet's bullying nor Myrtle's gentle directions, had saved her from making mistake after mistake. As she had run hither and thither about the dining-room, and then the kitchen, and had sped upstairs to tell Kitty about Mrs. Sharman's warming pan, and dashed down again to begin clearing the table in the Little Parlour, and then raced up to the attic door for a second time in order to fetch Miss Harriet the key of the store-room, and finally trotted flat-footedly into the Little Parlour for the last trayload, her dry blanched lips had moved continually and almost without an attempt at concealment, as she prayed and prayed that God would save her even at this eleventh hour.

As it grew later, and still she was not finished with her work, it broke upon her distracted mind that God hadn't understood her prayers. She had pleaded that she might be saved from the part which Sarah had decreed that she must play. And now it seemed that she would not be free in time to do so. But that manner of salvation was quite useless. God must know that for Effie just not to be there would only infuriate Sarah and precipitate the hour of reckoning. To be of any good the escape must be miraculous and so ordered that Sarah's vengeance could be averted. But the moments had spun away, and no miracle had happened; there had just been these extra duties and unforeseen errands which were making her late and doing harm, rather than good.

"Oh, God," she prayed, as she passed with her rapid, burdened shuffle along the length of the passage between the parlour and the kitchen, "it ain't enough that I don't be there! You gotta save me some other way. If You don't do something right soon I'll be doing a sin that You oon't be able to forgive. Then I'll end in hell. Oh, please God, save me! Jesus Christ, take pity on me and save me!"

Beneath this constant pleading, which had, to tell the truth, become by constant repetition almost mechanical, her mind writhed in the grip of several torturing fancies. Not the least dreadful was the idea that she had suddenly conceived about Will's guest, Jonathan Smail.

When Harriet had told her that Will was taking supper in the Little Parlour and had bidden her to go set the table there, Effie, for a few brief moments, had imagined that the miracle had happened. Maybe, she thought, with the hope of desperation, I could go in there and tell *him* all about it. Maybe that is what God meant me to do all along. She had entered the room accompanied by a mental picture of herself confessing everything to her master, and of Will being kind and helpful. She had been so engrossed in it that she had not noticed that the tray Harriet had prepared with her own hands, bore evidence that two persons were going to share the meal. She had opened the door and found her master in the company of a stranger. So open confession upon her part had not been God's intention. The burden which had lifted slightly settled down sickeningly upon her tremulous heart. She began to set the table clumsily, so distraught by her thoughts that she could hardly tell a knife from a fork.

Then suddenly she had become aware that the other man was looking at her. Against her will she looked across the table and met his eyes. A cold and deadly feeling of fear seized her. For those bright reptilian eyes stared out of the ugly fat face with such malice and such an air of knowing all about her, that she was sure that this man whom she had never seen before was really no stranger, even to her inmost thoughts. Her dim mind made a bid for sanity; it was nonsense, she thought, no man could know about Sarah and her. But to think that way was like trying to cross water by a stepping-stone, her foot slipped and she was deeper in; for the words, "no man could know," carried a terrible implication. Every old story that she had ever heard about the Devil appearing in flesh to mortal men flashed into her feverish mind. Sarah had planned a devilish deed for this night, and Effie was pledged to help her. What more likely than that the Devil himself should appear to take part in the act?

"Get along, Effie," said Will irascibly, glancing up and finding her frozen into immobility, staring at Jonathan as a rabbit stares at a stoat. "And for God's sake! Do you think we're left-handed?" He altered the position of the cutlery with jerky fingers. From behind him his guest's lipless mouth widened in a smile which almost made Effie faint from horror, so mirthless it was, so malicious, so knowing. Then he looked away and, released from the trance of his stare, Effie bolted into the passage with her heart thudding against the thin wall of her chest as though it would burst free. Hell, often present in her mind these days, altered its imagined appearance as a pit of flames, and became merely an endless age spent in the company of that dreadful smile, that searing stare. She was halfway along the passage before she could muster enough control to re-commence her monotonous prayers. On both the errands which had taken her subsequently up the dim stairs to the cold attic floor she had expected to see Jonathan Smail's bulky figure barring her way at every step. But, of course, she reflected crazily, as she made both journeys safely, he was waiting. All eternity was his.

Now, as she edged her way through the door of the Little Parlour and closed it behind her, hopelessness shut down upon her heart and mind. She must wash up these dishes with as much speed as possible and then go to face Sarah. There had been no miracle. Evil had triumphed. And there in the Little Parlour sat Evil in the flesh, gloating.

In the room which she had left a subtle change had already taken place. Smail rose heavily from the table, loosened the top of his trousers, and moved towards the sofa close to the dancing wood fire, the sofa where usually Harriet sat plying her needle. Will took his own chair on the opposite side of the hearth; but tonight there was no easy relaxation in his pose. His body was tensely braced, his eyes alert and troubled.

"You do yourself proud, no mistake about that," said Smail, reaching for the glass of port wine which he had moved to the edge of the table. His broken voice was pitched to the tone, half mocking, half ingratiating, in which he had conducted the conversation during the meal. "Christ! To think that it's twenty years since you and me sat down to eat together. And if we could have looked forward and seen ourselves tucking into such food and sinking liquor like this . . . well, well, well!" He stared at Will searchingly. His manner became rather more assured. During the meal he had felt rather like a hunter who had, with infinite patience and difficulty, tracked a dangerous beast to its lair, and who, though delighted with the success of his hunting, is now not quite sure about his ability to deal with his quarry. The yellow pallor of Will's face and the slight tremor of his hands were comforting to see.

"Well," he said again, "here we are. And I can't say that you seem very glad to see me."

"Did you expect me to be?" There was great bitterness in the question. "Our common experiences were not of the sort that make pleasant memories."

"I dunno," said Smail cautiously. "I've been through so many worse since that I've often looked back and wished myself on that bloody boat again. As for the old *Ethiopian Queen*—why, she looked like heaven!"

He shifted in his chair like a badly-set jelly. "And to think that all this time you've been sitting here, well fed and well-to-do, free to come and go. Jesus, God!"

"What happened to you was none of my affair," said Will harshly.

"So *you* think. You always was the lucky one. When I think of the luck you've had. . . ." His voice rose squeakily. "If you'd been the sort that a man could of stuck to I'd have got home, too, with my share in my pocket. I might of had a place like this." He swept a glance about the cozy room, a glance that included all the things that he could not see. "Whereas," and there were tears of self-pity in his voice, and in his eyes, "I've been a slave . . . a slave I tell you, for twenty years. I've been treated worse than any animal, Mike Latter; I've been starved and beaten. There's been things done to me . . . ."

Pity, unwilling, laced with disgust, coloured with hatred, but pity none the less, showed on his listener's face.

"I know," Will said. "There's no need to tell me." He was silent for a moment, reflecting upon the rough justice of Smail's fate, and when he spoke again his voice was harder. "But you can't blame me for any of that."

"I do," said the fat man hysterically. "You left me. You was the one who wanted to go on alone. I'd of stuck to you. I always knew you was lucky. How'd you have explained about old Peabody if things hadn't turned out the way they did? The very box was put in *your* hands. You always did have all the luck. I'd have been all right with you."

"Oh, well," said Will with an air of dismissing an unimportant matter. "If you think that, and have been thinking it for twenty years, there's no point in arguing further. There's one thing I would like to know though. How did you find me?"

He had been longing to ask the question; but he himself

had said, "Talk about ordinary things." And Smail had obeyed him all through the meal while Effie was in and out.

The fat man now drew out a vivid coloured dirty handkerchief and dried his pouchy eyes. Over the handkerchief he looked at Will maliciously.

"Ah," he said with relish. "You always thought you was the clever one, didn't you? You and young Peter Dunn. Stupid you said me and old Peabody was—stupid. But when it comes to following a trail twenty years old and staler'n cask meat, I can show you a thing or two. How did I find you? Listen, Dr. Latter. Last year they bombarded Algiers. Maybe you read about it. And they let about a thousand of us out; freed us after ten, twenty, forty years. Some was glad and some was sorry, wondering what they'd do now. I didn't know how to feel. Lately I'd had a good crib, plenty of food and easy work. But I came with the rest.

"In London some kind charitable people,——them, had got up a Rehabilitation Fund. That's a long word for a little thing. Fifteen pounds, a suit of clothes, and a Bible is what they give me. That was to last the rest of my life and make up for what them——s has robbed me of. And what could I do? I was a sailor. And who'd want a sailor that'd been ashore for twenty years and got slow and fat and fond of easy living? I was desperate, I tell you, desperate. And then I thought of you, Mike Latter." He paused, refilled his glass, and rolled the wine around his mouth. He eyed Will glaringly.

"Yes, I thought of you. And I started remembering things. You used to talk very free to that young milksop, Dunn. You told him all about your wife and the dear little house at Budleigh, and the rowan tree in the garden and the flower-pots in the window. I used to like to listen to you and Dunn yarning away, using all them long words and sounding so high-falutin'. I wasn't that stupid that I couldn't remember it all. And you told me once that when you was little and sick you'd spent a month in East Anglia and thought it was the best place in England. And another time you said that your father or somebody'd kept an inn, and as a boy you'd had an itch to do the same. Just bits and pieces, but worth remembering when you'd got fifteen pounds and a bloody Bible between you and starvation.

"So I took coach to Budleigh, and mow me down if there wasn't the little house with the rowan tree in the garden and the kitchen window catching the morning sun, just like you'd said. Any seaman could of found it blindfold. That much was common sense; but I admit that the next bit was lucky enough to have been your sort, not mine. I knocked on the door and a woman came." He giggled. "She'd lived there a long time, and she'd never heard of anybody of the name of Latter. But there was a woman, she said, that did a bit of washing for her now and again, and this woman had an old mother that used to work, a long time ago, for another lady who'd lived in that house. She remembered that because the washer-woman had said, "It's in our family to work for this house." So I thanked her and set my course for the wash-erwoman's house, and there, sure enough, was an old crone by the fire, blind as a beetle and wrong in the head. At least, that was her daughter's tale; but she was only wrong in the head like a lot of old folks are, think they're back in the past all the time. This old faggot couldn't have told what day of the week it was today, but she remem-bered Mrs. Latter all right. Ah, she could tell me what colour her hair was and how small feet she had." Once again he halted his story and looked with intense gloating at his listener.

Will said, "All right, Smail. That'll do. You tracked me through the old woman. That's all I wanted to know."

"Ah . . . but I haven't told you half! Remember, I'm the chap you thought was so stupid. The old dame re-membered this pretty Mrs. Latter, whose husband was at sea and whose little girl was about two years old. And she remembered the gentleman who used to come all the way from London and stay in the house, which the old woman never had thought very nice. But at that time Mrs. Latter had plenty of money and was free with it. Then the gentleman stopped coming, and soon you could see what was wrong with the young lady, and her husband had been away for more than a year. . . ."

"That'll do, I said," said Will in a voice quiet with menace. The fat man shifted his position slightly and dropped one hand to his side.

"So you don't want to hear it. All right. We'll go on to the night when the new baby was a few days old and there wasn't any money, and the old woman was just staying with the poor dear out of pure charity, and a tall thin man with a face like a gypsy came back in the middle of the night and gave the old woman a gold piece and sent her off. And the next morning, very early, when the crone went back to the house to snout round a bit, it was empty. The dark man and the pretty lady—only she wasn't so pretty any more—and the little girl and the new baby, they'd all gone. And till I walked in asking for Mrs. Latter, she'd never heard word of them since.

"No. I haven't finished yet. Look at this." He pulled out of his pocket the little book which he had studied in the coach. He turned the pages as he continued.

"I asked myself what you'd do. Five hundred pounds you had, same as I did till them———s collared it. And you couldn't take to doctoring no more, I reckoned. And you wanted to keep an inn, and you liked East Anglia. So I thought, fifteen pounds won't do much for me and Mike Latter, if I can find him, will. And I mapped out this. . . ." He thrust the page of coach routes across the hearth and held it under Will's eyes. "There's your stupid common sailor. Man, I've been over the eastern counties like a bloodhound. See there were four more places and then I was done. Look. . ." He dived into another pocket and fished out a handful of small change. "Twenty-seven shillings between me and beggary, and four more places to visit. Christ, when I saw your yellow face come out of that passage . . ." He dropped the money back into his pocket and brought out the handkerchief again, mopping his brow, his upper lip and his palms. "Ah," he said, with deep satisfaction, "that minute made up for it all."

Will was thinking. Only this morning Harriet had begged him to remain in bed. He would probably have done so if this had not been Michaelmas Day. And if he had, Smail would have seen the name Oakley over the door; he might, since he was following a preconceived plan, have tried to take a look at the landlord, but Harriet would not have allowed that. And the critical moment would have slipped past, the danger have missed him by a hairsbreadth. But he hadn't stayed in his room. He had felt better, and he had come down to take his share of the day's work. It almost looked as though Destiny, as well as Smail, had been working out a plan. But it was no use thinking that way. He had to consider, not how the crisis might have been avoided, but how it might best be met.

"Well," he asked, "what now?"

Smail tittered. "The same old Mike, blunt as they're made! What now? You're the one to answer that, I think. I take it that it's worth something to you not to have it blazed abroad that Will Oakley is Dr. Mike Latter, late ship's surgeon on the *Ethiopian Queen*. Twenty years is a long time, but the Admiralty people would be interested to hear the full story, I reckon."

"As told by the mate, twenty years after?" But even as he spoke he knew the answer to that, knew that any kind of argument was futile, knew that Smail had him at every point.

"While I was in captivity I couldn't make a statement, could I?" asked Smail, softly. "And when I got back wasn't the first necessity to find you if you were to be found? And haven't I done it?" He fumbled in his pocket with the hand which had never been far from it during all the talk, closed his hand about some object within and so sat, eyeing Will warily. "I wouldn't put it past the Admiralty to be pleased with my sense of duty. I might rake in a thousand pounds."

A short bark of bitter laughter came from Will's lips.

"There's no point in my bargaining with you then. I can't offer you anything like that."

"And why not?"

"For the simple reason that I haven't got it. To buy this place took every penny I had, and I borrowed money beside. I've only just finished paying it off."

The fat man reflected on this statement. He did not, oddly enough, question its truth. Nor was he either disappointed or angered by it. He said slowly:

"That's your affair. But it's a good spot. I can see that. Anybody'd lend you money on it. I'm not asking for a thousand down, though it'd only be fair if I did, since I know where I could get that much. But after all, a man can only eat one meal at a time, and I'm looking for security in the future. I'll take a hundred and fifty now, and the same every six months. How's that?"

"It's every penny of profit the place makes."

"That's your affair again. You'll have to find a way to make more. There's my offer, a damned generous one. Three hundred pounds a year for the safety of your neck. . . ."

There was a long tense silence. Dampness glistened on Will's face. Watching it, and the expression that dawned in the tortured eyes, Smail drew his right hand from his pocket, showing it clenched about the butt of a short black pistol. Almost casually he said:

"And no violence, Dr. Latter, please. I've kept my aim, and this stays by me." He waited another moment and then said, "Well?"

At last Will spoke. "I haven't the money in the house.

But I could give you a letter to a man in Norwich who would advance it."

"That'll suit me. You can write it tonight and I'll take it myself tomorrow." Remembering the look that had come into Will's eyes, he told himself that the sooner he was away from th*e Fleece* the easier he would feel.

Retaining his grasp upon the pistol with the right hand, he reached out with his left and clumsily filled his glass, slopping the wine upon the polished top of the table. As he did so the thought of his own power went to his head in a dizzying rush. To think that when he landed in England there had been nothing ahead of him except the alternatives of menial work or the poorhouse, and within this short space of time, by the sole aid of his own wits, he had assured himself of comfort and security for the rest of his life. Another thought struck him. Will might die first. And a third thought came, causing his face to wrinkle with that smile which had so affected Effie Stevens. Brilliant, he thought. With one proposal he could make the future both more comfortable and more certain, and at the same time show this fellow how far his power extended.

"There is one other thing. That pock-faced wench of yours. I'll marry her."

"You'll *what*?"

"Marry that yellow-haired girl I talked to this afternoon. Why, what's wrong with that? She wouldn't be anybody's pick. But I could do with a woman to see to my comforts. And an attractive piece'd be no use to me. I'd enjoy taming her, too. . . . Look out. I shall shoot."

"Shoot, then, you——!" said Will between his teeth, and was halfway across the hearth, undeterred by the fact that Smail had raised the revolver and that his finger was at the trigger, when, behind the fat man's chair the door which formed the second, seldom-used exit from the Little Parlour opened, and Harriet herself swept into the room.

Only her eyes betrayed that her arrival was not due to accident; the grotesque painted mask of her face covered all other sign of emotion. And her voice was as steady as the red and white of her false complexion as she said:

"I'm sorry to disturb you, Father. But I thought Mr. Smail ought to know that his room is quite ready."

The fat man, with his right hand in his pocket again, turned and leered at her. "Thank you, my dear," he said. Over the top of her head, for she had moved to the hearth and now stood between the two men, his eyes met Will's. His glance was hard, implacable and significant.

"Is there a lock on the door?" he asked, lowering his eyes to Harriet again. "I've been particular about locks since I was robbed one night."

"There is a lock and a key," said Harriet.

"I think I'll retire, then. It's been a trying day for me. Good-night, Oakley. I'll see you in the morning." He moved with surprising nimbleness to the door, where he halted and leered back at Harriet. "Good-night, my dear."

"Good-night, Mr. Smail. I hope you'll find the room comfortable."

He closed the door sharply behind him, and they could hear his first few footsteps, almost running, in the passage outside.

Harriet and Will, standing on the hearth, stared straight into one another's eyes for a long moment. The stare was as eloquent as speech. Sympathy, horror, curiosity, reproach, despair and enlightenment informed it in turn. Then Will, dropping limply into the chair from which he had leapt with sheer murder in his mind, put his head in his hands and groaned.

Moving quickly, but without haste, Harriet went to the sideboard, and, with her back to Will, measured into a glass two fingers of brandy, pouring it with the same precision and care as she would have given to the pouring of a dose of medicine. She touched Will's shoulder and said quietly, "Drink this," standing by him until he had done so, and then taking the glass.

She glanced at her usual place on the sofa, remembered that Smail had been sitting there, and pulled forward a little elm elbow chair. She sat down, her feet together, her skirt smoothed over her knees and her hands primly folded.

"I was in the lobby," she said after a moment's silence. "I got there through the back of the store-room. I heard everything."

"My God, Harriet! I'd have given the world to have kept you out of this."

"No," she said. "No. I think it's better as it is. I heard rightly, didn't I? I mean I understood properly? *I* was that other baby. I'm not your child at all?"

"No, Harriet. But that doesn't matter now. In fact, after the first hour or two, it never *has* mattered."

She leaned forward a little, inclining her body stiffly and directing at him a gaze of intense earnestness.

"It matters now . . . in this way. You've been very good to me." The trite phrase lost its triviality as she said it. "For twenty years. Fed me and clothed me, given me your name. I'm very grateful. And for that reason, unless we can think of any other way, I am willing to marry that man."

Will's haggard face turned towards her sharply. Astonishment showed upon it, and then horror.

"Never," he said. "Why, Harriet, my dear, you don't know what you're saying. I'd sooner see you dead. I'd far rather hang than that. Oh, far!"

"And would you? That is one thing I must know. Suppose we did nothing. Could he enforce his threat?"

"I suppose. . . . Yes, Harriet, I think he could. Everything is in his favour. And besides, the main part of the tale he would tell is, in essentials, true."

"Oh! Then . . . then what can we *do*? Except raise the money and well, the other thing?"

"I could raise the money. But your marrying him,

Harriet, is entirely out of the question. Don't even think about it. It's obscene. It would take Smail to think of that."

"You mean because of my face?" asked Harriet, in a curious suppressed voice.

"Great God, no! Because of *him*. Because he isn't fit to breathe in your presence, or in the presence of any decent person. He was always vile, cruel, bestial—and what has happened to him since has made him worse." He got to his feet suddenly and began to move about the room with rapid, nervous steps. "There must be a Devil, there must be! To have kept that creature alive all these years and brought him here to do this to us." He swerved round towards Harriet and said in a changed tone, "But you're not to worry. Do you hear me? You're not concerned in this—except that you saved me from killing him just now. In the morning I'll offer him more money—four, five hundred a year. I'll buy him off somehow. And probably the other, that infamous suggestion, wasn't meant seriously. The last turn of the screw. Kind of thing he would think of. Forget it, Harriet."

Harriet studied him, her eyes narrowed. It was as though she were seeing him for the first time. This tall, thin, slightly stooping man, with his yellow face, heavily lined, his startlingly blue eyes, his thick black hair, streaked with white, his lean, fever-shaken hands, he emerged all at once out of the anonymity of accepted fatherhood and became a stranger. And that past of his, which had always been a mystery, was simultaneously transformed in a vital, important, *present* thing.

"There is one question that I would like to ask you, if you don't mind." He looked at her without speaking, but signifying his willingness to answer. "This Peabody . . . was he my father?"

"My dear child, no. Peabody was the man I killed. He was captain of a ship called the *Ethiopian Queen*, chartered to take a load of convicts to Botany Bay."

Then how did you . . . ? I mean, where did you meet

him? And what has Smail to do with it?"

"Smail was mate, and I was a surgeon on the ship. You heard him say 'Doctor Latter,' with a sneer. That's what I was." He halted his steps by the sideboard, poured some more brandy into the glass which Harriet had replaced there, and drank it as though it had been water. "Yes," he said, with a touch of that wryness which always puzzled Harriet, "I was reckoned a brilliant fellow in my time. Head man of my year in the final examinations. That's why, Harriet, to your annoyance, I don't always follow old Weatherall's prescription to the letter."

"And what happened? Why did you go to sea? And how did you kill this Peabody man? Did you make a mistake, doctoring him?"

"Oh, no. I went to sea because things went wrong and I couldn't get a job ashore. You see, Harriet, my own father died when I was very young, and my mother married again; a very decent fellow who kept the Ludlow *Feathers*. But she didn't want me to be an innkeeper, and as I grew up she got a relative of hers, a doctor, to take an interest in me. He was a jovial old man, with a very lucrative practice and no children of his own, and he took to me, and started me. It became—in the course of years —an understood thing that as soon as I was qualified I should go to live with him and take on the heaviest work. I had besides a little money left me by my mother—she was dead by the time I was eighteen; and with that and such settled prospects it didn't seem unduly reckless to marry during my last year, especially as your mother was very unhappy in her home. The old man, who I called Uncle Sydney, though the relationship was not, as a matter of fact, so close, invited us, your mother and me, to stay with him for a short holiday just before my final examination. Clarissa was very lovely, and I had told her to make herself charming to the old man. He'd been very handsome in his time and very attractive. It was difficult for him to realize that he was old, almost senile. I think

he tried to hide the fact from himself by . . . well, silly
behaviour. I was studying for a great part of the day, and
he used to take Clarissa about with him. One day I came
upon them . . . maybe the thing wasn't so important, but
I was young and hot-headed and head over heels in love.
There was a row. I took Clarissa away and Uncle Sydney
never spoke to me again."

"So then?"

"Well, then the prospects were gone, and owing to the
way we had been living, so was most of my capital.
Myrtle was born before we had married quite a year, and
although I had passed my examinations so well I just
didn't seem able to get a job. I couldn't afford to wait, you
see. And just as it began to look as though I would have
to take to another trade, I met a man I had studied with,
and he told me about the *Ethiopian Queen* wanting a surgeon. The government had just become concerned because
so many convicts didn't live out the voyage, and a ship's
doctor and the promise of a bonus for every one landed
sound and well were the obvious steps to take to remedy
the evil. I took the job, borrowed some money on the
strength of it, and settled your mother and Myrtle in a
tiny house at Budleigh, and went away in good heart."

He paused, plunged in memories. And Harriet, her
curiosity still unsatisfied, waited a moment and then said:

"And Peabody was the captain?"

"That is so. He was a bad, cruel man. His doings are
not fit for your hearing, Harriet. He'd sailed transports for
years and always mishandled the convicts. Now, with this
new idea for preserving them in life and health and sanity,
he seemed to make up for it by ill-treating his crew."

"And Smail helped?"

"Smail was the worse of the two. I hated him from the
first. Though, and you'll hardly credit this, he was extremely good-looking, slim and spare and tanned all over;
and he had wonderful hair, a tangled mass of curls, reddish
gold. . . . It was partly his hair that. . . . Look here, Harriet,

you don't want to hear any more of this. . . ."

"Just why you killed him."

"Well, it's difficult to explain without a lot of revolting details. You see, they weren't just cruel, they delighted in cruelty, some people do. I tried. . . . I'd just finished a course of studies which had borne in on me what a wonderful thing the human body is, such a wonderful piece of mechanism, so sensitive, so resilient, so easily injured and yet so adaptable. I hated to see it ill-used—hated it, I suppose you might say, professionally. And, in addition, cruelty revolted me, it still does. It's a negation of good, a worship of evil, as, I think, no other sin can be. . . . But that's all by the way. I was young and not very wise. I allowed Smail and Peabody to perceive my feelings; I even voiced them, and was met with ridicule—and worse. For, since they could not physically ill-use *me*, they derived immense pleasure from saying and doing things in my presence which were calculated to sicken me. Many's the meal they ruined. Four of us ate together generally—Smail, Peabody, myself and Peter Dunn." He paused again, and Harriet said, "Yes. I heard him mention Peter Dunn."

"He was a young man who was going out to the Bay in some minor official capacity. He shouldn't have been on the transport at all, but he had been prevented from taking passage three weeks before by an attack of jaundice. He was not completely well and consulted me professionally, and so we became friendly. Otherwise, perhaps, I should never have got past the barrier of his cold, shy reserve. He was a peculiar young man, remote, self-absorbed; but he hated Peabody, too, and, of course, Smail.

"Before we reached the Cape—where we watered and took on supplies of fresh food—I was sick of the ship. I had learned, however, to keep my mouth shut, since for me to take any man's part was tantamount to asking for that man to be increasingly persecuted. I would gladly have left the ship at the Cape, but that would have meant forfeiting my salary and the share of the bonus which I had been promised. Two men did desert there. And two others were taken on, one of his own free will, and the other dumped aboard unconscious. There, as elsewhere, there were men who lived by what amounts virtually to stealing seamen and putting them, drugged or pole-axed, on to ships where the captains are short-handed.

"This fellow, who was brought aboard insensible, was the cause of all the trouble. His name was Wade, or Wady. And he was—apart from the blow he had received on his head—an extremely sick man. I was interested in him, because I had never seen such a case before. He had the slowest pulse, usually, that I have ever tested; hard knotted lumps in his neck, armpits and groins, shallow respiration and very sluggish reactions to external stimuli. Every evening he fell into a state of high fever, and he was always sleepy. I have, literally, seen him sleep standing.

"Smail and Peabody, not unnaturally, attributed his sloth and apparent idleness to resentment at finding himself on the ship and unwillingness to perform his duties— if you can call them duties. They followed the usual procedure with such cases, a brutal, but perhaps necessary form of breaking in and intimidation. But they failed to inspire activity or wakefulness in Wade, and when I had, with some difficulty, obtained permission to examine him I told Peabody that such measures were useless, since the man was plainly sick.

"He asked me what he ailed, and of course I could not name the specific complaint because it was new to me. I did tell him, in plain language, such as I have used to you, the symptoms which I had noted, and suggested what had occurred to me, namely, that it was some disease, or form of disease, peculiar to Africa, where, on his own showing, Wade had spent some years. Peabody, backed by Smail, dismissed this as rubbish; and from that moment the wretched devil was never given a moment's peace. He was, obviously, no use as a seaman, and never would be. And he would probably have been shoved overboard one dark night, save that he served the purpose of being a stick to beat me with. They hated me because I opposed them; and baiting me had become a sport. The thing went on for some days. Every bit of ill-treatment meted out to Wade was either ostentatiously done under my eyes or meticulously described to me. Finally, the man fell asleep on some duty or other, and Peabody ordered him twenty lashes. He also demanded—and was within his rights to do so—that I attend the execution of the sentence."

Will stood still, staring at the wall, and drew a deep, unsteady breath, as though labouring again under the emotion of that far-away hour. "I went, of course. And I spoke to the captain, civilly. In fact, I begged for Wade. I told Peabody that I was aware of the purpose of the punishment, and that if he could derive equal pleasure from having *me* beaten, he could do it. He laughed, as though it were the best joke he had ever heard. The thing started . . . and Wade began to squeal. Peabody shouted to the man who was yielding the rope's end to lay on harder and earn his rum ration. And I went mad. I took Peabody by the throat and shook him. He was a big man, tall and stout and active; and I suppose Smail, who stood near, was quite certain that he would make a mash of me in no time. Anyway, he danced out of the way and stood grinning. We strove together for some seconds and then his foot slipped and he went down, taking me with him. His skull cracked like a coconut, but I was too mad to notice that. I kept shaking him and demanding that he give the order to release Wade. It was some minutes before I realized that I was shaking a corpse."

"But that was pure accident," said Harriet in a tone of genuine relief. "Nobody could hold that against you. Surely, Smail and anyone else who saw it, must have seen that it was an accident, not murder."

"Manslaughter. Yes, that was what I thought. And although, of course, it is a very serious offence to lay violent hands on a ship's master, I felt that a court might, in the circumstances, stop short of exacting the extreme penalty. Anyway, I hoped so."

"Then why must we bargain with Smail?"

"Ah, but you see that is not the end of the story, Harriet. I made sure the fellow was dead and past all aid, then I said to Smail, 'The best thing for you to do now is to assume charge of the ship, and put me in irons and charge me with homicide as soon as we touch land.' He stood there gaping and seemed afraid to approach me. Finally, however, he took me to my own cabin and shut me in. In the evening Dunn came down to see me, brought me some food and liquor, and sat for over an hour discussing whether I should be wiser to go on and face the charge, or to try to escape by boat. He assured me that it would be a simple thing to get away, sice everything was in wild confusion and Smail's authority very shaky. The argument against the plan was that I was no seaman, had no idea how to handle a boat, or in what direction to steer. Dunn was slightly in favour of taking the risk, he said, since he thought it likely that I might hang. Judges, he said, were less sentimental about flogged seamen than they were convinced of the sacredness of authority. I said I'd think it over until the next evening, and he said he would see that a boat was victualled and watered.

"I spent the next day—an endless one—in a torment of indecision. There was so much to be said for and against either procedure. But the choice was not mine. Dunn came down to me—not excited, for it was not his nature to be that—but alert and out of himself as I had never seen him before. He was wearing his heavy top-coat, and carried mine over his arm, and beneath his arm, half hidden by my coat, a heavy little box with such thick brass corners and edges and studs that the wood of it hardly showed. He told me to follow him at once. The convicts had mutinied and broken loose. Smail had failed to control the situation, the whole ship was over-run, most aboard her were drunk, and her course had been already altered, and there was talk of taking her to America.

" 'They'll not do it, of course,' he said. 'They'll set her afire or run her on the rocks. In any case, the food will give out. So I'm going with you. I have a boat all ready, with enough food and water for a long time. It's a desperate chance, but we must take it.'

"I followed him out of the cabin and on to the deck. The ship might have been deserted for all the evidence to the contrary—to the sight, that is—for from the big cabin, and from the fo'castle, there came the loud senseless din of drunken merry-making; and there was a smell of cooking from the galley.

"On deck, however, there was a man at the wheel. We moved quietly over to the boat which Dunn had prepared, and as we drew near saw that somebody was already at work lowering her. Dunn swore—the only time I ever heard him do so. There were three men, Smail, quite sober, and two others not so sober. They were opposed to our joining them, but Dunn had a pistol and at the point of it made them take us. Smail took the oar and thrust it against the the ship's side, and as he did so one of the other men giggled and said something about letting them burn now. And it was true. The smell of burning was not from the galley.

"We saw the ship burn through the hours of darkness."

"And then?" said Harriet as Will again fell silent, staring at the wall.

"Well, there were five of us in a boat provisioned for two. And we were at sea for eighty-four days. We rowed, and then we drifted and we starved and we thirsted. The two men who had been with Smail, died, one after the other. Then Dunn died. The last thing he did was to sign to me—he was too weak to speak—to take the box. Smail and I were left. We were bad friends still. He blamed me, not without reason, for the whole affair. There had been some convicts at exercise on the deck at the moment when I killed Peabody, and that, Smail said, had started the

mutiny. That may be so. I opened Dunn's box and found
that there was just over a thousand pounds in it. It sounds
a strange thing, but both Smail and I had hoped that he
had stored a reserve of food in it. The money, when we
saw it first, mocked us. We would have given it all for a
loaf and a mug of water. But it did . . . in a way . . .
unite us. He said that if I would give him half, if we ever
reached land, we would bury the whole story of the
Ethiopian Queen. It wasn't my money, I suppose, but I
agreed to share it. We landed, after eighty-four days and
indescribable sufferings, in the Dutch East Indies—that
was Smail's doing. At his worst, he was a navigator of
no mean order. We were lucky enough to be received
kindly and questioned by a man who could, it is true,
speak English, but whose understanding of it was ele-
mentary. And I was, by that time, so sick of Smail that
I would not be taken back to Holland in the same ship.
I went in a small trade vessel to India, and then home, on
a tea clipper. And that's the whole story. And you can
see, Harriet, that, as Smail would tell it, I am damned.
He can always say that he intended to denounce me—that
may indeed have been his intention. His twenty years of
slavery gives him a perfect alibi, while my behaviour is
entirely consistent with guilt. I came back to Budleigh, I
took you all away in the night. I bought the *Dun Cow*
with what might be called the proceeds of crime. I do,
indeed, stand in a far worse position than I should have
done twenty years ago if we had gone on to Botany Bay
and I had given myself up. And that is why, puerile as
it may seem, I am obliged to barter with this blackmailer.
I'm afraid we are going to be very much poorer, Harriet."

"That doesn't matter a bit." How foolish, how feeble the
words sounded. "My God!" she cried. "What does the
money matter? If only we can keep him quiet. But can
we? Can we?"

"I think so. He has, after all, no certainty of a reward

for his story. I am the only person to whom it has value.
I think he knows that."

"And can demand anything from us." Between their
thickened lids her clear grey eyes darkened. "But you're
not to fall out with him on *my* account. Remember that.
The whole thing began with your being sorry for other
people. Don't put yourself in his power again because
you're sorry for me. I should make *him* sorry. I promise
you that. If he sticks to the point and I have to marry him,
he'll regret it!"

Will, who had told her his story in a controlled, even
slightly pedantic voice, now said passionately, "Harriet,
that is a contingency which I will not even discuss. I
have, from a desire to spare your feelings, said little about
this man's character, habits or condition. But I must insist
upon your understanding, once and for all, that if I were
dying for lack of air and my next breath was dependent
upon your spending an hour with him, alone and unpro-
tected, I would die willingly, gladly, rather than breathe
at such a cost." He swallowed and said more calmly,
"After all, my dear, I'm forty-five. The better half of my
life is behind me. It's full of mistakes, not without sorrow,
but I've had my share of pleasure." God, he thought, he
was getting maudlin, sentimental. He shrugged his thin
shoulders. "That's all rot, of course. I don't really think
the question really arises. Smail knows his market. Tomorrow I'll settle him finally. Five hundred a year. He'll
take it. So you're not to give it another thought. You go
to bed, and remember that if you hadn't gone in for eaves-
dropping, you'd have known nothing about this at all. I
wish to God you hadn't . . . though it's a relief to talk
about it! However, off you go to bed and forget all about
it."

That's right, thought Harriet, dismiss me as you would
a child . . . as you would Myrtle. Brace up your shoulders
and bear the whole burden, as you have always done, you
dear, foolish, saintly fellow. Her hard little heart suddenly

melted, her slow imagination quickened. She could see
his whole life, as though it had been a map laid out before
her . . . the young, ardent idealistic young man who had
married a girl who was lovely to look at, and unhappy at
home; the busy young student who had quarrelled with
his benefactor because of a situation for which Clarissa
was, at least, half to blame; the anxious, harassed young
father who had a distasteful job in order that Clarissa
might live in comfort; the sensitive, hot-headed young
doctor who had been inspired to murder by the sight of
cruelty. And she saw him now, middle-aged, ailing, desperately worried, standing between her and some fate
which she did not properly understand, just as he had
stood between her and bastardy all these years, trying
to shoulder the whole burden, saying, you go to bed
and don't worry.

She stood up suddenly and faced him:

"I've always envied Myrtle," she said in a voice utterly
unlike her own. "I've envied her for being so pretty and
so carefree and so . . . so lovable. But tonight I envy her
a thousand times more. From my heart I wish that you
were my father."

"Ah," he said, misunderstanding, "you mustn't feel like
that, Harriet! I never knew your father. Your mother
was too ill for questioning. But of one thing you may
rest assured. He would not be a person of whom you
would be ashamed. You mustn't think hardly of *her*. She
was young and beautiful, and very affectionate, and alone.
But she had taste, Harriet. Your father, whoever he was,
was a better man than I am in all likelihood."

"But she had known *you*," cried Harriet.

"That is why I say that," said Will, with his wry, self-
derisory twist of the mouth. "Look here, Harriet. All
this is old and best forgotten. Go to bed and try to sleep.
There's nothing for you to worry about, believe that.
Leave me now to think things out."

"Promise me one thing."

"What is it?"

"Don't lose your temper with him again, whatever he says. He would shoot if you frightened him."

"All right. I'll try to keep my temper. Now you go to bed and don't think about it, if you can possibly avoid it. There's nothing that thinking will do. It looks to me, Harriet," he added with a flash of that light-hearted irrelevance that she always found so disconcerting in him and Myrtle (and, ah, now she knew the reason of that puzzling difference!) "as though you and I are going to work twenty-four hours a day and live on pease pudding to keep Smail with cakes and ale. We mustn't undermine our strength with worry and bad nights."

Harriet rose from her chair, stood hesitant for a moment, and then, stepping close to him, put her beautiful hands upon his bowed shoulders. Her grotesque face twisted itself into a grimace that might have been a smile, or the prelude to tears, her grey eyes looked straight at him in a dumb, eloquent, almost dog-like gaze.

"You know," she said after a moment's silence, "I'm no good at saying things. But I am grateful, very grateful."

He held her close for a second and then, stooping his head, kissed her scarred painted cheek.

"My dear, that is no word for you to use to me. You've been the greatest help and comfort always." He gave her a gentle push, and Harriet, with pride and pleasure surging up through all the mingled emotions of the last hours, turned and walked to the door.

Effie

It was almost with a sense of relief that Effie climbed the steep attic stairs at last, shuddered in the draught that raked along the dim passage, heard the rattle of rain on the roof and set her swollen fingers on the latch of the door. Complete despair settled upon her heart and mind and body, bringing a kind of calm with it. There had been no miracle. Instead, things had gone as she had, in her most secret heart, often suspected they would. Once you started to do wrong you sank lower and lower until you took your punishment and ended in hell.

Sarah lay, uneasily prone, upon the tumbled bed. Earlier in the evening, when she could be certain that the attic floor was uninhabited, save for herself, she had allowed herself the small relief of pacing the floor and groaning occasionally. Effie, on her earlier visit, bringing news that Miss Myrtle had heard some noises and attributed them to a ghost, had put a stop to that. And for the last hour Sarah had been very conscious of the cook's presence in the attic next door, and of the other girls coming, one by one, to bed. So she had preserved a Spartan silence.

"You hain't half bin a long time," she said in an angry whisper as Effie entered. "I thought you'd hoofed off."

"I got stopped," Effie whispered back. "I come as soon as I could." She gave Sarah one long, frightened glance in which hatred and unwilling pity mingled with fear, and then, stooping stiffly, slipped off her shoes and put on her old comfortable pair.

"Did you eat yer patties?"

"One I did. The other sorta stuck in my throat. You might give us a drink of water. I ain't dared stir since that old swine come up to bed. Oooh! That wuz a twister! I say, Effie, how long do this go on?"

"Depend how bad they are. The real bad uns don't last long. Maggie Baker wuz three hours."

"I bin longer than that."

"Nut real bad, you ain't. You wuzn't real bad time I was up here afore."

"——!" said Sarah softly, gripping the side of the bed. The spasm passed, and after a second's silence she said in a firm, sibilant whisper, "Now look here, Effie Stevens, for the last time, afore I git any wuss, you know what you got to do.?"

"Yes," said Effie.

"And tomorrer morning, if so be as I ain't right fit to go down, you're to say that I towd you I might stay till noon. I reckon that'll gimme time to pull around." She drew her breath sharply. "That other mawther you did for. How long wuz she afore she got about?"

"Maggie Baker died."

"Fine lot of help you must of bin. And a fine look out for me," snorted Sarah with admirable fortitude. "But I ain't gorn to die. I'm gorn to get rid of this and marry my Bill when he come home for Christmas. Oooh!——! You'll see if I don't."

Effie wanted to say, "I hope you will." She had a certain animal patience herself, and bore things, like weariness, aching feet, cracked knuckles, and chilblains with an almost unconscious fortitude; but she lacked real physical courage, and had as a result a vast and exaggerated admiration for it. But she was not at all certain whether she ought to admire Sarah, who was obviously a bad, wicked girl. Moreover Sarah, as part of her wickedness had made Effie lie for her, and steal for her, and made Effie swear to perform a deed beside which lying and stealing looked almost virtuous, and she had lost Effie the hope which had supported her through long years of toil and penury —the hope of heaven. So Effie would not say, "I hope you will," and so associate herself with Sarah's plan to deceive the young sailor who was coming back to marry her. But she did permit her grudging admiration to find voice in the heartening words, "You oon't to be long now." And as a pledge of the promise she took off the almost clean apron which she had donned for her work in the dining-room, and rolled her sleeves up over her knobby elbows.

"Did yer say all I towd you about my owd mother?"

"Yes. Every word."

"Did they swaller it?"

"They seemed to."

Sarah swore again, and gripped the side of the bed, and then, as though there had been no interval, resumed her inquisition.

"What d'yer mean, 'seemed to'? Either they did or they din't."

"Mrs. Sharman believed me—you wuz there, Sarah. You must of see how I spook up for yer. But arterwards, when Miss Harriet got on to me that worn't so easy. I hatta make up a hool lotta things about hulling gooseberries afore she'd take it in."

Sarah shot a distrustful glance at Effie and was about to tell her that she'd better just repeat what she was told. What the hell had gooseberries to do with this? But before she could voice her remonstrance the final pang had her in its grip, and instead of rebuking Effie she was glad to accept her assistance.

The chilly, draughty attic seemed to grow hot and stifling as Effie worked. And now, in this last moment, she realized that after all her despair, there *was* still time for a miracle. The baby might not be born alive. God must know, since He knew everything, that there would be no sense in lending it breath just for a moment.

Yet, even as the hope flashed through her mind, she was assisting, with all the gentleness of her hard cracked hands and all the strength of her wiry body, the safe passage of the child, and in a surprisingly short space of time she had perfomed the rite of accouchement. Once more the mystery was performed. The tiny fleshly tabernacle was completed and separated; and from some place afar off the visitant soul which had been awaiting its earthly dwelling moved in and took possession. The tiny lungs filled spasmodically, and as Effie cleared the little face the baby gave a shrill gasping cry.

The triumphant sound, which might have been so eagerly awaited and so welcome, brought no joy to either woman. Sarah, whose careless conception and unwilling gestation had been thus concluded, stirred on the bed and

muttered something which Effie did not hear. She had no
need to. She was staring down at the child, knowing that
her very last hope was now shattered. Despite the grim
measures which Sarah had taken, first to obtain an abor-
tion, then to conceal her state, the infant was alive and
perfectly formed. One glance told Effie that, and she
thought wildly that if it had been maimed or marred in
any way her task, though then not an easy one, would
have seemed less dreadful. She might have persuaded
herself that death, with life so short a tenancy, was to be
preferred to existence as a cripple pauper.

As it was she might, had she been in a mood to reason,
have carried that thought to its logical conclusion, and
asked herself for what fate she now desired to spare this
apparently healthy little body. Born unwanted to such a
mother and in such circumstances, what, indeed, could its
life hold of promise? But Effie did not ask herself that
question. She was obeying something far more powerful
and primitive than reason as she gently wiped the small
body and wrapped it in a piece of flannel which had once
been her petticoat, and which she had saved for patching.
She laid the little bundle on the chair by the bed and turned
back to Sarah.

"Hev yer done it?" Sarah asked in a breathless, but
inexorable voice.

"Nut yit. Gimme time. I got something to do for you
first."

"That'll yell agin in a minnit," said Sarah, voicing
her most urgent fear.

Effie said nothing. She was experiencing another mad
revival of hope. Suppose the child did cry out again, and
someone heard it, and came in. . . . Then she would be
saved. But when Sarah said ungratefully, "There, that'll
do. Now you git on and keep your sworn promise, Effie
Stevens," and she stepped back and lifted the baby again,
it was still alive. And now the moment had really come.

Relief more poignant than that afforded by the cessa-

tion of her pangs poured over Sarah when Effie lifted the
child again. Up to that moment she had secretly doubted
the extent of her ascendancy over her room-mate. But as
Effie stepped back, so meekly and without a word of protest, the big girl relaxed for the first time. There . . . she'd
done it, diddled the lot of them. Her coarse, insensitive
spirit soared upwards in a burst of self-congratulation.
She remembered two village girls over whose fates she
had pondered a good deal of late. Mary Dyer had put
herself into Lownde Pool; and Aggie Drew had suddenly
married old Jim Gathercole and lived a dog's life ever
since he discovered how she had tried to fool him. None
of that for Sarah Cross. All you needed, she told herself,
was enough guts. Then the luck would follow. And she
had had both: guts enough to carry on without a word
to anyone until last July, when luck had given her a hold
over that poor tool Effie; and then again guts enough to
go on with her job right up to noon time today. Now, with
Effie's help, her temporary absence was explained; and in
the morning her strong body, relieved and lightened, refilled by a lust for living, would be her own again. Nobody
but Effie would ever know about this little happening. And
at Christmas she would marry Bill.

But something had happened to Effie as she stooped to
the chair and lifted the negligible weight. Unconsciously
her ungraceful arms had closed about the child in a gesture
that was fond and maternal. The little round head, brushed
with silver down, rolled on its stem of a neck and fell
against her flat bosom. The hands, small and beautiful
as petals, rested on the edge of the flannel wrapping.

"Thass a boy," she whispered. "Don't you even wanta
look at him?" Surely if Sarah would just look she would
see the helpless loveliness of it and change her mind.

"No, that I don't," said Sarah harshly. "Thass give me
enough bother already. And don't you stand there making
sheep's eyes at it either, Effie Stevens. Git on. I thought
you wuz done."

Yes, she thought, this was what she had feared all along. She reared her towsled head and stared at Effie, but Effie and the baby and the candle swung in a dizzy arc before her eyes and she fell back on the pillow. She only just managed to say:

"Go on. What you waiting for?"

Effie drew in a loud sobbing breath. She lifted one hand and stroked the child's cheek with her finger. So soft and warm. She looked at its tiny mouth and almost non-existent nose. How could she put her great rough hand over these sources of breath and choke out the life— as she had promised to do? She knew that she had promised the impossible. Come what might she could not kill this little thing. And yet, as she thought come what might, she remembered hearing a man in the yard describe an execution—the cart, the gibbet, the rope, the jeering crowd, and the kicking, struggling body at the rope's end. Every detail of the horrible scene had been vividly described, and had made an indelible impression upon her mind. She let out another long shuddering sob, but when she spoke her choked voice had a ring of utter finality in it.

"Thass no good Sarah. I can't do it."

"You gutless little sod," said Sarah in a vindictive voice, but remembering, even in this extremity, the nearness of the other attic-dwellers. "Arter all, you promised me. Go on, snuff it out. T'won't take but a minnit."

"I can't! I can't!"

"Then Dick'll hang. You know that, don't yer?"

"I can't help it."

Sarah saw, in a red flash, all her careful schemes brought to nothing.

"Damn you then. Give it here to me. I'll do it myself."

"Oh, no!" cried Effie, and backed away until her sharp shoulder blades struck the wall.

Sarah, moving like a great animal couched in sticky mud, began to heave herself nearer to the edge of the bed.

The effort made her so dizzy that she was compelled to close her eyes. But after a second she opened them again and fixed them compellingly upon the shrinking Effie. She spoke in a calmer and more controlled manner.

"Listen to me now, Effie. And don't go for to do something you'll regret all your days. 'Less you hand me that baby now, this minnit, your brother Dick'll hang for a common highwayman. And a nice sister he'll think you are, when they put the noose over his neck, knowing you coulda saved him with one move of yer hand. And you oon't do the baby no good. Soon's ever I git off this bed I shall smother that brat, and you know it. I ain't done all I done lately just to be made a mock of. I'm desprit, thass what I am. Nothing and nobody's gorn to stand in my way *now*. I ain't arsting you to do anything, Effie. I allust knew you wuz a lily-livered little fool. I just want you to gimme that baby. Thass mine, ain't it? I kin do what I like with it, can't I?"

"Thass murder," said Effie.

"So is handing Dick over to the justices, ain't it? I'm surprised at you, Effie Stevens, allust making out you wuz so fond of that brother of yours. You cast yer mind back to the night when I see him, riding master's Katie and meeting Jemmy Mace on Foxley Heath. And in the morning we heard about Mr. Wedderburn been set on and robbed. And you see Dick with gold guineas that very day. Din't you beg and pray me nut to say nothing about it? You think what a state you wuz in then. You remember how you promised you'd do anything for me if I helt my tongue. And I did, din't I? I never split on your precious brother. Then you treat me like this. When all I arst is that you put my own baby here on the bed by me. Come on, Effie. That'll all be over in a minnit and Dick'll be safe."

Effie stood silent, except for the muffled sobs which shook her, for a long moment, and Sarah imagined that she had won. But at last Effie burst out, "Thass murder."

"So is what you're doing to Dick, ain't it? Which is wuss, you daft mawther? Nipping off a pingling bit of a brat thass going to die anyhow, or giving a good strong healthy chap to swing at a rope's end?"

"Oh," cried Effie, distracted. "You woon't do that, Sarah. Nut really. Look, I'll take all the blame. I'll say I fount the baby. I oon't say nothing about it being yours. I'll say I fount it."

"You bloody fool," said Sarah. "Who'd believe you? Old Sharman'd guess in a minnit. She a had her eye on me for weeks. There ain't gotta be no baby about here, and I gotta be up and doing tomorrer with this piller under me clothes. And you ain't going to baulk me either, you snotty little bitch. Gimme that baby. Thass mine, ain't it? I can do what I like with it, can't I?"

"Not that, you can't," said Effie stubbornly. "I ain't gonna do no murder, nor ain't you."

"I'll show you," said Sarah in a whisper. Gathering her strength she took the post of the bed in a strong desperate grip and heaved. Her thick bare legs came slowly but with deadly certainty over the edge of the mattress, and her feet touched the floor.

"You'll kill yerself," said Effie wildly.

"And that'll be your fault. Thass two good folks you'll kill for the sake of a bloody little bastard."

She raised herself and stood upright, still clutching the post of the bed. Then, swaying dizzily but moving with unfaltering intention, she loosed her hold and took a step forward.

Effie let out a little cry, a high terrified squeal like the cry of a trapped rabbit. Then, still clasping the baby in her left arm, she pushed out with her right and thrust Sarah away from her. The edge of the bed caught the thick legs at the back of the knees and Sarah sat down heavily. Effie made a dart for the door.

"Here, Effie! Come back here. I oon't do it. I oon't do nothing. You can keep the baby and I oon't tell on Dick

neither," said Sarah, aware now of her weakness, and
knowing that once the baby was over that threshold the
secret would be out. But Effie, who had looked Satan in
the eyes twice that evening, never even hesitated. She
opened the door, stepped into the passage, closed the
door again, and tested it to see that the latch was in place,
then, bending her head, she gnawed like a rat at the string
which worked the primitive contrivance. When it was
severed she drew it out and dropped it on the floor. The
taste of it, a mingling of tar and ancient dust, was bitter
upon her tongue. But Sarah was safely imprisoned.

The darkness was thick and black in the passage, and a
demented wind was howling. Its cold breath, sieved
through a hundred crannies, struck at Effie's heated face
and sweating body. But she only pulled the old petticoat
more closely about the child, and putting out her right
hand for guidance, felt her way to the top of the stairs.

Step by step she followed exactly the journey which
young Hester Roon had made on just such a blinding
black night a half century before. (Perhaps Hester herself, ripened and fulfilled, loved, wealthy and respected,
paused suddenly in the sunshine of her West Indian afternoon and remembered the stairs and the passages, and
wondered why she should think of them just then. Perhaps her spirit, again young and curious and reckless,
made the journey anew, guiding with its unburdened hands
and lighter feet, this woman of a later day who sobbed
and groped and stumbled.)

Near the head of the stairs that led into the kitchen
Effie hit her left elbow sharply against the corner of the
wall. The jolt disturbed the baby and it began to cry. A
high-pitched wailing lament which seemed to voice all the
despair and sorrow of the world. Cuddling it closer and
murmuring to it in a thick choked voice, Effie took the
last stairs in a blind reckless rush, pushed open the door at
the foot and entered the kitchen, warm with the stored
heat of a thousand fires. From the cavern of the great

hearth the last embers of the fire glowed red in the darkness. Effie lifted a twig from the heap of kindling drying on one hob and plunged it into the heart of the glow. When she withdrew it a flame flowered at the tip. She reached up and lighted a candle. The baby's thin, incredibly piercing cry went on. Effie looked at it for a moment. Maybe it was hungry, she thought. But it would have to wait a little. She wrapped it more securely in its flannel and laid it on the rag rug before the fire. Then, bracing her thin shoulders, she shuffled rapidly to the outer door of the kitchen, shot back the bolts and disappeared into the darkness of the yard.

Julia

As she wrote the words, "To my aunt, Mrs. Melinda Bell of Norwich, my diamond and emerald ring," Julia remembered that the jewel in question was still upon her finger. She slipped it off, pulled the open jewel case a little nearer to her, and laid the ring with the others on the white velvet bed. Then, with her pen still poised, she sat for a moment thinking. If Aunt Bell had this, her best ring, Aunt Stephanie, to whom she had planned to leave the ruby and pearl one, might be hurt. She could imagine the two stout, kindly, property-conscious women meeting, shedding a few tears together, and then going into the matter of their souvenir-legacies in the same spirit of competition as they brought to their clothes and their furniture and their social positions. Perhaps it would be better to leave the most valuable ring to Cousin Bridget, though it seemed rather a waste; Bridget never cared what she wore or what she looked like. But if she had the emerald, Aunt Bell and Aunt Foxe would not be able to make Julia's action the ground for another of their recurrent little quarrels. And after all, she was bothering to go through this stupid business of sharing out her personal property in order that there should be no rancour, no squabbles. She sighed, dipped her pen and amended the sentence, and added another. Bridget would have the emerald, Aunt Foxe the pearl and ruby, Aunt Belle the sapphire. And that was all.

She laid down her pen and read through the long list, of which these three debatable items had formed the final bequests. She thought she had remembered everyone. She hoped so, for she had certainly disposed of every article of value she possessed. It was an odd experience, this deliberate slow stripping of oneself of the treasures one had gathered through thirty years, and visualizing them in the possession of other people. She had a flashing mental picture of her little rosewood piano in Cousin Betsy's drawing-room, of her fur cloak warming Sylvia Cray's thin old shoulders, of her gold watch shining upon Cook's vast alpaca covered bosom. As far as possible, she had disposed of her goods according to the need or the nature of the recipients; and if the aunts chose to wonder why in the name of goodness Bridget should get the best ring, well, it would unite, not alienate them, and Bridget wouldn't give a fig for anything they might think or say.

She folded the sheet of paper and enclosed it in one already written, heated the red wax in the candle by her elbow, and sealed the edges. A third sheet of paper, bearing only a few lines of writing, she merely folded so that the side, addressed to "The Landlord of the *Fleece*," came uppermost. Upon it, pinning it to the table, she placed five gold pieces. Then she locked the jewel-box and the sealed letter and went over to the bed upon which lay her valise, open but not unpacked. Letter and box were placed inside, on top of the carefully folded clothes, and then, moving her fingers to the side, she drew out a white birchwood box of the kind which physicians and apothecaries used for the putting up of pills.

Fastening the clasp of the valise and taking a last look

round to see that everything was tidy, she moved across to the hearth where the fire she had neglected to replenish was dying in a heap of soft powdery grey ash.

She sat down and opened the white box. There were eight round white pills inside it. Old Dr. Bluett had made them, and many more like them, and prescribed them in order that she might sleep. They were very efficient. While she had taken them she had certainly slept. But even through the heavy drugged blankets of slumber in which they had lapped her, the evil dreams had penetrated. The wretchedness of her waking thoughts and the misery of her haunted nights had, between them, torn down the last defences of her health and sanity and fortitude. Dr. Bluett had, with obvious reluctance, given her a week's supply of the soporific pills before she left Norwich for her visit to Charles's mother at Westerfield; that seven, with one she had already saved, made eight. Judging from the effect of one of them, that should be enough.

Now the moment had come. A little resolution, a few last movements of the throat, and it would all be over. This mind and this body, mystically allied by birth, which had been called Julia Henderson and then Julia Foxe, which had loved Charles, who had died at Waterloo for the freedom of Europe, and which had borne Charlie, who had died because his mother had tried to help those who had been so wronged, this mind and this body now, by common consent, were about to sever their connection. The mind would go down into unconsciousness, blissful by its negation, and the body would rot. Here would end the longing for Charles, the grief over her son, the be-wilderment of a thinking mind lost in the maze of a world where there was neither justice nor mercy. And the sooner it was over the better.

One by one, for they were largish and difficult to swallow, she put the pills into her mouth. She dropped the box and the lid into the grate, but the fire was too low to catch even at so revivifying a fuel as the thin birchwood. Then, leaning her head against the needle-work panel at the back of the chair (Harriet's handiwork, an offering to the best bedroom), she waited.

A gentle soothing lethargy began to creep about her body. This was how, after the legitimate dose, slumber made its gradual approach. How long since she slept properly? Months. It had been May then. The scent of lilac had come up from the garden through the open window, and a nightingale had been singing, icily-sweet, in the thick of the newgreened trees. She had lain, as for almost a year she had lain every night, thinking of Charles, sadly, regretfully, longingly, yet without despair; for on that May night, which now seemed so long ago, and separated from this moment by so much more than mere time, she had believed in God and Heaven, in the resurrection of the body and the re-union of true minds. It had been amazing, during these later months, to look back and remember how simple and unquestioning her beliefs had been; it was even more amazing to realize that although her own faith had been shattered so completely, there were still, at this moment, a host of happy credulous people who cherished those beliefs. Happy people, even when they were in sorrow, as she had been happy on that early summer night when she had lain down to sleep, with a thought for Charles, and another for the child Charlie (slumbering, flushed of cheek, dewy-lidded, quiet-handed at last in his cane cot in the next room), and a third thought that she must be early in the morning since she had promised to help Susan Coke with some charitable work next morning. She had slept then peacefully, and had awakened refreshed, to go out and look into hell.

Against the embroidered chair back her head turned uneasily. Not again, cried her mind, not again. I have ended it all. I have given up. I have left, of my own will, the world where such a thing can happen.

Must my last thought dwell upon those children? Think of other things. How often had she bidden her mind think of some other thing? How often, how vainly. And how vainly again. There they were: the little children with their starved, stunted bodies, with their hollow cheeks and frightened eyes. They were so young; they should have been rounded and rosy, full of laughter and high spirits, confident, trustful, happy. But they had been martyred for money. They had been starved and over-worked and beaten. They had been kept from sleep, and from fresh air and sunshine, kept from play, until to look at them was to know, beyond all possibility of doubt, that there was no God, no mercy, no justice in all the earth.

There! That was over once more. It was always the same. As soon as she settled herself for sleep that moment had to be relived to its ultimate bitterness. And the first moment was always the worst of all, as though she were seeing and thinking and feeling these things for the first time. The second phase followed inevitably. You admitted—like the fool in the Bible, only was He such a fool?—that there was no God. Then life on earth was an accident, and the blue span of heaven, the coloured sunset, the rose-hued, fleecy dawn, and the night fields sown with stars were accidents, too. Think that, and you could hear the winds of mortality howl down the corridors of time, dark, empty, senseless. Think that, and your love for Charles was no more than the mating of two rabbits; think that and your love for Charlie was no more than a mother cat's affection for its kitten. And Charles himself was a heap of rotting bones manuring a foreign field; and Charlie a smaller heap decently buried in St. Peter Man-croft churchyard. Go on, think the thought to the end. Think that there can be no God because if there were He could not have endured to watch what had happened to those children and thousands like them, and you see that Christ Himself was only a deluded dreamer Who had died with a cry of disillusion upon His lips.

It was hopeless, she thought. She'd never sleep this way.

She must take one of Dr. Bluett's tablets. No, she was
saving them. She was going to save them until she reached
the halfway-house of her journey, some inn, where her
death would cause no distress to anyone. Then she would
never have to go back to the house in Norwich, so silent
now that Charlie's pattering footsteps and childish voice
were stilled. . . .

But . . . but this was the place, this was the inn; and
she had swallowed all Dr. Bluett's pills. And she was
sitting in the fireside chair because she would not die on
the bed. The inn people might never like the bed again.
There was a prejudice against sudden death of the kind
which she had chosen to die. People who hadn't had the
thoughts that she had had couldn't see that suicide was
the inevitable, logical conclusion. They would think that
she was mad. Which was stupid. The mad people in this
world were the people who very seriously said the Lord's
Prayer every day, asking God for their daily bread and
really expecting to have it given them; ignoring the fact
that every day, somewhere, people starved to death. The
mad people in this world were those who prayed for rain
but exonerated their God from any blame for the drought.

And she had caught a glimpse of that horse trying to
pull the coach this afternoon. That was new. Just another
fragment of tormenting memory. Lame and limping, being
whipped along. Trying hard, and limping and being
whipped. And that wasn't the only one.

True, John Savory had got down from the coach and
chosen to walk. But there weren't many like him. And
even if he gave an example and taught people, it was too
slow, it was foolish. Because if children in mills and
horses in coaches were treated better in future, it didn't
help the ones who had been broken while people were
learning.

Dark spaces about the stars. Accident. Thinking animals
who made themselves a god because they couldn't face
up to the dark spaces about the stars and the thought of

death and the knowledge that there was nothing afterwards. Poor human beings who had to have something to cling to because of the space and the darkness. Poor John Savory with his arguments, deluded like Christ, Who had said why hast Thou forsaken Me? Because it was all made up, all made up, because people couldn't face the dark and the space and the thought that there was nothing beyond the stars while children were being broken in the mills to make someone a shilling, and lame horses were being whipped along the road so people could get to inns where nobody knew them, and wouldn't worry if they died suddenly, because they couldn't bear it any more with no God and no Charles and no little boy, who was very sweet, just beginning to talk and say his prayers. Very silly, because he might have been a little pauper that they would hit with a billy roller to keep him awake after twelve hours' hard work, if he hadn't had a mother, and in the end there was nothing, only the cold and the dark, the cold and the dark.

Charlie was crying. She raised herself in the chair, but restrained herself and sat down again. Poor old Sylvia would resent it so much if she were forestalled. And she was so slow; nearly eighty, poor old thing. She had been pensioned for years when Charlie was born, but nothing would satisfy her but that she should be given charge of the new nursery. And she was very good in many ways, never ruffled, never alarmed by any symptom, never wanting to go out. But it was terribly easy to hurt her feelings and make her feel old. So Julia waited. The crying continued, growing fainter, but never for a moment ceasing its shrill lament. It was queer, the extreme passion with which children cried . . . as though they knew that there was a great deal in the world to cry for.

Sylvia was deaf, that was the truth of it, though she would die rather than admit it. Another moment and she would go herself, offence or no offence. "Sylvia!" she called. "Sylvia! Charlie is crying. Shall I go to him?"

There was no answer from the little room which Sylvia occupied, next to the nursery. And that was strange, because the old woman hardly ever went downstairs at all, and never without making sure that someone was within hearing of the child. Sorry now that she had waited so long, Julia rose to her feet and, moving towards the nursery door, walked straight into massive tallboys, striking her forehead, just above the eye, a sharp, dazing blow upon its edge.

She reeled backwards and put her hand to her head. Then, almost frightenedly, she looked about her, noting the strange furniture, the unfamiliar pattern of the carpet and the door which opened in an unexpected place. Where was it? A doubt as to her own identity seized her, but one glance downwards showed her the well-known lines of her heavy black travelling dress with the velvet bands on the skirt, and there was her own hand, her thin white hand with the wedding ring, hanging below the edge of the sealskin cape. Yes, this was herself, and somewhere, not faraway, she could hear Charlie crying. She must go to him at once.

She opened the unfamiliar door and peered out into the darkness. She must have the candle, and turning back she lifted from the table the special candlestick, the silver nymph, bearing the candle like a torch, which Harriet had assigned her because of her clothes and her gentle voice. With it in her hand she went to the door again, and then, after listening for a second, turned towards the sound of the baby's crying.

She was in a passage, so long, so wide, so high that the candle could only light a tiny section of it at a time. So shines a good deed in a naughty world. Naughty was a tolerant, almost playful word. Charlie was often naughty. Words had changed a little since Shakespeare's time.

Sounds had changed, too. There was so much silence around her that her footsteps were as loud as drub beats, intolerable, shattering, combined as they were with the loud hissing cackle of the candle burning, and the violent screaming of the child. "I'm coming," she cried, and her voice sounded like the harsh tearing of a strip of calico. "I'm coming, my precious!" she said more softly.

The walls were pale, almost white. And at intervals in the endless stretch of them there were doors, or pieces of furniture. Some of the pieces lurched out at her as she passed them, and she was obliged to dodge out of their way. Once, in order to avoid the sudden attack of a vast reeling linen press she found herself in a little alcove before another door. Peculiar sounds came from behind the door, sounds as though two heavy bodies were wrestling together, panting and stamping. She could hear some stiff resistant material being torn into shreds.

But through all the noises which battered upon her senses she could still hear the child crying; and she kept on, past the lurching furniture, between the walls which pulsed in and out, over the floor which rocked and tilted, moving always towards the place where Charlie awaited her.

Presently, when she seemed to have been walking for hours and was sobbing with impatience, and fright and bewilderment, she reached the top of a flight of stairs which stretched away, endless and steep. She set her foot on the top stair and then the whole flight contracted under her weight, pleating themselves together, so that her next step, a painful one which twisted her ankle, found her at the bottom of the flight, pressed against a door. Her candle was broken, hanging downwards and spilling hot grease on her fingers. But she found the latch of the door, pressed and pushed and found herself in a vast, gloomy apartment with a strange red glow at its farther end.

The child was crying now with a violence that rent her eardrums.

"Darling, darling!" she cried. "I'm coming. I'm here." But the floor of this place was even more treacherous, strewn with boulders which caught and tripped her feet, and it was only after hours of climbing and stumbling that she reached the mouth of the cavern where the red glow was and fell on her knees beside the child, lifting him to her bosom, holding him close and murmuring, "There, there. Mother's here. Don't cry, my precious! Mother has you safe. There, my lovely! There."

She twisted her legs under her so that she was sitting on the rag rug, and lowered the child into her lap, looking at him hungrily. Only just born, poor lamb—and she had felt nothing, that was strange—and quite bare! She replaced the flannel and dragged off her cape, wrapping the child in the warm folds of it. Comforted, he hushed his wailing, and with the cessation of the deafening noise, she could suddenly think clearly again. It was as though a thick fog had lain over her mind and then, all in a moment, split, lifted and rolled away. She could have cried from relief and excitement and remorse. How could she ever have doubted? How could she ever have thought that life and consciousness could end with the ceasing of the heart-beat? It was true, completely and beautifully true, that belief which men had cherished since the beginning of Time—death did mean a renewal of life, and a reunion. Already she had her baby in her arms again, and soon, soon, Charles would come. She was so certain of that, that the sharp opening of the yard door behind her made her turn her head quickly, a rapt look of delight and love and anticipation upon her ghastly face.

But it was only Effie who shuffled into the kitchen.

Effie was feeling better. The worst had happened now, and she had three things to be thankful for. The sin of murder was not on her conscience. She had been in time to warn Dick. And since Katie was not in the stable—to Dick's voluble and blasphemous regret—she had not, by warning her brother, lost her master his beloved mare.

Now, if she could just sit by the fire for a little while and hold the baby and think up some story which would account for its presence, she might even be able to stay Sarah's tongue. Then Dick's absence, though difficult to explain, would be nobody's business, especially as he had not been able to take Katie.

So, in better heart than she had been for months, Effie flung open the door, and had taken several rapid shuffling steps towards the hearth when her breath stopped and her feet rooted themselves to the floor, as she stared at the apparition by the fire. Julia's black dress was indistinguishable from the darkness of the rug, and in the dim light only her deathly white face, the narrow strip of her white collar, and the pallor of her hands upon the fur-wrapped bundle, showed to Effie's eyes. Her first impression was of a bodiless face and a pair of hands floating on the darkness near the floor. A paroxysm of superstitious terror seized the girl. If she could have lifted her feet she would have fled back into the yard; if she could have moved her tongue she would have screamed and wakened the whole house. But she was paralysed and speechless, and could only stand and stare.

Julia, to whose drugged nerves all noises seemed immensely exaggerated, said in what she thought was a nomal soothing voice, but was in reality a mere shred of a whisper:

"I'm afraid I startled you. Don't be frightened."

Effie heard no words. It seemed to her that the face on the hearth was gibbering at her. She turned dizzy, her knees began to sag, and she would have fallen to the floor had not Julia, with a great effort, got to her feet, still clutching the baby, reeled across the uneven floor and put her arm around Effie's waist.

The touch of her body, human flesh and blood, the frail but willing support of her arm, and the sound of her voice, audible now that she was so near at hand, brought Effie to her senses. No ghost would speak so soothingly, and in a moment the girl realized, with another shock, but a reviving one, that this was a human creature; not only human, but, by the feel and sound and the smell of it, a lady. She moistened her blanched lips and gasped out, "I'm sorry, mam. You give me a bit of a turn, thass all. I'm all right now."

Julia, whose arms were being dragged from their sockets by the double burden, released Effie and sat down suddenly, this time in a chair.

"Dying *is* . . . quite an experience," she said in that muted voice.

Effie merely stared. Then she said, in nervous explanation of her behaviour. "I thought you was a ghost for a minnit."

"I expected that is what they would call me. And you, too. Yet you look perfectly ordinary to me. It's strange, isn't it? It's quite different from anything I had expected. So dark. Yet, when I think of it, I remember that people have always spoken about the Shades and the Shadow of death. I expect it is just a matter of adjustment." She noticed Effie's look of utter bewilderment, and added, "You look rather puzzled. I expect you haven't thought about it much. I have. More or less, the question of death has been with me ever since I lost my husband. Of course, being young, you wouldn't have given the question much consideration. Or is it . . ." a new thought struck her . . . "is it that you are puzzled by me? By my being so interested? Have you been here longer, perhaps?"

Poor thing, to be so mad, thought Effie. All fear had left her, and all class consciousness, as she realized Julia's madness. Deranged wits were no new thing to her. The person with whom she had come nearest to establishing any intimate human relationship was the village idiot, an afflicted creature known as Daftie. Effie's sympathies had been enlisted in his cause on account of the cruel teasing which he suffered, similar in kind, though fiercer in degree, to the treatment meted out to her in the old days in the *Fleece* kitchen. Now Daftie knew her quite well, and would brighten when she spoke to him. He often shared in her largesse, and he had taught Effie how to deal with the crazy—they must, above all things, be humoured.

So, picking out from Julia's words the one sentence which seemed to her to have any meaning, Effie answered it:

"I bin here ever since I wuz a little mawther."

"Oh, I see. You died young. Poor little thing. But no, perhaps I am wrong to pity you. Perhaps you have been happy here. . . ."

"Since Mr. Oakley come. Afore that I din't hev much of a time. You see, I wuz ony a pauper."

The dread word seemed to raise a faint, disturbing echo in Julia's mind. Her hands tightened about the baby's body, and she shot a glance of horrified pity at Effie.

"You poor mite!" she whispered. "But it is over now, isn't it? It was that . . . I remember now . . . it was the poor little paupers who upset all my ideas . . . and spoiled my life."

"They coon't," said Effie bluntly. "They coon't do nothing to nobody, the paupers coon't. It wuz other folks did things to *them*."

"I know. But it is all right now, isn't it? I mean . . . now that we know that we don't just die. It makes the other things unimportant." She looked down at the baby again, and then up at Effie with a smile. "It is wonderful, isn't it? To find him again so quickly. And so young. You see, his father never saw him, he was killed two months before he was born. And it does seem so perfect that now he will be able to see all his pretty little ways, and hear his first words. . . ." A slight shadow of anxiety clouded the pleasure of her face. "You think he will come? He may have gone further in the dark, of course; two years is a long time, but where things are all so different. . . . I have missed him so very much. I am delighted to have found the baby, but oh! now I am impatient. I do want Charles, too."

Effie had reached the limit of her ability to humour the

mad, and to support this crazy conversation any longer. She really must get this poor soul out of the kitchen and begin to think what to do about the baby. Time was getting on. She looked at Julia, and was about to make some sensible suggestion about getting back to bed, when, even as she looked, a dreadful change came over the gentle, ravaged face. Julia's lips had turned blue, and sagged stiffly away from her teeth; her eyelids had fallen so low that her eyes were mere glassy slits; and her arms had released their hold on Sarah's baby and now hung limply among the folds of her skirts.

Effie lifted the baby and laid it back on the hearth. Then, diffidently, she took Julia's arm in her hand.

"Mam! Mam! Wake up and I'll get you back to bed." There was no response from the limp figure. Even the convulsive frightened grasp of Effie's hand and the shake which it administered waked no sign of consciousness. Really frightened now, Effie stepped back a little, stared wildly at Julia for a second, and then, with a gasp, turned and went clattering up the stairs.

It was significant that she ran straight to Harriet's room. That was the rule of the inn. In any crisis one thought immediately, not of kind Will or affable Myrtle, but of Harriet, who would be brusque and harsh, but unshakable, able to deal with anything. She would ask questions, thought Effie, blundering along the passage, and she should have the truth. Yes, the truth. And then at last the whole thing would be finished.

But the end was not yet. For although she called Harriet by name and tapped on the door, softly at first, then vigorously, there was no answer from within the room. Once, indeed, as she listened she thought she detected a sound, a grunt, or a snore or a groan. She could not tell which, or whether indeed she had actually heard it. It was not repeated. She took the knob of the door in her hand, turned it, and pressed. But the door was locked.

Who'd have thought that Miss Harriet would have slept so sound?

Turning sharply and ricochetting off the side of the alcove arch, Effie continued her headlong flight along the main passage to the very end, where, at the top of six steps, was the room over the gateway, which was Will's. Stumbling up the steps, she assaulted the door, caring nothing now if she waked up the whole house.

"Mr. Oakley, sir! Mr. Oakley, wake up! This is Effie. You're wanted in the kitchen."

She was still calling and hammering on the door when it opened so much sooner that she had expected, that the impetus of her onslaught carried her into the room with the door as it swung inwards. Will caught her by the elbow and balanced her on her feet.

"Why, Effie," he said, "what's wrong?"

"Most everything," gasped Effie. "There's a woman in the kitchen mortal bad. Oh, sir, please come quick!"

"I'm ready," said Will, turning back into the room and lifting his candlestick. "What woman is it, Effie?"

Effie was staring about this sacred apartment, the room where *he* slept. She could see that the bed had not been slept in. And her master was fully dressed. Had nobody been to bed this night?

"I dunno, sir. She din't come from outside, her shoes was dry as a bone. But she was crazy, sir, sitting there and telling me a lot about being dead and cuddling Sarah's baby and saying it was her'n. Then she went all stiff and stark like, and I run for Miss Harriet, but she din't answer."

She shuffled along beside Will, gasping out the story as they moved rapidly back to the head of the kitchen stairs.

"I a got a lot to tell you, sir, one way and another, about the baby and Sarah and Dick."

"It'll keep, I expect," said Will shortly. He ran lightly down the stairs, followed by Effie clumping close behind.

Julia sat where Effie had left her. She looked like an effigy of a woman carelessly flung into a chair. A little blob of white froth had formed at each corner of her stiff blue mouth.

Next day, when Effie, momentarily enjoying an unwonted popularity, told and re-told the story of the night's adventures, she reported that no doctor could have done better than Mr. Oakley. Lingering lovingly over each detail, she described how together they had worked for a quarter of an hour, walking the poor lady up and down, shouting in her ear, dashing cold water in her face and pouring scalding coffee down her throat, even smacking her sharply on the hands and wrists.

It was more drastic treatment than Effie would have dared to apply to a seemingly dead body, though, for the rest of her life, anyone who lost consciousness in her presence was in danger of similar handling. For it worked. It worked amazingly. Soon Julia's feet, instead of dragging limply about the floor, steadied themselves under her weight. The blue colour left her face, and presently her eyelids, tinged with the violet of sleeplessness, fluttered wide open and she looked about the kitchen and at Effie and Will with eyes which really saw.

It had been only another dream, that long walk through the corridors of darkness, and the finding of the child, and the momentary expectation of Charles's arrival. She was still in the inn, the place where she had chosen to kill herself; and these strange, officious people who were looking at her with such kindly interest, had found her and dragged her back into life she had tried to leave.

A low sound, half moan, half speech, burst from her lips.

"You should have let me die."

"So irrevocable a decision was not ours to take," said Will, stiff with embarrassment. The innate courtesy which had dictated her actions since childhood, even to the last choice of a place to die in, asserted itself immediately.

"Of course not. I'm sorry. I shouldn't have said that. I'm sorry to have given you so much trouble."

"It was not a trouble. I'm glad Effie fetched me in time."

"Are you a doctor?"

"No. I'm the landlord."

Her gaze moved from his face to Effie's, smudged and exhausted.

"But I've seen you before." There was bewilderment in her voice.

"A course you hev, mam. I bin here with you all the time. I ony went off for Mr. Oakley when you flung that there faint."

"In my bedroom," said Julia, puzzled. And then, in a sharper, more definite voice. "But there *was* a baby."

"A course there wuz. Thass here still, poor little mite," said Effie, stepping aside and pointing with her finger at the bundle near the fire. Julia eyed it with astonished repulsion.

"I dreamed it was mine," she said in a tone of horror.

"Whose is it?" Will asked.

"Sarah's."

"What Sarah?"

"I towd you," said Effie. "Sarah Cross. You know, sir." She straightened her drooping shoulders and fixed her wild hare's eyes on Will's face and began to speak in a rapid gabble.

"Thass what I wanted to tell you, sir. You see, soon arter Sarah got here she got into trouble. And her young feller is away to foreign parts, him being a sailor, and she didn't think he'd marry her when he come back like he promised if so be he knew what she'd been doing of. I worn't going to hev nothing to do with it, ony one night, sir, back in the summer, when she wuz a-coming back from visiting owd Mother Fenn for a dose, she see my brother Dick a-riding your Katie, Mr. Oakley, a-longer Jemmy Mace. You know, sir, that wuz the night Mr.

Wedderburn wuz kilt out Winwood way. Then she come
to me and she say, if I don't help her in all she want to
do, she'll tell about Dick and he'll hang. . . ." Effie paused
for breath, drew a harsh gasp, and then rattled on, this
time in a more emotional voice, and with her big red
hands clasped almost dramatically in front of her hollow
stomach. "Oh, Mr. Oakley, I a had a terrible time all
alonga the things she made me do. She got that hungry she
made me steal stuff for her every day a'most. She made me
do her jobs and tell sich lies when I wuz caught at it. But
when that come to doing in the pore little owd baby, Mr.
Oakley, my heart that did fail me, and I jest coon't do it.
Not no way I coon't. And I won't let her do it neither.
She got that riled with me and say she'll see Dick hang.
But I brung the baby away and I brook the string on our
door so's she coon't git out; and then I tolt Dick to hoof
it quick's he could, and made up my mind to tel you. So
now you know, sir. And all I done, all the lies I tolt, and
all the food I stole, thass all wasted. I might as well done
nothing and saved myself from hell."

"Just as well," said Will, speaking to himself rather
than to Effie. But she, thinking that there was menace in
the words, took a step forward and reached out her
ruined hands and cried passionately:

"Oh, Mr. Oakley, don't set them after Dick. Oh, please,
don't I beg you. He ain't a bad boy, sir, he ain't really. He
allust done his work well, and he didn't do you no harm,
'cept jest to ride Katie now and then. He ain't no more'n
a boy now, Mr. Oakley, and he never had much chance.
He got into bad company, thass what he did, and there
worn't no one to tell him different, ony me, what he
woon't give no heed to. Oh, please, Mr. Oakley, sir, if you
jest oon't set them after him I'll work for you all my
days. I oon't want no wages and I oon't eat hardly
nothing. Don't you send a young boy like that to the
gallows, Mr. Oakley, and I'll serve you all my life."

She had never, in all her unnumbered years, spoken at

such length, or so passionately. The effort drained the last dregs of her strength, and she was obliged to grip the edge of the table. She swayed as she stood there, staring at Will as though he were her only hope, her only link with sanity. With an uprush of fellow feeling of which the tortured girl knew nothing, Will moved round the table and pushed her gently into a chair.

"Effie," he said gently. "Effie. Listen to me. Stop shaking now and listen. Of course I shan't set anyone after Dick. Do you hear me? Do you understand that? What you have told me—and why the hell didn't you tell me at once?—is strictly between ourselves. But we will see whether we can't get him out of that man's clutches and set him straight again. For your sake, Effie. There now. Don't cry. We've had almost enough upsets for one night. That's a good brave girl. It'll all come right. I promise you."

Effie gave a gulp and a shudder; then, with the fortitude native to those whose emotions have never been a matter for sympathy or interest to those about them, controlled herself and, after a second, was able to speak, with a jerk of the head:

"What about her?"

Julia was sitting in the chair in which they had placed her as soon as the need to drag her up and down the kitchen had passed. She had given the little scene a fragment of her attention, had listened to Effie's confession and pleading and heard Will's reassurances, rather as a person might sit in a theatre and watch a play while all the time his mind deals with some problem of his own. At Effie's words she roused herself and said, with gentle, pathetic dignity and utter lack of truth:

"I am all right now. I'll go. I just didn't like to disturb you. Thank you both, so much . . . for all your trouble."

"Effie is shut out of her own room," said Will. "I wonder . . . since it is too late to make other arrangements, whether you would let her sleep with you." His glance quenched the words of protest on Effie's startled lips. "It would be company for you. And a kindness."

"Of course," said Julia. She nodded her head as she spoke, and two heavy tears which had hung suspended from her lashes for a long time shook off and fell upon her cheeks.

"What about the baby?" asked Effie.

"Ah, the baby!" said Will. "Let's have a look at it."

He lifted the little bundle and inspected the evidence of Effie's homely but efficient midwifery. "You do this, Effie? A nice tidy job. Well. What about him?"

"We'll take him," said Effie eagerly, forgetting in this moment of sweet relief that she was no one to make suggestions. She would have undertaken anything at that moment. The dark cloud which for so long had obscured the sun of her happy contentment had been rolled away. There remained only to make her peace with God; and she had been thinking, while Will inspected the baby, that if a man—admittedly a man out of the ordinary, but a mortal man for all that—could be so kind and understanding, she could trust her Heavenly Father to be kind and understanding, too. She was impatient for the moment when she could fall on her knees and begin to pray.

She shuffled about, collecting the milk that she had warmed, how long ago, and a shred of white linen.

"He's quiet now, but he's sure to be hungry. We'll feed him soon's he wake," she said. She took the child from Will's hands and then, as Julia raised herself from her chair, proffered him to her.

"If you like to take him I'll give you a hand up the stairs, mam." But Julia, remembering the joy, the hunger, the passion with which she had clutched this strange child to her breast, shrank away.

"Oh, come on," said Effie coaxingly. "I know he ain't yourn; but he's a nice little owd chap. Pore little bastard, he ain't got nobody to care for him. His mother took

agin him right from the start. He's one of them you wuz
making out you wuz so sorry for."

Julia stared for a moment at Effie's ugly rabbitty face,
and suddenly enlightenment, blinding and dazing as the
light which smote Saul on the road to Damascus, burst
upon her. Negation and disbelief would never cure the
sickness of this world. You could never defeat evil by
retreating from it. It must be faced, and fought and overcome. Action, not futile sorrow, was what was needed. She
thought, in that one moment, of the big house, so empty
that she had feared to face it, of the money which would
have kept her and Charlie all their days, and still have
left an inheritance for Charlie's children; of the jewels
which she had been earnestly bequeathing to old women
who had more than enough of their own. Dear God,
how blind and selfish she had been! How foolish!

"Give him to me," she said softly.

"Thass right," said Effie, hooking her thumb through
the handle of the milk mug and closing her fingers round
the body of a candlestick in a manner possible only to
those who habitually carry more than they should. "Now,
you take holt of my arm, so fashion. And mind not to let
go of him. Good-night sir, and thank you ever so much."

"I have to thank you, too," said Julia. "I may not seem
very grateful, but I think I shall be—in time. And I feel
that I owe you an explanation. . . ."

"Please," said Will. "That's quite unnecessary. I trust
that you will sleep."

She stood hesitant for a moment, a strange figure in the
disordered kitchen, her soft brown hair drifting about
her pale blotched face, her eyes swollen with tears, her
rich gown creased and damp with water and spilled
coffee. This kitchen, she thought, which she would never
see again, and which might have been the last place on
earth to have met her mortal sight, had been a place of
revelation, as significant as that barn where she had first
seen evil face to face and known the scaring force of

pity. She might have died here; instead she had been re-born, not as she had deliriously imagined, miraculously, but actually, naturally, from within. Charles and the child were gone, irrecoverably, and she was still lonely and sad, a little bewildered in her new state as the re-born must ever be. But the core of bitterness, the heart of despair, had melted and vaguely she perceived where she was going, and why.

"Good-night, then," she said. "And thank you."

Linked together, so that in the grotesque shadow cast by Effie's candle upon the whitewashed wall they looked like one strange inhuman figure, the trio, lady and serving girl and new-born bastard, moved out of the kitchen and up the stairs.

Will dropped into the chair which Julia had occupied and put his head in his hands, resuming the train of thought which Effie's frantic summons had interrupted. But now there was a new element in it; and although he had forgotten Effie and the whole affair into which she had dragged him before she had reached the top of the stairs, it was some word of hers, innocently and desperately spoken, which had clarified his mind. "All I done . . . thass all wasted. I might as well done nothing. . . ." Mightn't any man, in the power of the blackmailer, say the same? Wasn't blackmail like a cankerous growth, breeding as it fed? First it was three hundred pounds a year, then it was three hundred pounds and Harriet. Would it stop there? Not likely. There was hardly a man born who could be trusted with complete indisputable power over a fellow being. And of all men on earth, he who had once resorted to blackmail, was the least to be trusted. For blackmail, once established, seemed to acquire a life of its own and grow, like a cancer. Even a common, ignorant slut of a girl like Sarah, unresourceful and uninventive by nature, had found the means for making Effie's life a hell of misery. What hope then was there for the man who lay in the power of a creature like Smail, sadistic, cunning, perverted, doomed to a smarting sense of self-pity, out to avenge his own wrongs upon any helpless thing he met. And that he himself was helpless, Will dolefully admitted. He had sent Harriet to bed with—he hoped—words of comfort. But he had, in his inmost heart, little hope of buying Smail off by an offer of more money. Beyond the standard of comfort and security which Smail himself had set at three hundred pounds a year, money probably held little interest for him. He had said himself, "a man can only eat one meal at a time"; and he had also said, in words that roused sick memories in Will's mind, "I'd enjoy taming her." Smail had had seamen in his power for years, and then . . . whom? Fellow slaves? Poor creatures of some harem? God knew! But there had been somebody to keep the old lust alive, and now his eyes had lighted upon Harriet, detecting instantly, with some damnable second sight of their own, that Harriet would offer good sport, resist, fight, retaliate . . . and be broken at last.

But though it cost his life Will would save Harriet. *His* life, and not his alone! There was, and in the back of his mind he had known it all along, only one way to deal with Smail. The violent, bloody way.

A great sigh tore its way out of Will's very vitals and died on the air. That will be the third, he thought. Three times a murderer. It was incredible. He looked back and saw himself . . . a little boy at Ludlow, protesting at the things that boys did to stray dogs, trapped rats, and frogs . . . a raw young student at his first dissection, squeamish, and yet absorbed, entranced with the magic intricacy of a mere lump of flesh . . . an almost qualified student watching beside the bed of a little seamstress whose needle-poisoned finger he had removed three days before. . . .

He had loved life, been aware of its wonder. Yet twice he had taken life and, it seemed, must take it again. He had killed Peabody in a fit of rage, and he had killed Clarissa in a fit of panic. He had been so anxious to leave the place where she was known by his name, so anxious to move her, that he had taken her too soon from her bed. In the eyes of God he was responsible for her death. And now he must kill Smail, not in the heat of the moment, not by accident, but coldly, deliberately, in a treacherous manner, when the man was under his roof, full of his food and wine.

For while Smail lived, nothing was safe. Whereas, with Smail dead, even if he himself were accused and hanged, the girls would be all right. The *Fleece* was his now. They could sell it and Harriet could start the school or the cakeshop for which, in her heart, she longed.

And what he had said to Harriet about having had the best of life was true enough. He'd had a happy childhood, a youth full of interest and promise. He had loved Clarissa madly. He had enjoyed every stage of growth of the little girls. There had been food and wine, books, trees and sunsets, happy hours on Katie's back. . . . Yes, he could afford to die in order to remove a menace from the world.

He raised his head and straightened his shoulders. Now, since the thing must be done, how best to do it? The door behind which Smail slept would be locked; but that was no obstacle. For in an inn keys were always being lost. Careless guests would take them away in their pockets, or lose them somewhere about the place. So, for convenience sake, there were always spare keys on a big hook in the passage, awaiting an emergency. Unless Harriet, in a moment of extreme possessiveness, had sought out and removed that other key, it would be a simple matter to enter Smail's room. And then. . . . It must be bloodless and swift. Relentless hands upon the throat of the sleeper; breath checked so suddenly that unconsciousness met sleep with hardly a pang between. For although he must kill Smail, he had no desire to hurt him. Smail was what life, tainted and warped in some manner, had made him. No man would choose, of his free will, to be what Smail had been. He was to be pitied, too.

Harriet

Softly and anxiously as any thief, Harriet entered the bedroom. It was not that she feared Myrtle's questions. Even if they were spoken they could be answered with a few snappy, unrevealing words. But she had, in every part of her, a deep and urgent desire to be alone. And since she must share a room, on this night of all nights, it was imperative that she share it with a sleeping, not a conscious, being.

She was outwardly calm. She herself was amazed at the steadiness of her own hand. The candle in it burned with an unwavering flame, yet every nerve and bone and vein in her body throbbed vibratingly. Even her stomach behind the rampart of its uncompromising whalebone corset seemed to quiver like an ill-made jelly.

She was twenty years old, and for fourteen years every thought of her mind and every action of her body, had in some way, conscious or unconscious, been connected with the marring of her face. And now suddenly she had been brought face to face with a situation which made all her despair and jealousy, and all her resultant efficiency, activity and accuracy of as little importance as the bits of straw that blew about the yard. She felt foolish, seeing herself like a child which has surrounded itself with toys, played with some and pretended to mourn over others, busy and absorbed in the path of a charging bull. Now the toys were all scattered, the joy and the sorrow seen for the empty simulacri that they were, and the child, bruised and frightened, was gathering itself together and wondering what to do.

Her brain felt raw, stripped of every protective layer which she had lain upon it during the course of the years. Yet some of the virtue which she had cultivated so earn-

estly, some of the pattern which she had rigorously imposed upon herself, remained, in this hour, to succour
and strengthen her. She was still practical, still self-con-
trolled, and still orderly, both in thought and action.

She closed the door quietly, raised the candle and looked
towards the bed. Myrtle lay where she had flung herself,
fully dressed. One slender white arm hung downwards,
and her fingers were lost in the warm soft mass of fur that
was Tabby and the kittens. The other hand, grasping a
sodden handkerchief, was pressed against her face, half
buried in the pillow. The very violence of her emotion
had worn her out and she was asleep.

Harriet found time to wonder what on earth had possessed her to go to bed like that. She came forward
cautiously and inspected the sleeper. There were some
strands of hay among the glossy disorder of Myrtle's
curls and the hem of her dress, as well as her shoes and
stockings, were splashed with mud. There was a wide
patch of dampness beneath her carnation-flushed face.
It was plain that something had upset her, and that she
had cried herself to sleep. Great God, thought Harriet,
suppose she had heard what I have heard tonight! What
sort of a state would she be in now?

She turned away from the bed and lighted, from the
flame of the one she carried, the two candles upon the
cluttered dressing table. Then she removed her dress and
washed her face and hands and neck thoroughly. Next
she lifted the box which contained the articles which had
lain in the locked drawer, and turning to the mirror, faced
the sight of which for years had met no eyes but her own,
her naked, horrible face. Tonight, for the first time in
fourteen years, she looked at it impersonally and began,
without wasting a second of time, to build upon that sorry
foundation, the mask with which she faced the world. With
sure, unfaltering, practised fingers she smoothed on the
thick layer of Mrs. Waterbury's paste, working until a false
surface had been laid over the pocks and scars, just as,

all over England, builders were laying a façade of white stucco over the flints and bricks of an older day. When she was satisfied with it she coloured its cheeks and lips carefully and powdered it with a lump of swansdown. Then she shook down her hair and dressed it anew, smoothing every strand with scented oil until it was as neat and symmetrical as a coiffure carved from pale stone. When the last pin was in place she stepped back from the mirror and looked at herself critically. As upon a thousand previous occasions, her reflection stared back at her, deceptive, at a slight distance, everywhere except about the eyes.

Then, for the first time, she paused and stood hesitant for a moment. Her glance moved from the dress which she had just hung across the back of the chair, and the one hook which she had cleared of Myrtle's clothes and used for her own. After a moment she had decided and, moving to the hook, took down a light, but bulky, garment and slipped off the cover of butter-muslin which protected its beauty from dust and friction, revealing a loose-sleeved, full-skirted négligé of blue velvet and cream lace. Neither material was good of its kind, for Harriet's stern good sense had forbidden her to spend much money on so useless and frivolous an object, but in the gentle light of the candles, against the background of Myrtle's cluttered room, the garment was suggestive of an incongruous elegance and luxury.

Harriet had made it herself, taking for her model a similar garment which she had once seen adorning the body of a very dashing young demi-mondaine, one of a party who had made the *Fleece* their headquarters during a week of races at Newmarket. She had bought the material and done all the meticulous work upon it behind the locked door of her room, as though she had been indulging a vice. Why she wanted it, and what possible service it could render her, she had not known until this moment, when, after months of secret and inconsistent existence it suddenly fitted into her plan in such a way that she wondered as she shook out the glistening folds, whether her apparent foolishness had not been inspired by Destiny itself.

That she was innocent of the robe's specific purpose in the matter of seduction, she proved by putting it on over her whalebone corset and stiff moire petticoat. Then she turned to the mirror again.

This time, with attention riveted upon her figure, she was pleased with her reflection. The long loose sleeves with their deep fall of lace were especially graceful, and made necessary a gesture which Harriet's hands performed to perfection, a little lift and a shake before the fingers were free for use. She repeated the lovely languorous movement twice. Then, bending forward, she blew out the two superfluous candles, took up her own and the little packet which she had taken from the box when she put away her cosmetics, shot a final look at Myrtle, who slept on, oblivious, and moved with graceful deliberation out of the room.

She set her candlestick down at the head of the stairs and tiptoed to the very end of the passage. There, in the darkness, she could see the line of light, not much thicker than a hair, which told her that Will had come up to his room. Satisfied, she tiptoed back and took up her candle. On the half-landing she raised it and studied the face of the tall clock. Only twenty minutes had elapsed since she had passed it before on her way upstairs.

When, like a pedestrian ghost, she passed the clock again she did not spare it a glance. She was intent upon what she carried in her hands, a heavy silver tray which bore, as well as her candlestick, the best decanter that the inn boasted and two of the best goblets.

At the top of the stairs she turned right and continued along the passage until she reached the alcove outside her own door. Once within its privacy she gave a little sigh of relief, and the tight hard lines of her face relaxed a little. Shifting the tray so that it was balanced between her hand and her body, she lifted her free hand and tapped, very gently, upon the door. From within the room came the creak of the bed, but no other sound. She tapped again. This time Smail answered, calling in a sharp nervous voice, "Who's there?"

"Ssh!" hissed Harriet at the keyhole. "It's only me. Harriet." Then, remembering that he might not know her by name, "Harriet Oakley. You saw me just now in the parlour."

"Who's with you?"

"Nobody."

"I don't believe you."

"Open the door and find out."

"Not likely!"

"Oh, please, Mr. Smail! I've got something I must say to you. For your sake, too. Am I likely to play a trick on you? After what Father has just told me?"

"What's that?"

"He said you want to marry me."

She heard his tittering laugh. "Please open the door. After all, you have got a pistol, haven't you?"

"That's right," said Jonathan, with an increase of confidence. "And I'll shoot if there's any nonsense."

"There isn't. Oh, do let me in before anyone hears me."

The bed creaked again. There was a shuffling sound and then the noisy grate of the key turned by an unaccustomed hand. Harriet stood still, and the door opened a crack, showing a section of Smail's face—one eye and a strip of cheek, and the hand which held the cocked pistol. He inspected her solemnly. Then, satisfied that this was not a trick to get the door opened, he swung it a little wider and said, "Come in quickly."

Harriet stepped into the room and set the tray on the glassy top of the chest of drawers. Behind her Smail closed the door smartly and locked it again. Then as he turned from the door and Harriet from the chest of drawers, they stood facing one another. He wore a soiled night-shirt of coarse striped flannel, which, stopping short just below the knee, left his thick white legs and huge splay feet exposed to view. On his head was a knitted nightcap beneath which his doughy face looked like a pudding which had split its bag. But to Harriet there was nothing comic in his appearance. She had to make an effort to keep her disgust out of her eyes.

He studied her with close attention for a moment, then he laughed.

"Well," he said, "you're a nice one, you are. Coming into a man's room alone, nigh on midnight."

A fierce unholy pleasure mingled with the nervousness in Harriet's heart. What did she care what he said or thought. She said, in her most dulcet voice:

"I hope you don't think me unduly bold, Mr. Smail. But I did feel that the occasion called for some little celebration. I thought we ought just to drink a glass of wine together." She raised her hand so that the veil of lace slipped back from her knuckles, and indicated the tray.

"Better and better," said Smail. "If you'd only tipped me the wink downstairs that you'd got this in mind, I'd have been in better shape to receive you, my dear. As it is, I've either to dress again or get back into bed."

"Please get back into bed," said Harriet.

He heaved his bulk between the covers. The bed creaked its protest. He settled into place and regarded Harriet with malicious delight as she moved to the chest and lifted the decanter.

"So you're pleased with your proposal, eh?"

"Naturally, I am delighted," said Harriet hardily.

"T'ain't every day you are so favoured, I take it."

"Not many people have your discernment, Mr. Smail. I am aware that my face is a disadvantage; but a man of taste should look for other qualities than beauty in a wife." As she spoke the pompous words she filled one of the goblets to within half an inch of the top, then she came towards the bedside with an unfaltering step and proffered the wine with a steady hand.

"It is my father's very best Madeira," she said. Smail giggled, lifted the glass to his lips and took a long, noisy swill of it. Harriet, back by the chest of drawers, raised her own and said formally, "I hope that we shall be happy."

"I'm damned sure we shall." He drank, meditating his next words. "About those other qualities you spoke of. What would you say *you* had to offer a man?" Ignoring the offensive tone in which he put the question, Harriet said gravely:

"Well, I'm a very good housekeeper. I can cook and sew. I'm very economical, too. They'll miss me here, I assure you."

"Modest, too, ain't you?"

"Who is to tell you these things if I don't?" asked Harriet, unperturbed. "May I fill your glass?"

"You may." He held it out, but as Harriet stretched her hand, instead of placing the glass in it, he shot out his other hand and seized her by the wrist. The lace fell back as she turned her arm so that the under part, with the blue veins threading the white surface, showed uppermost.

"You cry the wrong wares, you know," he said. "You've got a good figure and a nice white skin. You'd bruise easy."

"That's hardly an advantage," said Harriet, mastering the repulsion which sickened her, and forcing herself to speak lightly, though the last gloating sentence, chiming as it did with a memory of things Will had hinted, made her feel at once faint and furious. "Give me your glass."

"All in good time," he said; and still holding her wrist, looked her up and down again.

"How old are you?"

"Twenty."

"That's a lie. Why, by any reckoning you must be rising

twenty-three. Proper old maid, eh? How long have you had that face?"

"Since I was a child," said Harriet steadily. At the bidding of some atavistic feminine instinct she was going to add—and you're wrong about my age, I *am* only twenty —when she realized that he had made the mistake of thinking that she was Will's legitimate daughter. Oh, well, she thought, nothing in all the world could be of less importance. No word of this fantastic interview had any meaning, or would ever be repeated. She could afford to bear patiently whatever he might say.

"I reckon you'd give up all hope of getting a husband," he continued cruelly.

Harriet mustered her twisted smile and said, "Almost," with such a complete lack of chagrin that Smail, with a feeling of disappointment, suddenly abandoned the subject. He released her arm and thrust his glass towards her. "Fill it up," he said briefly.

While she did so he watched her with his bright pouched eyes, meditating his next attack. She was not sensitive about her age, or her ugliness; and he was about to hark back to the lack of decorum which she was showing by this visit, when his eyes fell upon her glass which she set down, hardly tasted, beside the candlestick on the chest of drawers.

"Here," he exclaimed, "what's that you're drinking?"

"Some light Canary," said Harriet. "Madeira doesn't suit me. It makes my head ache."

"So thats your idea of splitting a bottle with your intended, is it? That won't do my girl. Tip that wish wash into the slop jar and fill up with the real thing."

"I'd rather not. It would give me a dreadful headache."

And now, for the first time since the door had closed, shutting them in together, some genuine meaning and emotion informed the words that they spoke. Holding his glass away from him, Smail thought rapidly. Suppose Mike Latter had doctored that bottle and sent the pock-faced drab along to administer it with that spurious tale about drinking together. What's more likely? What's more easy? And he'd been sucked in like a fool.

"Come here," he said in a cold, terrible voice. "If you don't take this glass and empty it to the dregs, I'll rouse the house and swear you've tried to poison me."

Once again Harriet's mask saved her. Even the nervous stare of suspicion could detect nothing upon that painted face, or in those puckered eyes. And although her heart and her stomach seemed to sink away into emptiness, leaving nothing between her rapidly revolving mind and her shaking knees, she came forward calmly and without hesitation.

"Why on earth should I want to poison you?" she asked lightly. "Of course I'll drink it if you want me to. Only then I shall have to stay in bed all tomorrow."

"Much I care! Get it down!"

She took the glass in a steady hand and was going to raise it to her lips when even her will failed her. She would, at that moment, have drunk hemlock or henbane —was indeed prepared to do so, but she could not bring herself to put to her mouth the rim of the glass that had been between the lips of that toad-like mouth. She said weakly, with a fatal exposure of her weakness, "If I might have it in my own glass."

Eased of his most pressing suspicion, Smail gave a chuckle of delight.

"So you don't care to drink from my glass. Is that it? Mighty particular all of a sudden! Do you realize that just now you said you were delighted with the notion of sharing my bed and board? You ain't so young and innocent that you don't know the meaning of that, are you? Yet you baulk at sharing a glass with me. Go on, swill it down, or must I make you?"

"It was only that most people wouldn't care to share with *me*," said Harriet. "You see, the red comes off."

"That won't worry me. Bless you, I've shared a dirty

cup with women that couldn't have redded their mouths
if they'd wanted to, not having no lips. Where I've been
it was a custom to mutilate unfaithful wives so's no men'd
ever look at them again. I reckon I shan't be worried on
that score."

The shudder with which Harriet set the glass to her
mouth and emptied it in one long desperate draught might
have been attributed to the thoughts of the lipless women.

"There," she said, hard upon the last swallow. "Are you
satisfied that the wine is all right now?"

"That'll do," he said. "Now you can fill it up for me.
I didn't know but what you might have been mucking
about with a love philtre or some such rubbish. I know
what you women are." He was anxious now to deprecate
the very real fear that he had felt. He took another greedy,
noisy swig of the wine which Harriet had obediently
poured for him, and continued: "Not, of course, that
you'd think a love philtre necessary, a wench with a figure
like yours. You know, you'd have been a riot where I
come from. The ladies wear veils there."

"Indeed?" said Harriet, politely. "I shall look forward
to hearing about all your travels, you know. But now I
must go. It is getting late, and I am sharing a room."

A sudden cold fury seized the man. He found the calm
dignity which she had contrived to maintain throughout
the interview intolerable. In some obscure way he felt
that she had defeated him. She had come in this brazen
fashion to his room, late at night; she had borne unruffled
and unhurt the gibes and sneers he had launched at her;
she had been responsible for his moment of deadly fear;
and now she was preparing to take her leave precisely as
though she had been drinking a cup of tea with a harmless,
gossiping old woman. Her behaviour was insulting; it was
almost as though she knew. . . . Furiously he remembered
the contemptuous pity in the eyes of the young man who
had sat beside him in the coach; the unwilling pity which
had sounded in Mike Latter's voice when he had said,

"I know, there's no need to tell me." Pity for men, insults from women! He'd show this damned pocked bitch that there are other things to fear.

"Just a minute," he said softly. "Not so fast, my dear! We've spoke about that figure and that skin of yours; but maybe I'm getting a pig in a poke after all. Let's have a look at you. Take off that thing."

Genuinely frightened, Harriet instinctively clutched at the folds of the velvet, drawing the robe more closely about her. Then, not waiting to take up her candlestick, she took a hasty step or two towards the door. But before she could reach it she was seized and hauled back. The loose blue wrapper, wrenched from her clutch and deftly twisted, slipped from her shoulders and she stood with bare neck and arms in the painful, passionless grip of a monster.

She fought him silently, heroically suppressing the screams which terror and pain endeavoured to wring out of her. Her active life and Spartan habits made her less easily overcome than might have been supposed from her slight build, but she was outmatched. By sheer weight alone he could have overborne her and, besides, he had had, for years now, a vast and dreadful experience in the handling of women, women unwilling, women frantic, women beside themselves with temper and jealousy.

Still capable of coherent and logical thought, Harriet decided that the moment had come when she could be silent no longer. If only in the hope of frightening her assailant, she must scream and face the explanations and the exposure which would result. She had drawn a hissing, laboured breath when, from the other side of the door, near which their swaying silent struggle had carried them, came the sound of slow, deliberate footsteps.

Smail's cruel, searching hands fell away.

"What is that?" he asked, filled again with fearful suspicion.

"Someone looking for me," said Harriet wildly. "I'll make up some tale."

She snatched the robe from the floor and threw it around her shoulders, and this time had the cold key between her fingers when Smail's hand closed upon the back of her neck.

"Wait," he said. He jerked her backwards like a sack while he felt under the pillow for the pistol in which he had such confidence. Then, with his left hand, he turned the key, opened the door just wide enough to allow the passage of Harriet's body, raised his knee and thrust her out, slammed the door and turned the key again.

Impelled by that obscene push, Harriet stumbled forward, failed to regain her balance and landed on her hands and knees. For a moment she crouched there in a welter of shame and horror, then slowly she raised herself, and with one hand touching the passage wall, began to move slowly back towards Myrtle's room. Every bone in her body seemed to be wrenched out of position, every portion of her flesh felt bruised. Long vibrant shudders shook her from head to foot. And a deathly sickness was making itself felt at the bottom of the hollow where her stomach had been. But she staggered on, still driven and controlled and ordered by her will, which was now concentrated upon a humble focus—the slop jar that stood under Myrtle's washing stand. At all costs she must reach it before the sickness overcame her.

Fortunately, the key to Myrtle's room had been lost for years; Harriet had now neither to knock and await an answer, nor to fumble with a key. Blindly she made her way to the stand, pulled the jar from beneath it, and fell thankfully to her bruised knees. She was going to die, she was certain of that by this time, but she was still glad to think that in her final sickness she was being precise and tidy.

Myrtle awoke from the merciful sleep which had closed upon her shame and her sorrow. She did not at first re-

member that she was sharing her room with Harriet; but
she did remember Tabby and moved her hand over the
mass of warm fur, muttering a question in the language
which she used to her pet. Then, more fully awakened,
she identified the sounds which had roused her, retching
and gasping. Who? Ah, Harriet!

"Is that you, Sister?" she asked, raising her head from
the pillow.

A muffled sound, indistinguishable, but recognizable as
made by Harriet's voice, answered her.

"Are you ill?" Stupid question, she thought. "I'll get a
light."

She fumbled about for a moment, then, in the waxing
light of the candle that she had kindled, searched the
room for Harriet and found her.

"Oh, my dear!" she cried, hurrying round the bed. She
knelt beside Harriet and steadied her swaying figure, holding her head, as an old nurse they had had, long ago,
had held their heads during their bouts of childish bilious-
ness.

She did not speak again until, after a last violent paroxysm, Harriet leaned back against her shoulder, glad for
once of support, and lay there, supine, breathing in shallow gasps.

"Better?" asked Myrtle then, encouragingly. The head
against her shoulder moved in the ghost of a nod.

"Let me get you on the bed then."

"A moment," said Harriet.

They waited. But the sickness had spent itself, and
presently Myrtle said, "I'll lift you. You needn't do anything."

"Water first," said Harriet, and Myrtle, cursing herself
for not having thought of this obvious thing herself,
blundered to her feet and splashed some water into the
first receptacle that caught her eye, a tea-cup which had
stood on the washing-stand since the first day of Will's
illness. She had been carrying it downstairs, and had

stopped at her own room for something on her way, set the cup down, and forgotten it. Harriet had regarded it wih great distaste during her moving-in; but she was glad to drink from it now.

She emptied it twice. Then she said, "Thank you. You needn't lift me. Just help. I'm all right."

Myrtle half dragged, half carried her to the bed. The sight of Harriet, helpless, limp and suffering, had a strange incongruity.

"Whatever was it?" she wondered aloud.

"Oysters," said Harriet with weak assurance. There had been a consignment of oysters from Colchester on the coach; and oysters often poisoned people. Lying there, so dizzy and weak that the bed seemed to be falling to pieces beneath her, she congratulated herself upon remembering that.

"Of course," said Myrtle, relieved that Harriet's indisposition could be traced to so mundane a source. "I meant to ask Sharry to save me some, but I forgot." She loosened Harriet's shoes and drew them off, letting them drop to the floor and lie where they dropped. "Do you think a hot drink would do you good?"

"Just water," said Harriet.

Myrtle filled the cup again, and this time she remembered how that cup had come to be on her washing-stand; and how often in the four days she had seen it and thought about taking it down. And perhaps all the time it had been waiting there to serve Harriet in her hour of need. And perhaps all life was planned out like that, so that even your mistakes and lapses of memory were worked into a pattern. What a comforting thought! But not new. No. She'd had it before. Oh, yes, about the money she'd found, because Will had offered Lindy and Jerry the use of the haunted attic. And so she had found the money which had enabled her to make Roger that offer, and he had laughed; and she could see now that *then* was the moment when her mind was enlightened; and because she had seen by that laughter that he really meant her no good, she had cried out, just as Lindy had told her to; and so Dick had come, and she had had the wherewithal to buy his silence. Really, it was extraordinary. It made her dizzy to think of the infinite implications and ramifications of the thing. For relief she turned to Harriet and took away the cup.

"How do you feel now?"

"Much better," said Harriet in an almost normal voice. "Thank you very much, Myrtle. You've been kind."

"Rubbish!" said Myrtle. "You'd have done the same for me."

"Yes, I should. But I'd have been thinking why on earth couldn't you mind what you were eating; and wondering what on earth you'd do without me; and I simply couldn't have knelt down beside you like that and held your head so unflinchingly.

She said weakly, "Myrtle."

"Yes?"

"I'm sorry about all the times I've been nasty to you. And that isn't just because you've been kind to me now. I thought this afternoon how much nicer you were about sharing your room than I would have been. . . . In fact, you're a nicer person altogether. . . ."

"Oh, God!" said Myrtle. "If you only knew, Harriet! My character and my life are just like my room, messy and muddly and horrid. You don't know how I envy you, so clean and clear-cut and definite, even over the smallest things."

Harriet, lying flat on the bed like a doll that has lost most of its sawdust, closed her eyes and shuddered. But she did not mention the vision which the word "Clean" had called to her mind.

"It has all been because I was so jealous of you," she said. "Your face . . . and the way everybody loved you."

"My face!" Myrtle exclaimed bitterly. "That's made me the worst mess of all. *You* do at least know where you are. When people like you it is for yourself."

And the only person who does is the man who passes as my father. He would hang rather than hand me over to Smail . . . and I would hang rather than he should have to. I've proved that.

A warm comforting feeling ran through Harriet's exhausted body. She said more strongly:

"You'd better get into bed, Myrtle. I don't think I shall bother to undress any more, if you don't mind. I'll just lie here. We may be very busy in the morning."

Inside the alcove before Harriet's room Will stopped and drew a long steadying breath. Then, with hands more than usually tremulous, but with unfaltering purpose, he thrust the key into the lock and heard the other key upon the inner side fall to the floor. He had heard, in his imagination, that sound many times. Knowing that it must come, he had taken no especial pains to make his approach silent. Swiftly he turned the key, swung the door and entered the room, prepared for outcry, prepared to deal with it ruthlessly and swiftly.

But no outcry came. There was no sound at all. A candle guttering to its end, gave a feeble light upon the bedside table. Will plunged forward and set the light that he carried beside it. Then he turned to the bed itself, his hands already poised for the murderous stranglehold that he had planned.

Smail was dead. The most ignorant layman's eye could have seen that at a glance. He lay, grotesquely twisted among the tumbled bed-clothes, his nightshirt torn and muddled by his own agonized hands. Around him, upon sheet and pillow, were the traces of vomit by which his system, like Harriet's, had endeavoured to free itself of the poison. In the light of the candle his face had a shiny, tallowy pallor, tinged with green. His eyes were open and staring, dull now between the pouched lids which had darkened in colour.

Will stood for some time gazing at his dead enemy. He might have been posing as a model for Murder Baulked of His Prey, as his hands dropped to his sides and his face changed from resolution to bewilderment. He stared and stared, remembering Smail as the young man he had first know, the spare active seaman's body housing the dark sadistic soul. He remembered how often between the moment when the *Ethiopian Queen* had slid down the Thames, and the moment then she had been only a flaming shell on the face of the waters, he had felt murderously towards the young man; and how often afterwards, when they two alone had lain in that baking, tinder-dry boat, their moribund, desiccated bodies had still, at the bidding of their opposed souls, dealt weak blows at one another. And how tonight at a moment when fear and hatred had reached their cumulative point, he had come to do murder and found the big bloated body already a mere mass of carrion. It had not been required of him; it had not been decreed that he should kill Smail.

Who had? What had? Smail had walked out of the Little Parlour in perfect health. Now he lay, obviously poisoned. And he had eaten, bite for bite, dish for dish, with his host. Will reviewed the meal: oysters from the Colchester coach; goose; baked pears with cream; cheese. Oysters, of course. . . . But it was hardly feasible that, sharing a dish, one man should receive so large a proportion of bad ones that he should die, suddenly and horribly, while his fellow should suffer not even a mild inconvenience. No, Smail had been poisoned after he had said "Good-night" and hurried away to lock himself safely in this room. Then how? And by whom?

There was only one other person in the house to whom Smail's death would seem a desirable thing—Harriet. But what could Harriet know of poisons; where, at this time of night could she have obtained any; above all, how had she contrived to administer it? As though he expected the room to answer these questions, Will began to stare and to prowl.

He found the silver tray and the heavy cut-glass decanter upon the chest of drawers where Harriet had stood them. He recognized both articles as part of the inn's equipment which was only used on very special occasions; and it was Harriet who decided what exactly constituted a special occasion. Harriet kept the key of the cupboard where the best silver, the good glass, the nicest china were stored.

Yet, despite this adding of evidence to motive, his mind was still reluctant to accept the fact that Harriet was involved in this affair further than she had been when he had sent her to bed, bidding her not to worry. But when he found the two glasses, one with a mere dribble of Madeira in it, the other still more than half full of light Canary, and both bearing, in sticky red paint, the plain mark of a lower lip, he was forced to admit his conviction. That mark was a signature. It called up a vivid picture of Harriet's mouth, wry-lipped, stubborn, unnaturally scarlet.

There could be no more shuffling doubt. This was Harriet's work, and, like everything she did, it had been prompt and efficient. That it had not been finished off in quite her usual way was not to be wondered at; even Harriet could hardly be expected to remain calm enough to tidy up after committing a murder.

But such tidying up had to be done.

The thought brought Will back to himself with a start. There were two things that he must do immediately—the first to remove all trace of Harriet's connection with the business; the second, to decide what was to be done with Smail's body.

He realized, even as he set together on the tray the glasses and the blue candlestick which spoke Harriet's name as plainly as the lip marks, that although he had entered this room with murder in his mind, he had had no very clear idea of what he would do once he withdrew his hands from their stranglehold upon Smail's throat. He had sat in his room and weighed the alternative courses of killing the man or trying to bargain with him. It had been Effie's plaintive words which had tipped the scale in favour of the latter course. But his mind, as though exhausted from debate and the final choice of action, had dropped back, refusing to deal with this further vital question. Now, with the deed, already done and another person so deeply involved, decision must be not only unhesitating, but wise.

He stood still, midway between the bed and the chest, his head thrust forward, his lower lip pinched between finger and thumb. If he had strangled Smail, as he had planned to do, he would have had to hide the body, since it would have borne the marks of violence. But Smail poisoned was a rather different matter. It might be possible to call in old doddering Dr. Weatherall, mention the oysters, and trust that he would attribute Smail's death to them. There were great advantages in that plan. It solved the problem of the disposal of the body, which was the thing that brought most murderers to book. But there were risks as well. The possibility of questions being asked, not of Will alone . . . the possibility of suspicion being aroused . . . and, minor matter, but worth a moment's consideration, the bad publicity which would arise from the story, a guest dying horribly and suddenly after supper at the *Fleece*.

Will's mind, having completed this preliminary survey, darted off at a tangent. What had killed Smail? What had Harriet used? And then, like the impact of a blow, the significance of the two red marks struck him. Harriet, for some reason which he could not begin to guess at, had drunk from both glasses. Great God! She might herself be dead!

Hurriedly he lifted the tray, balanced it clumsily while with shaking hands he locked the door behind him, and set it down behind the linen press in the passage. Then, running, he made for Myrtle's room and burst in without ceremony. There was the same sour smell about it that he had noticed without realizing that he did so, in the room of the dead man, and as he recognized it he said "Harriet" sharply upon a note of panic. The voice from the bed, weak, but alert, saying, "Sh! I'm here. Don't wake Myrtle," was, he thought, the most reassuring thing he had ever heard in his life.

"Are you all right?"

"Yes. I've been sick. How did you know?"

"I guessed. I mean, I was afraid. Harriet, I've been into Smail's room."

"I see." The quiet, whispering calmness of her voice seemed to reproach him for the noise of his. Myrtle stirred, flung out an arm, and muttered in her sleep.

"I'll come," Harriet whispered. "We don't want Myrtle in this."

"No. You must lie still. There's nothing you can do. I only wanted to make sure that you were . . . all right."

But Harriet, with stealthy movements, was already turning back the one cover which Myrtle had spread over her.

"Let me hold your arm," she whispered.

Myrtle said clearly, "Tabby, be quiet."

As soon as they were in the passage Harriet tightened her grip on Will's arm.

"Is he dead?"

"Yes."

The sound that she made was expressive of relief, and her hold slackened.

"I left everything about. . . . I didn't have time. I had to get away. I had to get away to be sick," she said firmly. Never, even by implication, would she allow anyone to suspect what had happened in the last moments of that secret interview. "You see, he made me drink out of his glass, because he was afraid of being poisoned." An odd, shaky sound that might have been laughter came from her lips.

"And you drank it, knowing what was in it? Oh, Harriet!"

"I'm all right. I feel a bit odd; but I *was* very sick." Her tone rebuked the emotion with which he had spoken. "I've been lying there wondering how I could get the glasses away. How did you get in?"

"With the second key."

"Was there one? To *my* room? I didn't know that."

"Come to my room and lie down," Will suggested.

"What are you going to do?"

"I'm not quite sure. Harriet . . . what did you use?"

"Some stuff that old Mother Fenn sold me for my face. She said it was deadly poison, and to mind not to put any near my mouth. It was the only thing I could think of. It was all I had."

"I see." That meant that it might have been anything in the world.

"What are we going to do now?" asked Harriet.

"You are going to lie down. I must decide something."

"About *him*?"

"Yes. Whether it would be better to . . . well, dispose of it; or to call Weatherall in and trust to luck."

"As I had planned it," said Harriet slowly, "I was going to trust to luck. I had no choice. I meant to bring the glasses and the decanter—and my candlestick. And he would have locked the door behind me. In fact, he did. I reckoned that when he didn't come out in the morning someone would force an entry and find him. Who could be blamed? He'd eaten with you. . . . Effie saw that. Mrs. Sharman put the food on the tray and Effie carried it in. When he left you he went straight to bed, with a locked door. Besides—and this is the thing I thought of, all the time. Nobody knows why he came here. And he hasn't been robbed. Why should it look as though he was murdered, and why should anybody murder him? He had oysters and he was sick. I didn't have any, though I told Myrtle I did. I shall tell everyone that I did. In fact, I shall stay in bed tomorrow and have Dr. Weatherall attend me, too." All her old force and decision sounded in her voice. Then she added, with sudden diffidence, "That is, of course, if you think it is the best plan."

And suddenly, before Will's mental eye, the whole thing fell into pattern. With a feeling of relief, akin to that which followed the cessation of pain, he saw that Harriet—no, not Harriet, for she herself had been only Fate's tool, Fate itself had taken the whole situation in hand. If he had gone first to Smail's room he would have been faced with the disposal of the body which bore marks of violence upon it. Fate had prevented him there. And if Harriet had not been compelled (and how clearly he could imagine the scene of that compulsion) to have drunk from the deadly glass he would not have been concerned for her safety, and so have reaped the benefit of this clear-headed advice. And, deeper still, if that poor crazed creature had not tried to poison herself and so sent Effie in search of him, he would probably, lacking the inspiration of Effie's words, have spent the night in mere waiting for the morning, and would not have gone to Smail's room and removed the evidence of Harriet's action. . . . If, if, if . . .

Like Myrtle, a few hours earlier, he felt dizzy as he contemplated the intricacies of the plot which Fate had woven. It was like looking into the works of a vast complicated machine. In a way it was frightening, too. We're like marionettes, he thought, we think that we do things and decide things, but actually we only dance at the end of the strings. Mostly we are unconscious of them, but sometimes we feel the tug and know that the other end of the string is held firmly. And by whom?

(Effie knew. She had made Julia comfortable on the bed, and she had dribbled the warm milk into the baby's mouth and laid him in the crook of Julia's arm. Then she had knelt down by the chair on the hearth and buried her face in her hands. And when she had expressed, with monotonous repetition, her earnest thanks to the God who had arranged everything so perfectly, she elaborated the theme. "Oh, dear God," she prayed, "I do ask You to forgive me for what I was a-thinking about You time I was that worried. I did expect a miracle; I wanted a flaming grut angel to come down and do something about me and Sarah and Dick. I forgot like that You kin do things athout grut angels these days. I din't trust You like I oughta. I do hope You see Your way to forgive me. I oon't never worrit agin, acause I do see plain that You kin work things out the best way. I do thank You, dear God, and you, dear Jesus Christ, for fixing everything up so nice. . . ." She prayed on, asking forgiveness, asking blessings on Mrs. Foxe, and the baby and Will and Dick, until she fell asleep, still on her knees by the chair.)

Harriet's voice reminded Will that the time for abstract thought had not yet come.

"Have you still got that second key?"

"Yes."

"Then we'll get that tray away. What happened when you put the other key in?"

"The tray is out . . . on the floor near the linen press. His key fell on the floor."

"Did you leave it there?"

"Yes."

"So it still looks as though the door were locked from within?"

"Yes."

"It will look as though it fell out when the door was burst open. Don't do it yourself. I think if we could get Dr. Weatherall here to see me, first, quite early, and have him here when the door is opened. Do you see?"

"Yes, I see. Harriet, come and lie down. I'm worried about you." She was sagging heavily against his arm.

"I'm all right," said Harriet. "I want to wash those glasses."

"I'll do that."

"Properly," said Harriet, "and put them, and the decanter, and the tray, away in the oak cupboard?" That was the kind of dictatorial fussiness for which he had rebuked her. But he did not rebuke her now. He was seeing again, inconsequently, that morning after Clarissa had died. And he was standing, looking down at the days-old baby, the little bastard, the proof of his own cuckolding, the cause of his wife's death. He remembered how he had wondered, in that bitter moment, whether he could ever look upon the child without hatred, without being reminded of the most hideous hours of his life; and how, as he looked upon that piteous helplessness, that epitome of innocence, he had vowed that the child should never know. Whatever it cost him of effort and resolution, he would regard the little thing as his own, because, whoever was to blame—himself for leaving Clarissa, Clarissa for her faithlessness, the unknown man for his lust—the child at least was guiltless. So he had reared and cherished Harriet, in order that they might stand together at this moment, he physically supporting her, she mentally upholding him.

They had reached the bottom of the few steps up to his room. Stooping, he lifted her in his arms and carried her up the steps.

"You shouldn't do this," Harriet protested. "You haven't been well, remember."

He lowered her on the bed.

"I shall tell Myrtle that I came here because I felt ill again," said Harriet. "But I shall go back in the morning, so that Dr. Weatherall will believe me about being sick." She sighed. "It is such a comfort to lie flat out. You will wash those glasses, won't you?"

"I'll do it now," said Will. "And I'll send Davy for Weatherall as soon as it's light."

Across the little flame of the candle their eyes met and held for a moment. Both were conscious of things that were left unsaid; both aware that there was something almost uncanny about their lack of emotion, and the intensely practical way in which they were regarding the night's doings.

"And put them away. You know where they go," said Harriet, reverting to the question of the glasses.

"All right," Will said, moving to the door. There he halted, and looked back and said earnestly:

"Harriet. If anything should go wrong, you're to keep out of this, do you understand? Smail was my enemy. And I went to that room meaning to kill him. *If* anything happens about it, it's my affair."

"We'll talk about that when something has happened," said Harriet non-committingly.

"No. That would be too late. You're got to give me your word, your promise, *now*."

"If you'd just see to those glasses and things, I should be quite easy in my mind," said Harriet. "Oh, all right, I promise. I never saw Smail, if you like."

She closed her eyes as soon as Will had left her, and lay writhing in silent fury. If only that beast had let her alone, so that she could have cleared up properly, no one would ever have known. For years and years and years she had been tidy and neat and precise; she had cleared up after hundreds of guests, scores of sluttish maids, after Will and Myrtle, as well as herself. She had never left so much as a needle out of place. And then tonight, in the middle of the most important and serious job she had ever undertaken, she had been forced to leave things about. Her clear, but narrow, mental vision, studying only her own individual action, was blind to the fact that she had been only a link in a long chain, and that her very omissions were insignificant. Unlike Will and Myrtle, who had each been smitten by a dizzying sense of Destiny; unlike Effie, with her comfortable recognition of the hand of

God, Harriet only knew, with a mingling of satisfaction and chagrin, that she had begun a job well and ended it badly. It would have been so much better if she could have tidied up and kept her secret to herself. Still, there it was, and there was no point in worrying about something that could not be altered.

From anxiety she was curiously immune. She had already planned exactly what should be said and done in the morning; and throughout her life, she had been a believer in the value of forethought. True, her plan had miscarried tonight, but its failure had been due to Smail, and he, she thought viciously, would never thwart her again. He was the only person who had ever really frightened her, the only person who had ever made her swerve from the path she had set herself, and he was dead. He had ceased be a person and was now a mere lump of material. And never for one moment had Harriet doubted her ability to deal with a material thing.

She closed her eyes, deliberately relaxing every nerve and muscle in her body. She must garner what strength she could, so that she would be able to get back into Myrtle's room as soon as it was morning, and, once there, have power and vitality enough to impose her wishes upon Will and Myrtle. And to do that she must close the door between yesterday and tomorrow, salve her mind's hurts with the balm of unconsciousness. She must sleep.

MORNING

The Fleece

Effie, heavy-eyed, more leaden-footed than usual, but at peace with God and man, was engaged in the first of her day's tasks, the raking-out and relighting of the big fire. She was adding stick to stick upon the first precarious flame and bellowing furiously when, to her surprise, the yard door opened and Will himself entered. She was shocked by his appearance, he looked so old and ill. The slight tremor of his hands had become a noticeable, steady vibration.

"You got your fever on you again, sir?" she asked, sympathetically.

"What? no. No, thank you, Effie. Why, what made you ask that?"

"I thought you looked bad. Wuss than you did afore you took to your bed."

"I had a bad night. Miss Harriet was taken ill after you left me. I've just been out to send Davy for the doctor."

"There now," said Effie, sitting back on her heels and clasping the bellows to her stomach, "maybe I ought to of towd you. Last night, time I come to you, I went to Miss Harriet's room first like I said, and I did think I heard a kind of a groan. Ony that might a bin a snore. And I was that moithered in my mind I clean forgot it afterwards. Wuz she bad?"

"Quite ill. Yes." So Effie had heard Smail's groaning.

Thank God she had forgotten it and not included him in her rescue work.

"Oh, dear! I am sorry! I ought to of towd you."

"It wasn't Miss Harriet you heard. She wasn't sleeping there last night."

"Maybe it wuz a snore then. Or maybe somebody else took bad."

Suppose, Will thought, old Weatherall is awkward, and there's an inquest, that innocent statement of Effie's will take on the dignity of evidence. . . . He shivered slightly, and then controlled himself fiercely. He mustn't let his nerves get out of hand. Effie noticed the shiver.

"You're cold, sir. Thass cold these mornings, wholly raw. Kin I git you a hot drink? Cuppa tea, perhaps?"

A cup of tea was the one thing she longed for herself these mornings; it performed the miracle known to Effie as "pulling meself together." But the general supply of tea was locked away until Mrs. Sharman made her appearance in about half an hour's time, and the caddy of special Su-chong which Harriet kept in the Little Parlour was, of course, sacred.

"I could get the tea from the Parlour. Wouldn't take a minnit. A cuppa tea do pull you together wonderful," she insisted.

It would take more than a cup of tea to pull him together, Will reflected grimly; it would take a blind, comforting verdict from Weatherall, and four feet of soil over Smail, to do that. But he could detect the eagerness in Effie's voice, and he must do something until the doctor could arrive. He had helped Harriet back to the door of Myrtle's room; he had dispatched Davy for the doctor; he had nervously re-inspected the things which he had put away the night before; and he had, hundreds and thousands of times, evoked the memory of the room where Smail lay dead. Had he overlooked anything that mattered? He was driving himself mad. Better stay here and drink tea and talk to Effie. So he said:

"Well, thanks Effie. That would be very kind."

Effie bellowed furiously, threw on more sticks, and put the kettle in place. She shuffled into the Parlour and brought back the tea and warmed the pot and carefully chose a matching cup and saucer from the dresser.

"Don't you drink tea yourself?" Will asked, accepting the steaming cup.

"Well, yes, sir. If you don't mind. There's nothing like a cuppa tea in the mornings." She filled her own mug to the brim.

"By the way, Effie, how did you get on last night? How's our patient, and the baby?"

"They're both all right, sir. Pore lady! You know she ain't really mad at all. Clear in her head as anything arter I got her to bed. That seem as though that little owd baby made a right difference to her like. Full a talk, she wuz, all about she's a-going to start up a home for little children that nobody don't want. She got a grut house in Norwich, and she say she'll fill it from top to bottom. She's a-going to give them schooling, too. She say did I think thass all right for her to keep that little owd boy? Woon't Sarah want him soon's she realize. I tell her, the further that baby is away from his mother the better. Thass right, ain't it, sir?"

"You know best, Effie. I'm glad to hear the baby is settled."

"So'm I," said Effie, and fell into a reverie, remembering that part of Julia's conversation which she did not intend to repeat to Will. Julia had said how nice it would be if Effie could come back to Norwich with her and help her look after the children. And for one moment Effie, thinking no more Mrs. Sharman, no more Miss Harriet, no more dining-room, had wavered in her allegiance and agreed that it would be very nice. But that moment passed quickly. Will Oakley was at the *Fleece*, and as long as he stayed there and permitted Effie to do the most menial work in his kitchen, so long would she be there, too.

After all, what did Mrs. Sharman's impatience, Miss Harriet's bullying, and the occasional embarrassments of the dining-room count when weighed against Will's presence and rare, precious word of greeting? So she had refused Julia's offer, gently, without regret. And here was immediate proof that her choice had been right. Will was warming himself by the fire that she had lighted, and pulling himself together with a cup of tea which she had made. What more could she ask?

"Is there any more water in the kettle, Effie?"

"Plenty, sir. Will you have another cup?"

"No, thank you. I'll take it up. I'll shave before the doctor comes." Effie noticed the shakiness of the hand which Will stretched out for the jug, and thought, pore dear, he'll wholly cut hisself don't he ain't careful. Will, with much the same thought in his mind, determined to be very careful indeed.

Myrtle had greeted Harriet's return with the loudest of self-reproaches. "But Harriet, you know I would have fetched Daddy for you. Fancy trying to go to him when I was here, wallowing asleep. You make me feel so useless and ashamed."

"I didn't want to disturb you," said Harriet. "What are you doing now?"

"I thought I'd clear up a bit. You said Daddy had sent for the doctor. We don't want him to find us in *this* mess, do we?"

"Leave it alone," said Harriet. "I'll clear up later on."

But Myrtle, who had twice last night fallen asleep upon the thought that she was going to begin to be an entirely different person, was set upon putting resolution into practice.

"Honestly, Sister, I don't mind a bit. Tabby's often sick and I always clear up." Oh dear, now Harriet would be annoyed. That "Sister" had just slipped out in her earnestness. Had she noticed?

"Leave it," said Harriet, in whom the forbidden word had started feelings other than resentment. "Please, Myrtle, do as I say. Get dressed yourself and leave everything else as it is."

"But why?"

"Well, if you *must* know . . . I want Dr. Weatherall to see for himself that I *was* ill. I'm so much better that I think he'll be annoyed and think he's been got up early on a fool's errand. I don't want him to think that I was just imagining that I was ill."

"Great Heaven!" said Myrtle, staring in genuine astonishment. "Imagine minding what he thinks." It was almost the last weakness one would have suspected in Harriet, who, when Will was ailing, bullied the doctor as she did everyone else. Still, this unwonted sensitiveness to another person's opinion was probably a symptom of Harriet's illness; and she couldn't know how very sick she looked, or she wouldn't worry. The mask of paint was wearing thin in patches, and her scarred skin showed through lividly. The scarlet paint on her lips was cracked and flaking; and around her eyes shadows like bruises showed. Yet the old rasp of authority was in her voice:

"You get yourself dressed. That's the first thing. He'll be here soon."

Obediently Myrtle began to open drawers and fly from chair to cupboard, dressing in her usual muddled scramble. The clothes which she had thrown off after she had helped Harriet on the bed overnight, lay all together on a chair which she avoided sedulously. She would never wear any of them again. Effie could have the underclothes, but the dress must be disposed of so that it would never be seen again. That combination of hyacinth blue and clover colour would always have the power to stir a sickening memory. And Myrtle intended to forget; she was not going to spend her life looking backwards. She was going to be a different person, busier, more methodical. For twenty-two years she had lived within a rainbow bubble of dreams;

last night it had cracked and vanished. Harriet, watching from the bed, would have felt a little less anxiety about the immediate future if she could have known how practical and realistic Myrtle was feeling this morning.

Harriet was listening as well as watching. She caught the first hollow ring of the horse's hoofs as Dr. Weatherall turned in under the archway.

"Is that the doctor?"

Myrtle pushed the last curl away behind her ear and ran to the window. The wet roofs gleamed in the grey early-morning light, and a few last reluctant raindrops fell at long intervals into the pools between the cobbles.

"Yes. Daddy is just going out to him."

Will must have been as alert, as nervously tensed as she was herself, thought Harriet. Now . . . now . . . she counted fifty of her own heartbeats. Then she cried sharply:

"Oh, Myrtle!"

"What is it?" Myrtle wheeled from the window, expecting, from the sharp panic in Harriet's voice, to find her in a fresh paroxysm of sickness.

"Oh Lord! Myrtle, I've forgotten something most important."

"What is it? I'll do it. Don't excite yourself Harriet. I'll see to it for you."

"That man, that friend of father's, in my room. I promised faithfully that I'd call him at six. He said he had a lot of writing to do before breakfast. And I clean forgot. I didn't tell anyone because I knew I was sure to be awake. And then, being ill. . . ."

"I'll call him now," said Myrtle eagerly. "He'll be late, but that can't be helped."

"He said he slept extremely heavily, and whoever called him had to hammer on the door until he did answer. So bang hard . . . and Myrtle, ask if he'd like some tea. . . . That'll sort of make up for the lateness."

Myrtle hurried to the door. Tabby, who had been lying

watching her mistress, made a salmon leap over the side of the box and began to follow.

"Now don't go letting that cat out, and then talking to someone in the yard. Knock Mr. Smail first." The sound of double footsteps could be heard in the passage outside. Will and the doctor met Myrtle in the doorway. Myrtle, with a fleeting smile, slipped past them and was gone.

A glaze of cold perspiration broke out on Harriet's face, her palms were clammy, her stomach quivering. How loud would Myrtle knock? Getting no answer, would she just drift away and forget? How hideous it was that so much of a well-laid plan must depend upon other people for its execution.

"Well, young lady. Tired of nursing other people? Having a little attention yourself for a change, eh?" cried Dr. Weatherall breezily. He liked and admired Harriet whom he saw at her very best during Will's indispositions.

"I ate some oysters," said Harriet, straining her ears. Yes, there it was, the sharp rapping of Myrtle's knuckles on the door.

"Oysters! Disgusting bivalves!" said Dr. Weatherall, who detested all shell fish, which gave him nettle-rash. "Should have credited you with more taste. Let's have a look at you."

As he bent over the bed where Harriet lay shivering, with hot and cold waves chasing one another over her whole body, the rapping of knuckles changed to the steady hammering of wood upon wood. Good Myrtle, good girl! Another moment. Harriet glanced at Will, who stood between the doctor and the door. The glance carried a message of courage and assurance.

"Yes. You've had a nasty turn. A very nasty turn indeed. Undoubtedly the oysters were to blame. You'd do well to take nothing but milk for twenty-four hours—a little weak tea if you like: I know what you ladies are for tea. And stay in bed today and tomorrow, the rest will do you good." It was the kind of agreeable, easy, obvious advice that the old man had been giving, not without good results, for almost fifty years.

But Harriet was not listening. Down the passage came the sound of hurrying feet, interspersed with the sharp clatter of a shoe flapping loose at the heel. Myrtle burst into the room.

"Daddy, that Mr. Smail in Harriet's room. I can't make him hear." She looked at Harriet: "Honestly, Sister, I did bang hard! I took my shoe heel and simply hammered."

Harriet closed her eyes. "You must try again, Myrtle. He was most emphatic about being called."

"If that was your knocking it was fit to wake the dead," said Dr. Weatherall, instinctively taking Myrtle's part, as men always did, and would for many years continue to do.

"Harriet shouldn't be bothered now," said Will quietly. "I'll come and see what I can do. He can't have come down or I should have seen him."

"Perhaps somebody else has been eating oysters," suggested the doctor, half seriously.

"Mr. Smail certainly did," said Harriet from the bed. "He had a good many more than I did."

"Now, now, we can't have you upsetting yourself, my dear. You lie back and think what a lucky escape *you've* had. I'll come along with you, Oakley, and see. . . ." He began to sweep Will and Myrtle out of the room ahead of him, but Harriet said, "I want Myrtle."

The two men went out. Myrtle, looking agitated, said: "He couldn't be dead, could he?"

"I should hardly think so. Though I felt like dying once or twice myself."

"Poor Harriet . . . we didn't realize. Oh dear . . . and he did say you'd had a lucky escape. Harriet dear, how awful! Shall I go along and see?"

Every fibre of Harriet's body longed to cry, yes. And don't bother with seeing, *listen* and come straight back and tell me what that old dodderer *says*. But she remembered that although Myrtle might be able to deal with a sick cat she was nevertheless squeamish and impressionable; the sight which lay beyond the locked door upon which both Will and the doctor were now hammering with all their might, was not fitting for Myrtle's eyes. So with as much unselfishness as she had ever shown in her life, Harriet said, "You'd do more good, especially to my peace of mind, Myrtle, if you go down and help see about the breakfast. The store-room key is on the dressing-table. Take it with you."

"Of course. Don't you worry, Harriet. We'll manage."

"Go the back way. It's quicker," said Harriet.

As soon as she was alone Harriet pushed back the clothes and got out of bed. Her legs felt a little weak, otherwise she was not bad at all. She went to the window and propped herself against the wall at the side so that she could look into the yard without being seen. Perhaps she could tell by the way Dr. Weatherall parted from Will, what his verdict had been.

Of one thing she was certain. If anything did go wrong, if any suspicion were aroused, she would take full blame. They would believe her; she remembered reading somewhere that poison was a woman's weapon. As for motive, she would make up some story. She had been surprised to discover, within these last few hours, how fertile and inventive her mind could be.

Hanging, of course, was a hideous death, violent and public. But it was quickly over. And really, she thought, experiencing one of her moments of spiritual malaise, she had singularly little to live for. No hope of a house of her own, or a husband, or children . . . just years and years of working and scheming to serve other people . . . and being pitied, or scorned or hated.

Yet despite these renunciatory thoughts, she still took a healthy interest in Dr. Weatherall's departure, and felt something very near foreboding when she saw him come out of the door alone, walk to his horse, mount and ride away. It seemed hours since he had left her. Why had he been so long? And why had Will not gone with him to the yard as usual? Was it because he had said something— mentioned poison, or inquests, and Will had been too over- come to even walk so far?

In a flurry of panic, Harriet began to stumble towards the door; but it opened just as she reached it. Will had measured her anxious impatience by his own, had parted from the doctor at the foot of the staircase, and run straight up to tell her.

"Well?" she asked breathlessly.

"It's all right," he gasped. Harriet put out her hands and clasped his. They stood for a moment, each half supporting the other, and both panting for breath as though they had just run from some pursuing enemy.

"Yes. It's all right," Will said again at last. "He said it was undoubtedly the oysters, combined with alcohol. He attributes your escape to your healthier constitution, and the fact that you don't drink spirituous liquors. When he had said that several times, I told him that Smail was an acquaintance of mine, and that he had no family. I suggested that he should be buried here. Weatherall's going to tell the Rector as he goes home. And I'm going to send for the carpenter now."

Harriet released Will's hands and sat down in the chair piled with Myrtle's clothes. She leaned her head on the back of it and began to cry weakly. "No, no! I'm all right. It's only the relief. Give me your handkerchief, please." She sobbed for a few seconds, then resolutely blew her nose and dried her eyes. "There!" she said. "I'm a fool! And there's one thing," she went on in a different voice. "Nothing now would make that dear old man change his opinion. If every other doctor in England said that, well, you know . . . the truth . . . Dr. Weatherall would go on declaring and believing that it was oysters and port wine."

"I believe he would. You'd better get back to bed, Harriet."

"I'm going to get up. What on earth have I to stay in bed for? If I were you I should get the carpenter at once and have *it* tidied up as quickly as possible. And, while we are on the subject, can I move into the Blue Room?"

A pleasurable air of excitement and mystery stirred through the inn as breakfasts were cooked and eaten, muddy wheels scraped and coachwork polished, horses trotted out into the yard. A wild sea of rumour and supposition churned about the few outstanding rocks of fact. Miss Harriet had been taken very ill in the night; the doctor had been on the premises by seven o'clock; Dick Stevens had disappeared; Sarah Cross had gone off yesterday and had not returned; somebody was very ill, or dying, or dead in Miss Harriet's old room and Miss Myrtle, in a very businesslike apron, was acting in a manner altogether unlike herself.

But an inn, although it makes no vows, is dedicated to public service. Drama and mystery, even Death itself, may take lodging under its roof, but its main business is still concerned with the undramatic, unmysterious, very-much-alive traveller whose sole desire is to be out on the road again as soon as possible.

First in the dining-room, and first in the yard, were the farmers and their families, looking up at the sky and prophesying a fine day. Their wagons and carts rumbled out through the arch and into the muddy road to the accompaniment of lowing and bleating, cackling, barking and shouting. Next to leave were a few of the solitary horsemen whose business took them abroad early: Mr. Roper, the seedsman, with his big box of samples on his pillion; Mr. Crabbe, the Norwich breeches maker, on his way to make his annual visit to Newmarket, where for a week, in his little hired room he would measure and calculate and scribble hieroglyphics, taking orders enough to keep him busy until Easter.

The coach left next, bound for Norwich. There was a

fresh horse in place of the lame near-wheeler, and five new faces among the passengers. The fat man whom everyone had hated, the handsome young man with the scar, and the pale-faced young woman were no longer in the company. The middle-aged lady declared that the *Fleece* was, despite its name, the most comfortable inn she had yet stayed in.

Then the horsemen of the more leisurely class emerged, good-humoured from an excellent breakfast, dropping largesse of small coins as they went. Last of all, but still very early in the day, the smart little private chaise rattled out. From the kitchen window Mrs. Sharman could see Effie, who had been unaccountably missing for about ten minutes, helping the lady in mourning clothes to carry and lift into the chaise the most incongruous piece of luggage, a big white wicker basket with something fragile —eggs? china?—under its flannel cover. The kettle for Mrs. Sharman's own cup of tea boiled just then, otherwise she would have stayed by the window speculating on the reason for Effie's presence in the yard.

Julia, before she entered the chaise, spoke to her driver. "Go slowly, Frank, and try to avoid bumps. And keep a sharp lookout for the old gentleman we picked up yesterday. He'll be on the road, and we can give him a lift home."

Yesterday. It seemed ages ago. Yesterday, when John Savory had left her and plodded off to find lodging in some cottage, he had said, "God keep and comfort thee." And she had been kept, and she had been offered the means of comfort. God's doing? She could not answer that. She only knew that the chance birth of a bastard, the resource of an innkeeper, the word of a little kitchen slut, had combined to change despair into resolution and keep what was at least a will-to-kindness alive in the world.

She turned to Effie and took one of the swollen red hands which Effie was sheltering in her apron. "Good-bye, Effie. I shall never forget you. If ever you change your mind, or need a friend, remember me."

"I will, mam. All the same, I din't do nothing. That wuz Mr. Oakley."

Julia stooped and kissed her in the middle of her knobby forehead. "Bless you," she said.

Effie, overwhelmed with shyness, could only look down at her feet and mumble her farewell. But as the chaise moved gently over the cobbles and under the archway, she withdrew one hand and waved it, at the same time sending Julia a smile of such sincerity and sweetness that it transformed her ugly little face. Will, just leaving the back door as Effie turned to dive into it, was in time to receive the lingering impression of its sweetness.

"Well, Effie," he said.

"Oh, sir. I wanted to see you. That Sarah is still upstairs. Shall I let her out? And what are we a-going to say?"

"Oh!" said Will absent-mindedly. "We don't have to say anything about the baby, do we. That's settled. Where's the girl supposed to be? At home, eh? Very well. So far as I am concerned she *is* at home. You must settle all that between you. I take it she won't bully you any more."

Effie stared after him as he went on his way across the yard. That was all very well, and nice for Sarah, but it didn't help Effie much.

She went into the house, took her bucket, and was about to fill it with hot water from the copper when the desire to have done with Sarah and Sarah's business overcame her. She carried the empty bucket into the kitchen and moved about, ostensibly tidying up before settling down to scrub, but, under cover of these movements, collecting a mug of strong tea, a hunk of bread and a slab of cold fat bacon. She dropped them into the bucket and laid over them her mopping cloth, a cover well calculated to defy the most suspicious eye. Then, watching her moment, she made for the back stairs.

Outside the attic door she replaced the string and

worked the latch. Sarah lay in the middle of the bed, sleeping heavily, oblivious of the time. Effie shook her briskly by the shoulder. Then, standing back and watching consciousness return to Sarah's sleepy eyes, she said happily:

"I brought you yer breakfast. And I want to tell you I a-got the baby a good home. And I a-told the master all about Dick. He know about the baby, too. But nobody else don't. So what you say and do arter this is yer own affair. See?"

Sarah was humble. No longer able to extort service, she begged for favours.

"Just you run down, Effie, and say as how I towd you I might nut be back till dinner-time. That'll just gimme time to pull myself round."

But Effie was adamant.

"I ain't a-going to tell no more lies for you, Sarah Cross, nor for nobody else. I a-told lies enough and to spare. I a-done with it now."

She shuffled towards the door. Sarah called after her.

"Hi! Effie, wait a minnit. D'you reckon master'll tell anybody? What did he say about me?"

"He say so far as he wuz concerned you wuz at home. I don't reckon he give you much thought. He got other things to think about. He's a-going to get Dick back for me, too. So don't you go making mischief about Dick, Sarah Cross, because Mr. Oakley is all on his side."

It did not occur to Effie's simple mind that she was now in a position to bargain for Sarah's silence, that *she* was now a keeper of secrets, and could, if she were so minded, compel Sarah to slave for her as she had slaved for Sarah.

"Thass all right then," said Sarah, resolutely taking an optimistic view. She drained the mug of tea and set about the bacon voraciously. "I'll get up now and slink in somehow."

"I don't care what you do," said Effie from the door. Down in the kitchen again, vigorously scrubbing the floor, she parried the questions of Mrs. Sharman, and of Dolly and Clara, by a monotonous, stupid-sounding, but quite truthful statement, "Thass no good asking me." It was the best thing she could think of, since the blessed refuge of "I don't know" was closed to her by its falsity. When Clara, upon whose shoulders fell the heaviest burden of Sarah's absence, said crossly:

"You must know whether she came in last night or not, stupid!" Effie was able to say, without violating her conscience:

"I didn't sleep in my bed last night. I was a-helping the master with a pore sick lady." And then, more with the intention of diverting awkward questions than from a desire to boast, she told them about Julia. The resultant interest disposed of Sarah most satisfactorily. Once, however, Effie's strict adherence to the truth was in momentary jeopardy. Mrs. Sharman, who also cherished a romantic feeling for Will, and would have welcomed the chance to have worked with him for an hour, said discontentedly:

"And why, I'd like to know, was you the one to do all this?" Effie, ignoring the question, said dreamily, "And the lady kissed me afore she went off this morning."

They stared at her in boundless astonishment.

"She must-a-bin dotty," said Clara, speaking for them all.

Just on eleven o'clock Sarah, in her outdoor clothes, stole down the main stairs, out the front door, through the arch into the yard, and entered the kitchen from the back. Her face had lost some of its florid colour and her eyes were heavy. She moved languidly.

"Well," cried the cook, "you're a nice one, you are. Taking off on the busiest day, and then ambling in at bull's noon like this. Who'd you think you are, I'd like to know."

"I got soaked," said Sarah, meekly sullen. "I hatta stay home till me things was dry. Got a fine old chill I have, too. And the rheumatiz in me back something shocking."

"I know a right good cure for rheumatiz in the back, my fine mawther," said Mrs. Sharman unsympathetically. "And thass a good turn at the wash-tub. So get that daft hat off your head and set to."

Moving gingerly, Sarah hung her hat and cloak on one of the row of pegs behind the door and went towards the wash-house. Effie dried off the last square of bricks with her wrung-out cloth and scrambled to her feet. One glance showed her that Sarah's plan for wearing a pillow under her dress had been carried out. And once again her hatred and loathing of the girl who had terrorized her gave way to reluctant admiration. Lifting her bucket, she followed Sarah out of the kitchen, and in the privacy of the wash-house said gently. "Jest you puddle about and pretend for a bit and I'll come and lend you a hand soon's I git a chanst."

"Thank you, Effie," said Sarah, very humbly.

"I got the taters to do first," said Effie, and shuffled away with clumsy haste.

By the time the tall clock on the half-landing cleared its throat rumblingly, and uttered its bell-chime announcement of the hour, the *Fleece* had swung back into its smooth internal rhythm. As the clock struck, Harriet opened the passage door and stepped into the kitchen, greeted by an inaudible sigh from Mrs. Sharman. The false hues of health lay on her cheeks and lips, every hair was in place, her clothes were fresh and neat. If anything, she held herself rather more upright than usual.

"I'm glad to see that you're feeling better, ma'am," said Mrs. Sharman in a voice that held anything but joy.

"Thank you, Mrs. Sharman. I have quite recovered. Now, let me see, there was something I wanted to speak to you about. Oh, yes! Last night, when I went to the store-room, I found two sacks of sugar open. I wish you would remember not to open a new one until the old is *quite* finished and the sack removed. And another thing, I think it is time we opened the 1815 raspberry jam. It looked to me to be going sugary on top. I should suggest raspberry tart for supper tonight. What had you in mind, Mrs. Sharman?"

With the gesture and expression of a child exposing to its teacher a sum which it well knows to be wrong, the stout, middle-aged woman thrust under Harriet's eyes the slate upon which she had jotted, as she had been ordered to do, her suggestions for the day's menus.

"Mrs. Sharman," explained Harriet, after a moment's perusal of this peculiar record, "cold goose *and* cold mutton! What can have come over you? Certainly, I know that both the bird and the joint were hot last night. That's no excuse. People arriving this afternoon will hardly be interested in what was served twenty-four hours before. We'll have the goose in patties, please, with ham and hard-boiled egg; and the mutton in a shepherd's pie . . . in two pies, one with onion and one without, for those who prefer it so. And leeks in white sauce as well as potatoes."

"Very well, Miss Harriet," said Mrs. Sharman, who had planned herself an easy day.

"And raspberry tart. Don't forget that."

"That Sarah which you let off on Michaelmas Day walked in this morning nigh on eleven o'clock," said the cook, less from vindictive feeling towards Sarah than from a natural desire to remind Harriet of her lack of consideration, and to forestall any further troublesome adjustment in the feeding arrangements.

"Oh, did she?" said Harriet grimly. "I'll have a word with that young woman. Where is she?"

"Back in the wash-house."

Harriet turned towards the wash-house door, from whose crevices came frail wisps of steam and the scent of soapsuds. Then she hesitated. Sarah Cross was a rude, truculent creature, and she needed a more vehement scolding than Harriet at that moment felt capable of administering. What she had to say to Sarah would keep, she reflected grimly.

"I won't disturb her work," she said with dignity. "Mrs. Sharman, we'll have our coffee now. And the chocolate sandwich, if you please."

"Effie," said Mrs. Sharman, with sour resignation, as soon as the door had closed behind Harriet's rigidly held back. "Get my duzzy pastry board and bowl while I make this dommed coffee. And then do you do some onions and leeks as well as them taters. I thought that young vixen was safe a-bed for the day. That do seem to me a rare rum thing, you coon't make some people lay down, not if you took a hatched to their skull."

The weather-wise farmer who had studied the sky and foretold a fine day, had been right. Just as Harriet, doggedly holding the coffee-pot in both hands, succeeded in pouring the three cups of coffee, the sun broke through and sent a shaft of yellow light over the red garden wall and in at the window of the Little Parlour.

There was little to show that the twenty-four hours which lay between this morning's first visitant ray and yesterday's had been in any way momentous. The dreaminess had gone from Myrtle's eyes; the lines on Will's face were harsher; Harriet sat in the elm chair instead of upon the sofa; no one was eating cake this morning. But the real changes, the battle scars, the buds of new growth, the life-streams whose courses had altered, all these were hidden as Will and Myrtle and Harriet, all unusually talkative, because words can be shutters as well as windows, drank their coffee and sat in the sun.

Also by Norah Lofts

KNIGHT'S ACRE   X2685 $1.75

Sir Godfrey Tallboys, that reckless but endearing young knight, left his family and half-finished home to go to Spain for a tournament which promised great wealth. He had thought he would be gone months. He was away for six years.

Six long years. His lovely wife, Sybilla, was convinced that he was dead. Until he came riding home one day with a wild young beauty at his side.

NETHERGATE   2-3095-3 $1.75

To Isabella de Savigny, an aristocratic refugee from the French Reign of Terror, her cousin's magnificent English country estate promised sanctuary. But Nethergate became a prison to the high-spirited young woman. For its mistress, the cold-blooded and beautiful Lady Rosaleen, treated Isabella like a servant. When Isabella was seduced by Rosaleen's son and discovered she was to have a child, Rosaleen devised a cunning and vicious plot to get rid of her. In her own way, in her own time, Isabella took her revenge.

FAWCETT CREST
BESTSELLERS